The Dead Pennies

BY ROBERT FORD

CEMETERY DANCE PUBLICATIONS

Baltimore

— 2023—

Cemetery Dance Publications
132B Industry Lane, Unit #7
Forest Hill, MD 21050
www.cemeterydance.com

Prologue

DENNY SHIVERED INSIDE his weathered Army jacket. The older he got, the more the chill seemed to mess with him, and lately, he'd started to think of making his way south—Nashville maybe, or New Orleans—some tourist town where the dumpster pickings were better.

He stuffed his hands into his pockets and felt the half of a sandwich he'd found in the hotel trash can earlier. The things people threw away amazed him. So much waste. His backpack was filled with the bare essentials, but he was feeling his age carrying that around as well. The town shelters were full, and after scoping out several possibilities, Denny arrived at the enormous abandoned building in front of him, and thought he might have found the right place to bed down for the night. He stood in the gravel parking lot for a few minutes, watching for any security guard patrolling the area, and then cautiously made his way to the rear of the building. There he found a series of low, narrow windows close to the ground.

Digging through his pack, Denny pulled out his old Ka-Bar knife and worked the blade against the frame of a window.

I was a goddamn tunnel rat, you think a little window's gonna keep me out?

He chuckled to himself as he drew the sharpened edge along the frame to the corner of the window, watching the glazing crumble beneath the pressure, and chuckled as he felt the pane of glass pop and shift in place.

Denny dropped his backpack inside, and though it took a bit of effort to shimmy through the opening, he succeeded and landed in a crouched position on a cement floor.

Meww.

He turned in the darkness, listening closely.

Mew.

"*Awww,* come here little guy. *Pspspspspss.*" Denny pulled the soggy, half-eaten sandwich from his pocket, pinched off a piece of lunch meat, and waved it in the air. "That's right, you smell that, don't ya? C'mon, I'll share. *Pspspsspspss.*"

His eyes were adjusting to the low interior light, and Denny saw a flutter of movement in the darkness to his right. He smiled and spoke in a gentle voice. "Don't be scared now. C'mon, I'll share with you."

The shadow grew larger.

BOOK ONE

Chapter One

ONCE ABBY MADE her decision, it took less than three hours to pack up everything she owned.

Nick had been awake for the last three days on a binge and had finally gone to sleep in a sprawl after their argument. After he snapped, Nick had gone quiet and slinked away to the bedroom, while Abby had gone to the living room, sat on the couch and cried.

A little after 4:30 in the morning, she made a pot of coffee and took a Marlboro from Nick's half-empty pack, stepped out onto the balcony of their apartment, and enjoyed her first cigarette in almost a year. The mixture of nicotine and black coffee brought clarity to her mind, and by the time the cigarette was down to the filter and her mug was empty, she had gone beyond the crossroads and started down a new path.

One by one, she carried her things to her aging Honda Accord and arranged them inside. Her clothes were stuffed in trash bags.

Favorite books in a clothes basket, along with her near-empty jewelry box. She hadn't looked at her jewelry in a while, and seeing half of it gone had shocked but not surprised her. It didn't take a rocket scientist to realize where the missing items had gone.

Abby pulled the filled trash bag from the kitchen, tossed it aside, and then stacked DVDs and CDs inside the empty garbage can, with old photo albums and a folder of tax papers and other important documents.

After packing them in her car, Abby came back inside, stood in the living room and looked around. The sofa and loveseat were pockmarked with stains and burn holes. The TV she couldn't care less about. Photos and artwork on the walls, but nothing she would shed a tear over.

Everything else... screw it.

She grit her teeth, felt the urge to scream at Nick, and she got so far as to step next to the bed with her clenched fists at her side and glare at him. *But no,* Abby stood quietly, raging inside, and did nothing but stare at him while he snored.

His hair was greasy from not showering and he needed a shave. She could smell the meth stink on him from where she stood. Abby had seen this before, and knew Nick would probably be out cold for at least another ten hours, but she didn't want to take any chances. She glanced at the nightstand beside him: the glass rosette pipe, cheap lighter, and empty plastic bag. It made her stomach turn, partially because it was such a waste, but mostly because she had put up with it for so long.

Abby walked to the fridge and considered putting some ice cubes in a plastic bag to put against her face, but decided against it.

She peeled a sheet of paper from a notepad on the kitchen counter, and grabbed a pen.

You wanted the perfect high.
I wanted the man I fell in love with.
Guess neither one of us will find what we're after. —A

One last stop to use the bathroom, and Abby stared in the mirror as she washed and dried her hands.

Goddamn, this hurts. Son of a bitch really did a number on me this time. I might actually get a black eye. How do men know just the right way to slap you? Is it a merit badge in Boy Scouts or something?

She gently touched the swollen flesh, winced at the pain, and exhaled slowly. Pulling her dark hair back into a ponytail, Abby grabbed a tie to keep it in place. Her phone buzzed and she pulled it from her jeans pocket to check the screen.

Shit.

Abby had ignored the last several phone calls from her mother, and the voicemails were growing more agitated. Not urgent, though. No. *Urgency* would indicate some sort of concern from her mother. That wasn't the case—had *never* been the case. This was about getting attention.

She accepted the call and closed her eyes as she nestled the phone against her face and spoke in a low voice. "Hi Mom."

"Abigail! I've been wondering about you! Are you—"

"Mom, I'm okay, really. It's just… look, I was going to call and tell you or… I don't know, surprise you or something."

There was a hesitation on the phone and Abby counted out the moments of silent judgment.

"Are you coming to visit?"

"Maybe more than visit, Mom. I'm not sure right now."

There was a quiet pause on the other end of the call and Abby closed her eyes.

Here it comes. The avalanche of I-told-you-so's.

"Did you and Nick break up?"

"I'm leaving him, *soooo*... yeah, you could say that, Mom."

"From the first time I met that boy, I knew he—"

"Mom! Listen, I *know*, okay? *I know*. I'm in the middle of... look, I can't talk right now, but I will soon, I promise. Ok?"

Another quiet pause. Abby could visualize the pursed lips and expression on her mother's face.

"All right, then. I love you."

"Love you too, Mom." Abby ended the call and stuffed the phone back into her pocket as she walked from the bathroom toward the apartment door. Grabbing her sunglasses from her purse, Abby gingerly eased them onto her face. She took one more look around and stopped, smiling to herself despite the throbbing pain.

How could I possibly forget you, Marilyn? I would have cried if I had left without you.

Abby pulled the strap of her purse over her shoulder and walked to the mannequin in the corner of the room. It was a vintage figure, void of any real detail on the face and hands, but at some point, she had dressed the form in a denim jacket adorned with pins of her favorite bands, a black mini-skirt and fishnet stockings, and a pair of her well-abused Doc Marten boots. Her second year in art school, Abby had seen it in a dumpster near the Center City Mall and joyously retrieved it and brought it back to her apartment. She had dubbed her Marilyn, as the mannequin had the hourglass figure of Monroe, even if the face bore resemblance to no one, and it had been the focal point of many parties during college.

Flipping the body under one arm, Abby maneuvered through the doorway and pulled the door closed behind her. Marilyn went head first into the backseat, her booted feet protruding from the open window. Abby scooted behind the steering wheel and started her car. She tapped the dashboard twice with her hand. "Alright, Linda. You be a good girl and get us to Florida."

She stared up at the apartment building and the bedroom window. "Goodbye, St. Nick, you fucking asshole."

Chapter Two

THE LINE OF brake lights getting out of Philadelphia was the expected bumper-to-bumper traffic, but Abby knew once she got closer to the King of Prussia Mall it would ease up. She glanced at the Philadelphia Museum of Art, and the reflection of Boathouse Row in the Schuylkill River.

It brought back memories of first moving to the city, and the excitement she felt—exploring the strange shops and galleries along South Street, walking through China Town and Reading Terminal. Everything felt a million miles away from Clearwater, Florida, but more than that, it felt good being on her own. A little scary, yes, but it made her feel alive.

Being on the highway, even stuck in traffic, Abby felt those old feelings start to resurface, the sensation of taking control of her life again. The dead, numb emotion of being with Nick was a gradual thing, a stalking darkness, and before Abby realized, she was in the shadows.

Goddamn it, Nick! You fucking asshole! Why couldn't you get your shit together?

The tears sprung up out of nowhere and she angrily wiped them from her eyes.

Two years. Two goddamned years! How could I be so stupid?

She gripped the steering wheel with both hands, screamed in frustration, and shook her head with a scowl, forcing her emotions away. Abby pressed the buttons to lower both front windows, and then she turned the radio on. The mall wasn't far away, and traffic was already moving a little faster. The exit for the Turnpike was coming up, and after that, it was a long stretch of highway back home to Clearwater, Florida.

Her stomach roiled and Abby realized she hadn't eaten anything since the evening before. Nick had been hyped up when he got back home, but she recognized by the way he kept peeking through the window blinds and scratching his arms, he was on his way to crashing. He had continued to try to get in her pants all evening, and she had put a stop to that when he was high a long time ago. It had led to a screaming match ending only when Nick backhanded her, and then crept off to the bedroom to find sleep.

Thinking about it all, Abby felt her anger swell up inside her again, but she tamped it down as she paused at the Turnpike entrance, took a ticket, and tucked it into the cupholder of her console. She noticed Nick's pack of cigarettes in her purse as well, though she had no memory of doing it. Smiling, she pulled the pack out and shook a Marlboro loose, pinching the filter with her lips. She pushed the car's cigarette lighter and waited to hear the satisfying click when it was heated.

After taking a long, satisfying drag, Abby turned the volume up on the radio and sang out loud with Jim Morrison about *Roadhouse Blues*. She goosed the pedal and the wind rushed in from both windows, carrying the sound of her voice, and the past, along with it. Morrison changed to Tom Petty, then Led Zeppelin, and Lynyrd Skynyrd. Abby kept belting out the song lyrics and tapping the drum beats on the steering wheel.

The Turnpike stretched on.

When the gas gauge started to match the empty feeling in Abby's stomach, she began watching for the familiar highway signs for fuel and food. It wasn't much longer before she pulled into a rest stop and gassed up the Honda.

After putting her car in the parking lot, Abby went inside and got a chicken salad wrap, a large bottle of water, and a bag of Doritos. Sitting in the driver's seat, she uncapped the bottle and took a swallow, then moved her sunglasses to her head and pressed the cold plastic against her cheekbone. The sensation was painful and soothing at the same time, and Abby sighed.

Her phone buzzed and she winced. There was no way it was Nick—not yet, not after being awake that long—and even Mom should be holding tight after the phone call earlier. She peeled the plastic away from the sandwich wrap, took a bite, and then pulled her phone from her pocket. She smiled at the text message on screen.

She had known Hayden since eighth grade, and though he had gone off the grid for a few years after graduation, he was the only one from high school Abby still kept in touch with. Back then, Hayden kept telling everyone he was going to become a priest, and though she wasn't sure he would follow through, sure enough, he enrolled in seminary college not long after graduation.

At first, Nick had started calling Hayden her other boyfriend, but it hadn't taken long to start referring to him as *Altar Boy*, or *Pope Hayden*, and when Nick was *really* smashed out of his mind, he called him *Kiddie-Diddler*.

It quickly reached a point where Abby stopped speaking about Hayden entirely, and Nick seemed to drop the possessiveness. They still messaged each other, but a big part of Abby felt as if she had given up her longest friendship by hiding him.

She took a bite of her sandwich wrap and thumbed her phone to the text message.

HAYDEN: 'Sup, loser?

Abby texted back: Soooo… you know that thing I've been talking about for a while, trying to decide?

HAYDEN: Trying to grow a set to do it?

ABBY: My decision was made for me last night.

The ellipsis popped up on her screen as Hayden was typing and then disappeared, came back again, and then vanished.

HAYDEN: You okay?

ABBY: I will be. I'm on the highway with a car full of my stuff. Heading back home.

HAYDEN: Back to Clearwater? ARE YOU SERIOUS?? Stop by!!!! It's about the halfway point!!

She took another bite of her wrap, considering his words, and then typed.

ABBY: I dunno, Hayseed. I've got a car full of shit right now.

The ellipsis popped up on screen and remained there, the animation cycling for a few moments before his reply popped up.

HAYDEN: Look, you finally made a break and I'm proud of you. VERY proud of you! But it's time to live YOUR life. Swing by and stay a night or two. The stuff in your car's not going anywhere. Rhinesville is a great place to get lost, but it also might be a good place to find yourself again. Besides, you in a big rush to get back to your mom's house? =)

"Asshole." Abby whispered out loud to herself, but couldn't help but smile.

HAYDEN: C'mon Abs. Pull up your big girl panties and do it.

She put her phone in the cup holder of the center console, started her car, and had barely put her foot on the pedal when she heard the familiar *whoop whoop* sound of a cop siren behind her. Abby immediately braked and put her car in park. Red and blue lights spun behind her.

Shiiiiiiiiiit.

Abby raised her phone and took a selfie photo with the cruiser lights flashing in the background. She sent the photo to Hayden and then dropped the phone back in the cup holder. In the rearview mirror, she watched the officer get out of his car and walk toward her with the slow, purposeful stride only cops can muster.

"Uh… Miss?"

The cop was younger than she expected, maybe in his late twenties. He looked uncomfortable in the patrol uniform and had a confused expression on his face.

"Yes, officer?"

"I can't let you drive on the highway like this."

"Like... what?"

He took a step away from the car and Abby turned to see him pointing at Marilyn's legs poking from the window. His expression changed to one of slight amusement, bordering on a smile.

"*Ohhhh,* that. Yeah, I guess I wasn't really—"

"May I see your driver's license, insurance, and registration, please?"

Abby nodded and turned to her purse for her license, and then the glove box for her car registration and insurance papers. She handed them over with as genuine a smile as she could muster.

The officer gave a long look at her driver's license before walking back to his cruiser.

Her stomach swirled, and Abby looked into her rearview mirror as he sat in his driver's seat, the door still open. After a few moments, he returned and leaned down toward her, documents still in his hand.

"Remove the sunglasses, please."

Abby sighed and reluctantly took off her sunglasses, knowing her cheek and eye were still red and swollen. The officer's expression grew serious and she saw him flash a look at the rest stop building before returning to her. "Are you traveling alone?"

"Yes."

"Miss, are you okay?" He slowly handed her documents back to her, and Abby laid them in her lap.

She nodded. "Yeah, Officer, I'm ok. I'll be better than okay, soon. I'm heading to Florida."

The cop studied her eyes for a moment and nodded. "All right, then. You can uh... you can put your sunglasses back on if you'd like. Florida's a long way to go, so let's make sure your... *friend* here, doesn't choose a different journey on the road, okay?"

He smiled and grabbed the mannequin's legs, sliding the figure so Marilyn's head was on the passenger side floorboard and her feet barely stuck out from the window. He stepped back and studied the adjustment and then tied the loose laces on the Doc Martens.

Abby grinned as she watched him do that and then, for some reason, her eyes became glassy with emotion.

"Alright, I think you two are all set." He stepped to her window, gave a nod and a smile. "You be careful, now, okay?"

His gaze lingered on Abby and she thought maybe there was something else he wanted to say, but he didn't. "Thanks, Officer. I'll try."

The cop walked back to his cruiser, turned the lights off, and then pulled from the rest stop and onto the highway.

Abby picked up her phone.

HAYDEN: Oh shit! A ticket ALREADY?

She replied: Getting back on the highway now.

HAYDEN: Bad fine?

ABBY: No fine. I flashed him my boobs.

HAYDEN: I've seen your boobs. How bad was the fine?

ABBY: Asshole! I cried, okay? No ticket.

HAYDEN: Confession is good for the soul.

ABBY: WORST. PRIEST. EVER.

HAYDEN: I'm not a priest.

ABBY: Priest in training, then.

HAYDEN: Yeahhhh, about that... just get your heathen ass to Rhinesville. We'll talk.

Abby read the text and reread. Something was definitely up. Hayden had been in seminary school for the last three years. He had taken a lot of teasing his senior year of high school about wanting to become a priest but he shrugged it all off, steadfast in his choice.

It had been a while since they had really talked though. Things had gotten so bad with Nick that Abby had gone quiet with almost everyone. Hayden probably knew the most about the situation, and that wasn't a lot. He knew Nick was on meth and he knew she had been considering leaving.

Now I feel like a jackass. What has Hayden *been going through? I am* such *a shitty friend.*

She took a drink of water and capped the bottle, nestling it in the second cup holder.

"Okay Rhinesville, here we come."

Chapter Three

THE EMPTY BAG of Doritos and the water bottle had been tossed to the passenger side floorboard long before Abby's bladder began to protest. She held off as long as she could and finally gave in, taking an exit when she saw a sign for Rhinesville, SC: 43 miles.

She found a gas station that was small but clean, and went to the bathrooms in the back of the place. Abby pulled her sunglasses down and checked herself in the mirror.

Son of a bitch.

The flesh beneath her left eye and along the bridge of her nose had shifted color to a dark blue-purple tone.

That's the first and last black eye I ever get because of a man.

She pulled her phone out and texted Hayden: I'm about 45 minutes from your redneck town but I need an address, dinkus.

Hayden replied almost immediately with his address and a landmark to watch out for—Dippin' Wicks Bar and Lounge—and Abby was back on her way.

She had to admit, Rhinesville seemed pretty amazing. Art galleries and interesting looking boutique shops dotted Main Street. She passed through the town square and saw cute little café bars with outdoor seating. People walked around with smiles on their faces instead of expressions of distrust and barely concealed anger like Philadelphia.

At the end of Main Street, the scenery turned into farmhouses and rolling fields. She saw pastures with cattle and others with horses—not as posh and stately as the thoroughbred farms in Jacksonville, but much more charming. It seemed like the sort of place you could walk up to as a stranger and be invited to supper.

Rhinesville was a lovely juxtaposition of city and country.

On her left were freshly cut hayfields and the sweet, natural scent. She breathed it in and considered stopping along the roadside to truly appreciate the sensory overload the smell brought with it. It was intoxicating and such a contrast from the gray pavement and dirty alleys of Philadelphia, Abby felt emotion glaze her eyes for the second time that day.

She passed the building Hayden had told her to watch for—Dippin' Wicks Bar and Lounge, with its hand-painted sign and tin roof. The gravel parking lot held a handful of pickup trucks and motorcycles, and she had no doubt Hayden had been in there more than a few times. It was exactly the sort of place he would visit, turn on his charm, and within an hour, he would know the bartender's life story and have several of the patrons chatting him up and buying him drinks.

A long, lazy curve of road stretched past the bar and Abby glanced at the map on her phone. Up ahead, right around the bend, was Hayden's place. It had been roughly three years since she had seen him in person.

Funny thing, Abby thought, *I was in Philadelphia this morning, leaving a meth-head behind me, and now, I'm in a beautiful little town seeing my best friend again. It's only been hours but that apartment feels like a lifetime ago.*

Barrett's Feed Mill was painted in a swirling script on a two-story building with white paint peeling from the clapboard siding. A weathered wooden staircase was on the side of the building, leading to the upper floor. Golden hayfields, without a neighbor in sight, surrounded the place, only interrupted by a copse of trees on the far right. Abby pulled the car into the gravel parking lot and eased up to the building beside an old Buick. She put her car in park, killed the engine, and let out a long breath she hadn't realized she'd been holding—the satisfaction of arriving at your destination after a long journey.

A flash of movement caught her attention and Abby looked up to see Hayden coming down the wooden staircase. He hadn't changed a lot since high school, except now he sported a mustache and beard. Same surfer-boy tangle of dirty blonde hair. Same easygoing movement about him. Hayden reached the gravel lot and stopped, looking at her with a big smile, and Abby opened her car door and ran to him.

He paused, and looked her over. "Hey." His smile grew wider.

"Hey." Abby's voice broke as she uttered the single word reply, but it wasn't until she felt Hayden's arms hugging her tightly that the tears threatening to spill all day long finally came loose.

Chapter Four

T HIS ISN'T WHAT I pictured, Hayseed."

"What, you expected a baptism font and a six-foot cross hanging over an altar?" Hayden opened his refrigerator and withdrew two Coronas.

Abby laughed and nestled back into the sofa. "No, not that exactly, but... this place is pretty awesome. Not very... *priestly* though."

Hayden's apartment was an open loft with thick oak beams and tall, floor-to-ceiling windows making up the rear of the room. The floor was hardwood—not polished, but worn to a fine smooth finish by years of use. Framed photos adorned the walls. A flat-screen TV sat on top of an ancient and enormous wooden crate with WHEAT stenciled on the side of it.

Hayden popped the caps on the beer bottles and sat on the couch, handing one to Abby. "I found the place by accident. A friend of my uncle's has owned the building forever, but they finally shut the mill down about five years ago. They didn't want to sell it yet

because property prices are starting to skyrocket around here so…
I'm the caretaker."

"You?"

"I can be responsible!" Hayden grinned and took a swallow of his beer.

"I'm sorry, *how* many hamsters did you go through when we were kids?"

Hayden put his Corona down on the coffee table and pointed at her. "Those hamsters were freak babies of incest or something! Their blood is *not* on my hands!"

"And the rabbit?"

"That's not my fault, either!" Hayden put his hands up. "My dad left him in the sun too long!"

"You killed the Easter bunny."

Hayden reached for his beer. "His *name* was Cocoa, and it was a painful time for me. Stop bringing up heartache from my childhood."

Abby felt a giggle fit start to spiral inside her.

He feigned a sad expression but when Abby burst out laughing, Hayden joined her.

Tears streamed down her cheeks, and Abby leaned her head back against the couch cushion. Her stomach ached from the effort but it felt good. She wiped her face and shook her head as her laughter died down for both of them.

Hayden's eyes glistened as he smiled at her. "So, what's with the shades, Britney Spears? You avoiding the paparazzi or something?"

She closed her eyes, took a breath, and then Abby sat up, removing the glasses as she did.

Much as the officer on the Turnpike had reacted, Hayden's expression turned from amusement to seriousness. He glanced away from her, and then turned back and reached for her as he moved closer. Hayden tenderly put a hand against the uninjured side of Abby's face.

It made her feel completely exposed and vulnerable, and she cast her eyes away, unable to maintain the contact.

He spoke in a soft, low voice. "I'm not going to ask you what happened. I'm not going to push." Hayden gently brushed her hair back from the side of her face. "But when you're ready to talk about it, I'll listen. Alright?"

Abby nodded and closed her eyes. She breathed slowly. She didn't want to break down again. Hayden wrapped his arms around her and she let him. Then she shook her head and pulled back, forcing the emotion away as she had on the drive. She stood, lifted her Corona bottle by the neck, and took a swallow. "C'mon skirt. Finish your beer. It's heating up the room."

Hayden smirked at her. "*Ohhhh,* it's gonna be like *that* tonight, is it?"

She smiled and walked around the room. There were several photos framed and hanging near the entrance. Abby paused in front of one, staring at a teenage Hayden and herself, standing in front of a rollercoaster, and smiling. She studied the photo and turned to him. "When was this?"

"You're messin' with me?" Hayden stood from the couch and took a swallow from his Corona.

Abby turned back to the photo and shook her head. "No, I…" She let her words fade off.

"We went to Shepherd's Point Park in the summer after eleventh grade." He stepped closer and tilted his head at her, his expression almost one of hurt feelings. "You really don't remember? We ate soft-serve ice cream and almost threw up after getting on the pirate ship ride."

Abby felt a wave of sadness wash over her. It only served as a reminder of what a mess her life had been since becoming involved with Nick, and made her wonder what other happy memories she had forgotten about. She wanted to say something to Hayden, apologize for not remembering, but couldn't find the right words and turned her attention to another framed picture.

This held a black and white photo of adult Hayden, kneeling down beside a young boy. They both wore wide smiles for the camera, and the boy had his arm slung around Hayden's neck.

"South Africa."

Abby turned to Hayden. "That's when you vanished for a while?"

Hayden nodded. "I was there for about five months on missionary work. This little town called QwaQwa. That picture was taken after that little boy, Disebo, read his first Dr. Seuss book out loud. *Green Eggs and Ham*."

"Cute."

"Disebo was a great kid. He was pretty proud of himself for reading that book. Hell, I was pretty proud of him, too."

"Dr. Seuss books normally part of missionary work?"

"Guess I'm not a normal missionary." He tilted his beer bottle, finishing it off, and gave a slight shake of his head and continued in a softer tone. "His sister died while I was there, young girl, maybe... fifteen, sixteen at the most. Life's different there."

"How do you mean?"

Hayden sighed, walked to the fridge, and withdrew two fresh Coronas. "One day, you're teaching kids how to read or building wells so the villagers can drink fresh water, the next day, you're reading the Anarchist's Cookbook to learn…" He shook his head again, popped the cap on one bottle and then the next. "It's just… it's an entirely different world there. Life doesn't really mean much."

He crossed the living room toward the tall windows and popped a latch on one, nudging it forward. The window swung open like a door, and Hayden turned to Abby with a smile and a nod. "C'mon."

Beyond the open window, it opened up to a wide rooftop deck with a small table, several chairs and a wooden storage trunk. An assortment of potted plants lined the edges of the deck. The fields stretched off in the distance, the sunset casting orange over waves of rippling hay.

"So, what happened to Linda?" Hayden pulled two chairs away from the table for them to sit.

"Linda who?"

"I saw what you're driving now. That's not Linda."

Abby smiled and sipped from her beer. "That's Linda II."

"Why did you name your car after Linda Ronstadt anyway?"

Abby sat down and set her beer on the tabletop. "First of all, Linda Ronstadt is a freakin' national treasure, alright? But second, I didn't name my car after her. Well… not really. It was a play on words, it was Linda Thermostat."

Hayden sputtered laughter mid-drink, and shook his head, coughing.

"Go ahead and make fun! I busted my ass the summer I bought that car, and I had to replace the thermostat three times! It ate up my checks from KwikMart." Abby lifted her beer again and grinned at Hayden. "Not sure why the thermostat was such a big deal, it was summer anyway. Not like I needed a working thermostat to keep the car heater going."

Hayden stared at her a moment, then squinted his eyes. "You're messing with me?"

"What?"

"The thermostat... it's not... it's not for the car heater."

A confused expression came over Abby's face, and then she took a drink of Corona. The grin returned as she met his eyes again. "Gotcha."

"Asssssssss." Hayden laughed and leaned back in his chair. "Good one. Got me good."

"What memory, in that twisted mind of yours, made you think I'm that dumb?"

Hayden studied her a moment, his eyes full of amusement, and then he shook his head. "You're not dumb, Abs. Never have been."

They both turned toward the fireball sun sinking lower on the horizon. It gave both of their faces a warm glow. Crickets began to sing. Abby felt her shoulders relax, the tension easing at how incredibly peaceful it was here.

"So, what's going on with you, Hayseed?" Abby leaned back in the chair, pulling one leg up beneath the other.

Hayden sighed and stretched his legs out. "So, this lady goes to the doctor, freaking out. Doctor, doctor, there's something really wrong with me! I keep finding postage stamps from Costa Rica in my vagina!"

He tilted the Corona, took a drink, and then grinned at Abby. "Doctor makes her remove her clothes and takes a look around. Tells her, those aren't postage stamps. They're stickers off bananas!"

Abby laughed out loud and groaned at the punch line. "You're gonna be *some* kind of priest, I tell ya."

"Yeah, well…" Hayden reached behind him and lifted the lid of the wooden trunk.

Abby watched as he withdrew a half-empty bottle of Yukon Jack, spun the cap off, and took a swallow from the bottle before he sat it on the table, nudging it slightly in her direction. She took the bait and sipped from the bottle. She shook her head at the taste, which she hadn't experienced since high school parties.

Abby took a swallow of beer to chase the too-sweet flavor, and stared at Hayden as she lowered her voice. "You're not gonna be a priest, are you?"

Hayden offered her a thin smile and reached for the bottle again. He took another swig and cleared his throat. The sunset made twin campfires in his eyes. "The summer after seventh grade, I lived with one of my dad's cousins, Steven, and his girlfriend at the time. Lisa, I think her name was… always looked strung out on something."

"After your mom died?"

"*Mmmhmmm.*" Hayden nodded acknowledgement, though he still stared at the setting sun. "Her dying really messed my dad up, and he couldn't seem to pull his shit together while I was around, so he sent me away while he tried to do it by himself. I didn't really know Steven at all, but they were the only option, so… I stayed there for about three months."

Usually Hayden's voice held a touch of humor with every word or text message, but Abby noticed it had grown soft and serious.

"You remember me in seventh grade, skinny as a fence post and… well." Hayden cleared his throat again. "Only took me about a week before I realized something was just… *off*. They were pretty much trailer trash and I'm sure my father paid them to take care of me. But anyway, I started to get this feeling, you know? Something wasn't right with me being there."

"Like you weren't welcome or something?"

"No, not like… I uh…" Hayden shook his head and took a drink of Yukon Jack. He rested the bottle on his leg and stared at the label. "One night I woke up and Steven was… doing things to me."

Abby's stomach clenched as she listened. Her throat tightened inside. "Hayden…"

He took another, longer swallow from the bottle and exhaled slowly, still not making eye contact. "Over the next month or so it got worse, *way* worse, and I didn't… I mean, I knew my dad was dealing with things and I'm… hell, it was *my* mom who died, right? I didn't want to call my dad, and I didn't know what else to do, so it just… went on. I didn't say anything, y' know? To anyone. But when summer was over, Dad came and got me and I went home with him. Never told anyone about it and tried to just get on with life. I kept thinking maybe God didn't love me."

Hayden tapped his fingers against his temple to emphasize his words. "I had that shit in my head, right? I mean, first, my mother died in the car accident, and then I had to live with this sick fucker so my dad could get better and... I mean, how could God let that happen? It *had* to be my fault."

"Hayseed..." Tears spilled over Abby's cheeks. She put a hand over her mouth and her heart ached for Hayden. She hadn't *really* gotten to know Hayden until ninth grade, long after all of this had taken place, but he had never said a single word about any of it. "Why didn't you tell me?"

"I didn't know how, Abs." Hayden glanced at her quickly and then away. "When I went to live with my dad again, I started reading the Bible every chance I could. Went to church *with* Dad and without him. You name it, I was there. *Yaaaaaay, Team Jesus!*" Hayden reached into his pants pocket and withdrew a pack of Marlboros and a lighter. He shook one out for himself, offered the pack to Abby, and they took turns lighting up.

"All I wanted to do was get back in the good graces of God. How messed up is that? I was the poster boy for it all. I would be *more* than a faithful *servant*, I'd be a company man for God. A priest! He'd *have* to love me then." Hayden released a bitter laugh and flicked ash into an empty bottle. "Another beer?"

Abby was definitely feeling the pleasant buzz of Yukon Jack and beer and it felt like Hayden *needed* to do this, to unburden. She nodded. "Please."

He slipped inside and quickly returned with two fresh Coronas and sat them on the table.

Abby couldn't help but notice how unbelievably peaceful it was here. The darkening fields were speckled with blinking stars as the fireflies had come out. No sirens. No thumping bass in passing cars. She sighed contentedly and turned to Hayden.

"So, what changed, Hayseed? Back in high school, you were dead set on becoming a priest."

A pained expression flickered across Hayden's face for a second, and then his gaze returned to Abby and his wounded appearance was replaced with a grin. "I realized I like boobs *wayyyyy* too much."

"Shut up!" She laughed out loud and swatted his arm.

"I'm serious! Big fan. *Biiiig* fan." He chuckled, reached for the bottle of Yukon Jack, and took a sip, and then followed it with a swallow of beer.

Abby smirked at him. "And priests only... *y' know*... with little boys."

Hayden winced. "*Fucking ouch.* I mean you're not wrong...but ouch."

"After the joke *you* just told about banana stickers, you're offended by that? Seriously?"

He shook his head. "Yeah, but that joke's in the *past*. Let's focus on the now."

"You're terrible."

"I know."

"Hayseed..." Smiling, Abby rose from her chair and stepped closer. "You don't need to be a priest if it doesn't feel right anymore. You're going to be amazing no matter what you do." She wrapped her arms around Hayden and kissed his cheek. He smelled like fresh air and the outdoors and mildly of cologne. "I missed you." She whispered.

Hayden closed his eyes and put his arms around her waist. "Missed you too, Abs."

Chapter Five

ABBY WOKE TO the sound of sizzling eggs and the smell of bacon. She opened her eyes cautiously. The beer and Yukon Jack from the previous night had her spinning by the time she went to sleep on Hayden's couch. Her head wasn't throbbing at the moment, and Abby thought she might have avoided a hangover. The real test, she knew, would be sitting up.

Hayden, his back to her, swayed in front of his stove, and Abby was pretty sure he was humming the tune to *Sweet Home Alabama*.

Still wrapped in a blanket, she eased herself up to a sitting position. The sunlight in the room was bright enough to make her squint but her head wasn't complaining in protest and her stomach grumbled eagerly at the scent of breakfast. These were good signs she had dodged a bullet.

"Best. Host. Ever."

Hayden turned to her and smiled. "Hey sleepyhead." He cut the flame on the stove and after a moment, brought two plates of food and a pair of forks to the living room, and sat down beside her. "So... I was thinking last night."

"How? How were you possibly thinking after... what, four beers each, half a bottle of Yukon Jack and what the hell kinda weed was that?"

"Purple Kush, and I'm not an amateur." He grinned and crunched a strip of bacon. "I was thinking about you last night and this morning."

The smell of scrambled eggs and cheese drew her like a magnet, and Abby dug in as Hayden talked.

"I know you just got out of a pile of shit in life. I get that. And, hear me out... going home to Clearwater might make you feel like you failed or something."

"It didn't before you said that, thanks."

"*Shhhhh,* listen." Hayden set his plate on the coffee table and pulled his phone from his pants pocket. "You shouldn't feel that way. Screw that. I meant what I said when I told you it would be good to take some time before going to live with your mom."

He scrolled on his phone screen and held it out so Abby could see. The image was the interior of a modern loft apartment—cathedral ceilings, light hardwood floors, and lots of sunlight streaming into the room. Hayden thumbed the screen to a new photo of a kitchen with black granite counter tops and a tiled backsplash.

"Gorgeous place," Abby said. "You have any idea how much that would go for in Philly?"

Hayden nodded. "Oh, I'm sure. I was going to move into this place but..." He looked around the living room and spread his arms out wide. "I really kind of like it here."

"Plus, it's free."

"There's that, but…" Hayden held up his phone and grinned at her. "So is *this* place. And it's yours if you want it."

Abby forked a bite of eggs into her mouth and stared at him, confused. "Hayseed, what're you talking about?"

"My uncle Jack—"

"The bald one?"

"The bald one, yeah, but the bald *rich* one now. Uncle Jack is renovating this building and converting it into high-end loft apartments. They've been working on them for months and something got caught up in permits or something, I don't know really, but the work had to come to a stop. They have one unit completely done and it's the model unit to show off to people and get them interested in buying. While they're tied up in legalese with the permits, Jack needs someone to keep an eye on the place."

Abby chewed her food slowly. "Free?"

"One hundred percent, including utilities right now. They can't legally sell or build onto the units until the legal mess is sorted out and Uncle Jack needs someone there at night to… you know, watch over things. Make sure no one's breaking in to steal tools, keep teenagers from vandalizing shit. It'll be at least a year or two until the entire building is completely renovated."

Abby glanced at the photo on Hayden's phone, and picked up a slice of bacon.

"Wi-fi and internet is set up, and I know that's a deal breaker for you, but there's no cable TV. Electric's wired. Gas heat. Water. All included. And… *oh yeah, t*here's a pool, but it's empty. A hot tub is wired up, not filled yet, but that's easy enough. The water lines are there."

"A hot tub?"

"Yeah, in the natatorium."

"I'm sorry, a what?"

"The natatorium. It's the room the pool and hot tub is in."

"You're making up fake words."

"Am not. Though I did only learn that word a couple weeks ago." Hayden smiled. "This place is gonna be the absolute shit when it's finished. Like MTV Cribs without the... you know, basketball courts and fourteen car garages and shit. But for now, it would be all yours." Hayden put his phone back in his pocket and studied her.

Abby's mind drifted, thinking of how amazing it would be to live in a place like that, then she snapped back to reality. "Hayden, I can't. I have a car full of shit headed to Clearwater. What am I supposed—"

"Give me three *real* reasons why you can't." Hayden snagged the last strip of bacon from his plate and leaned forward on the edge of the couch. "Take a look at it. You've got nothing to lose."

Abby opened her mouth to speak but closed it again because nothing came to mind. She had no one to ask permission from. No one was depending on her to be anywhere. It had been three years since she had lived by herself and the thought was a little intimidating, but it was damn sure better to unpack her stuff in an apartment of her own—a *kickass amazing free* apartment of her own—rather than running back to Clearwater with her tail between her legs. Abby leaned back on the couch and shoveled another bite of scrambled eggs into her mouth instead.

"Good," Hayden's smile grew wider, "because I called Uncle Jack this morning while you were still sleeping and told him you were interested. You and me are heading over after you finish breakfast so I can show you the place."

She hadn't even seen the apartment in real life yet, but Abby's stomach fluttered with happy excitement at the idea of living there. "Hayseed… what am I gonna do with you?"

Chapter Six

THOUGH THERE WERE several smaller buildings, the enormous old-world brick structure was the center of attention. Massive white columns framed the entrance, and ornate moldings decorated the façade. Thick, aged Sycamore trees were spaced out along the front like sentries standing guard.

On both sides of the building, long fields stretched out, eventually meeting thick copses of trees that bookended the property. The landscaping was unkempt and needed some attention, but the property was breathtaking, feeling like an abandoned college campus in London.

"What the hell *was* this place?" Abby stood in the muddy gravel parking lot.

"I think some sort of school or something, but I'm not really sure. Uncle Jack would know." Hayden put his hands in his pockets and scanned the property. "Pretty amazing though, huh? This is going to be one hell of a cool place to live when he's done."

Abby reached into her car to grab her bottle of water, and something at the periphery of her vision caught her attention. A man was standing at the edge of the main drive into the property. His hair was gray and he wore a brown jacket and faded blue jeans. He stood still, staring at the building, his hands in his jacket pockets. Hayden caught Abby's gaze and turned to look at the old man. As they watched, the man freed his hands from his pockets and fell to his knees in the patch of grass.

"Sir?" Hayden started walking toward him, and Abby followed. "Hey, buddy, you all right?"

His gray hair was cut short and neatly combed. He shook his head at Hayden dismissively and Hayden started walking toward him faster. "Sir?"

The man pushed off the ground and rose from his knees, stuffed his hands back into his jacket, and started walking away quickly, bordering on a jog.

"The hell was that all about?" Hayden stopped and watched him go.

The man glanced back several times as he rounded the curve in the road and then walked behind a row of trimmed boxwood bushes, out of sight.

Hayden sighed and shrugged. "There's a rescue mission about a mile or so down the road. They do what they can to help, but there's lots of veterans there. Maybe he was having a flashback or something."

They walked back to the building entrance and Hayden flipped the lid of a metal box on the outside of the building. He tapped a key code into the LCD screen and there was a faint metallic clicking sound before he grabbed the door handle and pulled it open.

"It's not much to look at when we first go inside, but don't judge too quickly."

A weak glow lit the foyer, but other than that, the place was dim and void of outside light. Hayden flicked a switch on the wall to his left and the low hum of overhead lighting began.

The ceiling overhead soared several stories, and Abby's gaze followed it down to the marble floor and the other side of the entrance hall. A wide staircase of ornate woodwork led upstairs to a landing and then turned on itself, leading higher. To the right of the space, she saw the familiar frame of an elevator set into a wall of ornate wainscoting.

"Not that you have a reason to use it, but I wouldn't trust that elevator. Probably hasn't worked in decades."

"Noted." She turned to Hayden. "What's upstairs?"

"Going to be more units eventually, but I'm guessing more classrooms. I haven't explored the whole place." Hayden put a hand to the small of Abby's back and pointed to a hallway to their right. "Down this way."

The place smelled of plaster dust and paint, and the air felt overly dry and charged with static. Abby followed Hayden down the long hallway until he stopped, turned, and smiled at her.

"Here we are." He twisted the door handle and pushed it open to reveal the interior.

It's not an option to turn this offer down, Abby thought. *Not an apartment like this.*

Abby stepped into the living room she had seen in the photos and it was even more amazing in person. Tall windows let in sunlight that filled the place with a warm, inviting glow. An exposed brick wall gave the space a retro-feel, but the contrasting modern design of the kitchen and interior was the perfect balance. A beautiful brick fireplace had a thick timber mantelpiece that looked ancient.

"Does the fireplace work?"

"It's gas, so I have no idea why there's fireplace pokers, but yeah, it's hooked up."

Abby tried to keep herself from smiling, thinking about how amazing it would be to relax and read by a fireplace at night.

Hayden stood and watched her as Abby walked through the living room, trailing a hand over the sofa and loveseat. She paused, a smile growing on her face, and looked at the art and photography hanging on the walls, tasteful black and white shots, along with some modern art prints.

Moving ahead, Abby walked in to the kitchen—the space was modern and elegant—the backsplash made of thin tiles in shades of gray and black. Stainless steel appliances completed the high-end appearance.

She cleared her throat and nodded approval. "It's fully furnished…"

"Yeah, like I said, it's the model unit. Fully furnished, throughout. Jack hired some… stager or something to deck the place out, make it look as real as possible." He turned and nodded toward a flat-screen TV on a weathered Asian credenza. "Only thing that's not working is the cable, but like I said, the internet's hooked up, so you could probably stream stuff."

Abby leaned against the island, staring at him.

"Well?" Hayden put his arms out to his sides. "You're killin' me with the suspense here, Abs. What do you think?"

Butterflies filled her stomach, but Abby already knew her answer. A laugh escaped her, and she ran around the island and gave Hayden a hug, and that was answer enough.

The next few hours were spent bringing Abby's things from her car to the apartment and putting them in the right rooms to unpack later.

Marilyn was set up in the corner of the living room, close to the tall, oversized windows, her featureless face staring at the rolling hillsides around the building.

Hayden looked around the open space of the living room. "There's a place on the edge of Rhinesville, a second-hand shop, but around here second-hand is pretty damned good. If there's anything else you need or want, we can check it out."

"Sounds awesome." Abby walked from the kitchen and kissed him on the cheek. "But not today. I'm wiped out."

"Yeah, same, plus, I have to finish an essay on God's foreknowledge and the free will of mankind."

"Exciting stuff."

"That's me, all right." He reached for his car keys from the kitchen counter. "So, you're good?"

"I'm great, Hayseed. This place... I seriously can't thank you enough. It's amazing." She hugged him tightly. "Once I get set up, I'll cook dinner for you. *Many* dinners, I promise."

"Looking forward to it." He started toward the door, paused, and turned back. "Oh shit. I need to set up your key code. Come with me a sec."

Abby padded barefoot down the hallway from her apartment. The walls were new drywall with unsanded white patches of plaster over the screws. Sheets of canvas drop cloth lay here and there along the edges of the wall and a large bucket of spackling and some hand tools sat in the doorway to an unfinished apartment. Every ten feet, a rough-cut hole in the ceiling housed a recessed lighting canister.

At the end of the hall, Hayden opened a door and stepped into a small room with a basic desk and a desktop computer. He worked the mouse to wake the system from sleep. "Okay, it's a keyless entry system to the building, so you have to pick a four-digit code.

"Hmm... let's do 1999."

Hayden turned his head slowly to look at Abby as she began humming the song by Prince. He delivered the perfect expression of sarcastic disbelief at her code choice.

Abby laughed and smacked his shoulder. "Oh, that's *riiiight*. You were never into his purple majesty, were you? I believe you used to make fun of me for it."

"I was busy worshipping Tommy Lee and Mötley Crüe."

"Devil music." Abby snickered. "Explains a lot."

"Whatever!" Hayden laughed and finished the set up. "Okay, go outside and make sure it works."

Abby walked from the foyer and let the heavy main door close behind her. She tugged on the handle and it didn't move, so she turned to the keypad and screen to the left of the doorframe, typed in 1999. A soft *click* sounded and she pulled the door handle again, easily opening it into the foyer. She walked inside, gave a curtsey in front of Hayden, and smiled at him.

"Now you, me, and my uncle Jack have key codes. That's it."

"That's it?"

Hayden nodded. "Not even the construction crew have working codes anymore, now that work is on hold. I think Jack was afraid they would get pissed off and come back to steal things." He stepped back and crossed his arms. "You gonna be okay?"

"Yeah, I promise. I'll get all settled in by tomorrow, but I'm good."

Hayden hugged her again, tighter this time, and stepped outside. He caught the door just before it closed and paused. "Abs? I'm really glad you're here."

She smiled at him. "Me, too, Hayseed."

The hallway back to her apartment was long, stretching about half a football field, and in her head, Abby made a mental note to buy a flashlight. Overhead lights were spaced out, and each of them only gave off a soft glow. Straight line or not, walking this at night would be a challenge until the workers finished the ceiling light fixtures. Entrances to unfinished apartments were staggered left and right about every twenty feet, and the building was quiet.

Abby stepped inside her apartment, closed the door, and leaned against it.

Two days ago, I had a couch with cigarette burns on it and a bedroom that mostly smelled of cooked meth. And now...

Abby paused and took in her surroundings. *How is this my apartment?*

This place feels more like home than the place in Philly ever did. Like I'm supposed to be here.

Chapter Seven

E VENING CAME QUICKLY as Abby arranged things in the apartment. Her stomach begged for attention until she finally conceded and grabbed her car keys to go in search of food. It was a ten-mile drive, but an easy one, to the grocery store in town. Abby walked the aisles, getting familiar with the layout. The store was upscale with a great selection of produce and cheeses. An organic foods area appeared fresh and well stocked. There was a man behind a counter in the deli area making sushi, and the smell of baked goods made Abby's stomach growl.

The wine aisle was close to overwhelming. Even in the state-run alcohol stores in Pennsylvania, it was rare to find *this* kind of wine selection. She grabbed a bottle of Australian red wine called Tommy Ruff because it had a cool label design, and some Kung Pao chicken from the deli area.

The dinner and alcohol selected, Abby's logic kicked in long enough to remind her she needed some essentials. Paper towels.

Toilet paper. Utensils. She shook her head as she tossed a box of assorted plastic utensils in her cart and continued down the aisles. Everyday normal things she had back in Philadelphia, but had chosen to leave behind. It was enough for now. She'd make a *real* trip for supplies in a day or so and truly get settled in.

On the drive back, Abby was close to salivating at the steamy smell of Chinese food in her car. Abby parked in front of the building and stepped free of her car. Before she opened the door to the back seat, to grab her bags, she felt a chill run over her skin—that rush of breeze.

Abby stepped back from her Honda and felt the iciness curl around the back of her neck like a frozen hand. She turned away from the door to her car, still open, and noticed a figure standing at the edge of the property.

It was the same old man from earlier. He was standing at the edge of the lane, his hands in his pockets, staring at the building.

"Sir?" she called out.

Christ, what if the old geezer's having a stroke or something?

Abby closed the rear door of her car without picking up the grocery bags, and started walking toward him. He was wearing the same clothes from earlier—brown jacket and jeans, and was so focused on the building he didn't even look her way.

"Mister, are you okay?" Abby had closed the distance to a car length away.

He blinked with a jolt, and turned toward her with his milky blue eyes. His raspy voice trembled as he spoke. "What have you done?"

Abby stopped, noticing his eyes had the heavy film of cataracts and were rimmed red, as if he might have been crying. "I'm not sure what… sir, are you okay? Do you need me to call someone?"

"I knew something was happening. All these years it's been quiet, and now…" He glanced toward the building and his half-blind gaze snapped back toward Abby, and he scowled.

He pulled his hands from his pockets and flexed them open and closed into white-knuckled fists. "They get stuck to you, you see? They get *attached* like…like some kind of…" He was breathing heavy, almost panting. White flecks of foam gathered at the corners of his thin-lipped mouth. "What have you…"

Abby took a step back and instinctively glanced at the ground for something she could use as a weapon. Nothing but pebbles. No sticks. She slid her hand into her jeans pocket and felt her phone, and her keys. Abby eased them free and positioned multiple keys so they extended between her index, second, and third finger.

"Look, mister, I don't—"

"Whaaat have youuu DONNNNNNNNE?" His arms shot out stiff to his sides and his clenched hands trembled as he screamed. Flecks of spittle flew from his mouth and his eyes bulged. Tears spilled over his pale cheeks.

Abby planted her feet and gripped the keys, ready to throw a punch if she needed to. Her heart was thudding in her chest but she spoke in a calm steady voice. "Mister—"

He shook, his balled fists straight down at his sides, and then he turned away and ran, crossed the street from the drive and headed toward a rusted green Nova. Abby watched him yank the door open and fumble at the steering wheel for a moment. She dug in her pocket for her phone. The man's car sputtered to life and he made a quick u-turn as he floored the car. Abby lifted her phone and snapped a photo as he drove away.

"What in the *hell* is wrong with you?" She yelled and let out a long breath as she watched his taillights vanish around the curve back toward town.

Abby had to admit, she didn't know the town that well, but she didn't expect something like this to happen here. In Philly, something crazy happened weekly, if not daily. Homeless people walked around mumbling to themselves—some of them literally wearing tinfoil hats. Junkies in alleyways screamed at nightmares in their mind. That was life in the city, and she was used to it, but this old man looked *normal*. He wasn't disheveled or wearing dirty clothes; didn't have the cornered animal eyes of someone deep in the throes of mental anguish or the razor cheekbones of a sweat-slick junkie. He looked like a retired accountant. If Abby had passed him in the grocery store, she might have thought he was there buying some artisan bread to have with his wife for dinner.

Abby gathered her grocery bags and then punched her key code at the entrance to get inside. She waited in the foyer until the door closed with a heavy *thunk*, and then she walked down the long hallway to her apartment. The other units, under renovation, were all absent of doors, leaving a row of vacant holes on either side of the hall. Abby's shoes scuffed in the plaster grit beneath her feet.

The smell of the Chinese food made her stomach growl and she hustled the few remaining feet to her apartment. Once she was inside, it didn't take her long to dig into the chicken. She searched the kitchen for a corkscrew and grumbled to herself for not thinking of buying one earlier. The last drawer Abby rummaged through a wide variety of brand-new cooking utensils along with a corkscrew still attached to the cardboard product tag. *"Hellll yes!"*

Abby removed the cork from the bottle of wine, opened an upper kitchen cabinet, and paused, staring at the row of coffee mugs and assorted glasses. "Really did think of everything," she whispered out loud to herself. She took a wine glass, filled it halfway, and sipped. "Not bad, you crazy Aussies. Not bad at all."

She brought it with her to the living room couch, sat down and sighed with satisfaction. It would take her a while to replace some things she'd left behind in Philadelphia, but she was expecting payment soon on some freelance jobs.

This place is amazing.

Her phone buzzed and she checked the screen, saw it was her mother calling. Abby sighed and let it go to voicemail as she opened the cartons of Chinese food.

She pressed the speakerphone icon and played her mother's voicemail.

"Abby? This is your mother. I thought you would… Nick called and asked where you were. I didn't tell him, *couldn't* tell him even if I wanted to, because I don't *know* where you are. I'm only your mother. It's not a big deal or anything."

The agitated tone and ever-present guilt in her voice came through loud and clear. Abby released another sigh and stopped the voicemail from continuing. "I'll call you tomorrow, Mom."

Abby forked chicken into her mouth, closed her eyes and savored the flavor. Tomorrow she had to write four blogs and two articles for clients, but that shouldn't take long. Tonight, she felt as if she could fall into a coma of sleep.

The bedroom was an elegant set up with an unbelievably comfortable memory foam mattress. Matching nightstands and lamps, along with a very modern clothes dresser, made it feel like a luxury hotel room. As beautiful as it was, Abby felt so relaxed and comfortable on the couch, she didn't want to move.

Her phone buzzed and Abby glanced at the notification of a text message.

NICK: You really, realllllly need to tell me where you are.

Shit. It was a matter of time, I guess.

She took another swallow of red wine and sat the glass down beside her on the carpet.

Let's see. Tequila makes me mean. Vodka makes me... mean and then sleepy. Gin... nope. I fuckin' hate gin, it's like drinking Christmas trees. Annnd wine makes me get emotional and want to cry.

Abby picked her phone up and hit the message notification from Nick. She shut her eyes and reached blindly for the glass of wine, bringing it high and taking a double swallow before she set it back down. Abby hit the info button on the text message and blocked Nick's number.

The phone buzzed in her hands with another text message notification.

HAYDEN: Doing okay?

She started to text a reply but called him instead.

"Hey there, girly."

"Hey yourself. I'm doing okay, wiped out, but okay. Asshole just texted me."

"That's unfortunate."

"I blocked him."

Hayden sighed heavily. "Abs, you know it's for the best. I mean, y' know, ouch and all, but not really. You had to get away from him."

"I know." She chewed her lip, and reached for the bottle of wine again. "Oh, hey, that creepy guy showed up again."

She heard Hayden taking a drink and pictured him out on his deck. "The crazy ol' guy from earlier?"

"Yeah, hang on a sec." Abby texted him the photo she had taken, and then continued talking. "I just sent you a shot I took before he drove away."

There was a pause on the other end of the call. "That's strange to say the least. Let me know if he shows up again, okay? Like I said, he's probably harmless, but no reason to keep putting up with that."

"I will."

Hayden hesitated on the call for a moment. "You sure you're okay? I can come over if you want or... you can come over here."

"I'm good, Hayseed. I'm gonna crash soon anyway. Lots to do tomorrow."

"Okay, Abs. Get some rest."

"You, too."

After she ended the call, part of Abby itched to unblock Nick to see what kind of bullshit he was going to say. Her guess was a flood of apologies and professing how much he loved her, and saying he would get clean. Abby gritted her teeth and tossed her phone away from her to the carpet. She pulled down a soft throw blanket from the back of the couch and let herself sink into the cushions. The apartment was cozy, and quiet, and it wasn't long before Abby drifted off to sleep.

Sometime around three in the morning, Abby opened her eyes. Marilyn was still on the far side of the room, close to the window, but her position had changed. Her cracked face was angled at Abby.

Abby stared at the mannequin, blinked sleepily, and turned over to go back to sleep. By morning she had forgotten all about it, and Marilyn was back to staring out at the rolling hillside again.

Chapter Eight

ABBY HAD WOKEN early, enjoying the flowing rays of sunlight coming into the living room, but after shuffling to her kitchen counter and flipping the lid off the coffee maker, Abby realized she had never bought coffee grounds. "Shit."

Ten minutes later, she pulled up to the Gas 'n Go convenience store at the edge of town. A few men dressed like construction workers were inside, grabbing breakfast sandwiches and half gallons of tea. Abby made a beeline for the stainless-steel urns of coffee and filled a tall foam cup with steaming black liquid, hot enough that she had to put two cardboard wraps on the outside of the cup.

The teenage boy at the counter gave her an odd expression as he rang the coffee up and told her a price, but the only thing he said was for her to have a nice day. Abby lifted the coffee and gave him a nod and a tired, half smile as she left.

Abby eased her car into the main drive of the apartment building with some caution, scanning for any sign of the old man again, but there was no sign of Mr. Creepy. She grabbed the coffee, noticing it still had hot steam spilling from the small opening in the plastic lid.

There were emails waiting for her, she knew it. Work to be done. Money to be made.

Only now, there isn't anyone to steal it from me for drugs.

She typed in her code at the keypad and pulled the door open.

Get some caffeine in my system, and I'll crank out some work and Hayden and I will hang out later. I owe him a thank you dinner anyway. Maybe he can come over and show me the pool.

Abby walked the dark hallway as the foyer door shut behind her with a metallic click and a high-pitched noise.

No, that wasn't the door.

Abby stopped moving and closed her eyes, cocking her head to listen in the darkness.

Mewwww.

Her eyes snapped open and she strained to see the length of the dimly lit hall but there was nothing out of place except for the odd remnants from the workers. Abby took a few steps and paused again. "Here, kitty, kitty. *Sssspssspssspsss.*"

Mewww.

Abby spun around and stared into the black hole of one of the unfinished apartments. She strained her eyes to see any movement but couldn't detect any motion at all. Abby took a step into the room and fished her phone from her pocket. "Kitty? *Sssspssspssspss.*" The flashlight from her phone put a small spotlight on the interior and Abby saw painters drop cloths crumpled up beside cans and empty trays. The smell of plaster dust and paint lingered but there was something else—an underlying odor of something gone bad. Abby wrinkled her nose and looked around the room.

An aluminum ladder stood against the far wall, casting shadows as Abby moved the light around to see. The kitchen area didn't even have cabinets hung yet—only a counter top, sink, and an exposed brick wall.

"Pssspssspssspsss."

A soft shuffling noise came from a paint spattered cardboard box resting next to a pile of drop cloth and Abby stepped closer, smiling. "Don't be scared, kitty." She squatted down and eased open the lid to shine her flashlight inside.

The smell of decaying meat poured from the open box and hit Abby squarely in the face. She grimaced but the light of her phone cast the box's contents into view—a half-eaten sandwich, blue-green with mold and writhing with maggots. Abby yelped and jerked away from the box. She took a step away, shook her head, and willed herself not to gag.

Abby stepped back into the hallway, scanning her flashlight around the room, but still didn't see any sign of a kitten.

Poor thing's got to be starving and scared to death.

She thumbed her flashlight off and turned in the direction of her apartment.

The black silhouette towered above her, inches away. Abby peered into the darkness and screamed.

Chapter Nine

J UST *YOU, ME* and *Uncle Jack* have key codes, *that's* what you told me, Hayseed!"

"Abs, I swear—"

"I was trying to rescue a stray kitten and almost shit my pants because I ran into the *raccoon* exterminator!"

Hayden was laughing so hard he was breathless on the other end of the call.

"Is raccoon exterminator even a real thing? There's a need for that? It sounds like an army of wild raccoons are invading the country or some shit." Abby held the lidless foam cup of coffee in front of her and frowned at the empty feeling. She had dropped and spilled the entire thing in the hallway. "So is that it? You, me, your uncle, and the *raccoon* guy, or will there be anyone else showing up for a surprise visit? Squirrel wranglers maybe?"

"That's it, I swear." Hayden stuttered through laughter, breathing deeply to collect himself. "I'm sorry, Abs. I didn't realize Jack had lined a guy up to check in like that. Apparently, he'll be back in two weeks. I'll make it up to you, I promise."

Abby could actually *hear* him smiling as he spoke. She tilted the foam cup and a thin trickle of cold coffee ran into her mouth. "I would kill for some coffee right now."

"I'd bring you an entire coffee pot if I could, but I have to go to a class about man's search for meaning or some shit."

"Go find your meaning of life or something." Abby tossed the empty cup into the kitchen trash can. "Do you have to give yourself to God or anything later tonight?"

"Hadn't planned on it, but it's the first of the month and new pay-per-view porn starts today, *soooo…*"

"Pervert."

"Look, I'm made in God's image, but I gotta run. I'll see you later."

Abby put her phone on the kitchen counter and smiled.

It felt good to be around Hayden again. More *than good.*

She glanced at her closed laptop and though the smile was still on her face, she had a sudden flash where she felt like throwing a full-blown tantrum because she had no coffee. Instead, she let out a long breath, sat on the couch, and flipped the laptop open.

The sounds of Social Distortion filled her living room as Abby cranked the music as loud as it could go. She wrote a blog about replacement hip joints for her medical supply client, and then switched gears to post on social media for her credit union client. All the while, Abby sang along with the gravelly voice of Mike Ness.

Lack of caffeine or not, Abby felt the words flowing in a rhythm. It had been a while since she had felt like this. Being around Nick was like having some sort of energy vampire sucking the life out of you.

By the time noon arrived, Abby had gotten her projects done and was drafting emails to marketing directors, prospecting for new work. Three more clients and she would be living large. She grinned at the thought and belted out a chorus with the music.

A high-pitched dinging kept beat to the music and Abby bobbed her head to the melody for a few seconds before she realized it wasn't part of the song. She tapped the pause button on her laptop and the music stopped.

The sound did not.

Ding-ding-ding-ding-ding-ding.

The noise was sharp and pristine, not like a fire alarm, but richer and fuller, and seemed to come from everywhere and nowhere as it echoed off the apartment walls. Abby moved her computer from her lap to the coffee table and looked around the room.

Ding-ding-ding-ding-ding.

As she stepped toward her kitchen, the sound swelled against her eardrums, growing stronger. It sounded like wedding receptions she had been too, where the crowd taps their glasses in unison throughout the evening to make the bride and groom kiss.

Ding-ding-ding-ding.

Abby reached above the sink with both hands and swung open the cabinet doors. Two rows of wine glasses rested on the shelf liner beside two rows of coffee mugs.

Ding-ding-ding.

Abby flinched at the sound, stepped backward, and stared at the glasses.

The apartment was dead quiet. It felt like the end of an exhale—nothing but a silent, airless void. Abby stared at the glasses a moment longer, slowly closed the cabinets again, and looked around the living room.

"I need coffee. Yeah, I definitely think I… need… coffee." She grabbed her phone from the couch and swiped her keys and wallet from the coffee table. "I'm caffeine deficient, that's all." Abby slipped into her sandals, took one last look at the cabinets, and left.

For the second time in the day, Abby pulled into parking lot of the Gas 'n Go. Inside, she once again poured herself a foam cup of coffee from the tall silver urn. She fitted a plastic lid onto the cup and took it to the counter. The teenage boy studied the coffee and then Abby's face.

"Did you…" His expression had changed into a grimace. "Did you actually *drink* the coffee you bought this morning?"

"Yeah, I… well, *actually*, no, I spilled it when I…" She paused and shook her head. "Know what? Doesn't really matter, but the answer is no, I never got to drink it." Abby pulled some cash from her pocket.

The boy nodded and leaned closer in a conspiratorial way. His voice lowered. "*No one* drinks the coffee here. It tastes like Bigfoot's ass and I'm probably saving your life by telling you this." He took the cup from the counter and dropped it into a trash can. "Wouldn't do this for everybody, I'm just saying."

"Well thanks, I appreciate it." Abby couldn't help but smile at the boy. JUSTIN was written in black marker on his plastic nametag. "I'm Abby, by the way." She stuck her hand out toward him and he took it to shake, automatically.

"Oh. I'm Jus—"

"Justin, yeah." Abby smiled and nodded toward his nametag.

"Oh, the tag, yeah. You're uh… you're living up at the new lofts, right?"

Abby crossed her arms. "How—"

"Don't get creeped out or anything, it's a small town. Everyone knows everything." He pulled a Slim Jim from a cardboard counter display and peeled the top apart. "Plus, with *that* place, I mean…" Justin shrugged.

"What do you mean, *that* place?"

Justin took a bite of the stick of meat and looked at Abby with a blank face. "You don't…" His expression shifted to one of amusement. "Look, go down Main Street a half block to the Bump and Grind coffee house. It's a cool place to hang and the coffee is awesome. Go ask for Stacy, she's my sister. Ask her about the girl from high school and the Ouija board. She'll know."

"Ouija board?" Abby smirked. "What're we, eight years old at summer camp?"

Justin waved his hand. "Yeah, yeah. Just go talk to Stacy. I was still eating glue and finger painting in school when it all went down, so I'll screw it up if I try to tell you."

Abby pulled her phone from her pocket. No word from Hayden yet, so he was probably still in the middle of jotting down notes from the mouth of God or something.

"Okay. I'll go talk to your sister." Abby pointed at the boy and smiled. "But the coffee better be *damned* good or else I'm coming back."

Chapter Ten

B UMP AND GRIND was, true to the boy's word, a cool place to hang out. Abby thought she might bring her laptop to work here if she needed a break from the apartment. Exposed brick walls surrounded several weathered leather sofas and chairs with tables in front of them. The place smelled heavenly, and when Abby looked around, she saw a wide glass window that showed the warehouse portion of the building. A massive coffee bean roaster stood like a monolith as workers bagged beans and piled them onto wooden palettes. An older man sat in one corner of the room, a folded newspaper held in his grasp.

"You must be Abby." A pretty brunette girl a few years older than the kid at the Gas 'n Go, stood at the counter.

"And you must be Stacy. Word spreads fast, huh?"

"My dork brother texted me that you might show up." She used a hand towel to wipe the counter off. "What can I get you?"

Abby ordered a caramel macchiato and pulled cash from her pocket, waiting as Stacy worked her way around the counter. She laid a ten-dollar bill on the counter and nodded to a tip jar beside the register. "Just put the change in the jar."

"Thank you!" Stacy slid the macchiato onto the counter. "I hope you like it."

Abby opened a straw, speared it through the whipped cream topping. She closed her eyes as she took a sip, savoring the smooth caramel and well-roasted coffee.

"Oh yeah. I can't tell you how much I needed this." Abby had been dodging a headache all morning and figured it was from missing her morning dose of caffeine. She relished another sip of the drink.

Stacy smiled and slid a plate with a croissant on it toward Abby. "Justin told me to hook you up with something tasty."

"Sweet kid."

"He's a dork." Stacy laughed. "A *sweet* one at times, but still a dork." She glanced over at the older man in the corner and lowered her voice. "So... did Justin explain why he sent you my way?"

"Besides his *very* colorful description of how bad the coffee is at the Gas 'n Go, he told me to ask you about a girl and a Ouija board." Abby took a bite of the croissant. It was flaky and buttery and tasted mildly sweet. She nodded at Stacy. "Is he full of shit?"

"Usually, but not about this." Stacy wiped the counter with a hand towel and then slung the cloth over her shoulder. "Over the summer, before junior year of high school, there was a big blowout party before heading into senior year. Parents out of town and someone's older brother got kegs of beer and liquor and shit. People showed up that weren't even invited, you know the kind of thing. The whole party was just… epic."

Stacy leaned against the counter, almost whispering. "So, the drunker everyone got, the crazier they became. This girl, Laurie, found a Ouija board in a closet with a bunch of other board games and shit."

"Let me guess, somebody got possessed or something?" Abby smirked and drank from the coffee again.

"Not… *exactly*. Laurie and a few others stumbled out of the party and walked to Harper's Grove." She tilted her head at Abby. "They broke inside and started messing around with the Ouija board."

"Where's Harper's Grove?"

"You can't be serious." Stacy straightened and crossed her arms. She spoke slowly, her tone communicating her disbelief. "The lofts… where *you* live."

"So?" Abby shrugged. "It used to be some old school or something. So what? Every town has something like that." She shoved the last of the croissant into her mouth.

"Not a school. A hospital. And not like *this*, they don't. Harper's Grove was—"

"Food service delivery is arriving soon. Maybe you should focus on making sure there's room to stock the shipment, eh, Stacy?" The stern voice came from the older man sitting in the corner of the room. The left side of his newspaper was drooping down and he peered at Stacy a moment longer, then flipped his paper back in place.

"Yes, sir."

Stacy positioned herself so that Abby was blocking her line of sight from the man, and silently mouthed the words "That's my boss." She grabbed a photocopied menu from beneath the counter, scribbled something at the top, and then folded it and handed it to Abby. Her normal speaking voice returned, full of sunshine and loud enough so her boss could hear. "Thank you, Miss. Have a great afternoon."

"You, too." Abby smiled at her. "I'll be seeing you, Stacy."

Outside, Abby set her coffee down on one of the wrought iron café tables, unfolded the menu Stacy had given her, and read the scrawled handwriting at the top:

Search for this video! Ghost scratches girl after Ouija board goes wrong at Harper's Grove.

Abby groaned but folded the paper and shoved it in her pocket. She checked her phone—still nothing from Hayden—and ran through her mental rolodex on what kind of dinner she could make for him later, arriving at shrimp fajitas. The very idea conjured up the scent of it cooking and Abby's mouth watered.

She hefted her cup and noted it was almost empty. For a moment, Abby considered going back in for another, but she took a sip, savoring the flavor, and decided against it. She'd stop at the grocery store on the way back and grab some supplies, including coffee.

It was time to buy some *real* supplies, get settled into the new place, and make it *really* feel like home.

Chapter Eleven

"THIS SANGRIA IS freakin' amazing." Hayden took a sip from his glass and shook his head. He leaned back into the plush cushions of the couch.

"Mom's recipe."

"Of course, it is." Hayden grinned. "How is Mom anyway?"

"*Ohhhh,* she's... about the same. Full of piss and vinegar and still capable of instilling the kind of passive aggressive guilt only she can put on someone."

Abby smiled at him from the kitchen island. She scooped two handfuls of sliced onions from the cutting board and put them in a skillet on the stove, where they began sizzling. She turned to the island again and repeated the process with thin strips of red and green peppers. After adding a small bowl of sliced jalapeños to the mix, she gave it a stir with a wooden spatula and added in a pile of peeled shrimp.

"That smells absolutely amazing, Abs. Mom's recipe too?"

"Not this one, Hayseed. I had an amazing neighbor in Philly that taught me. Carlita. Single mom with two kids that had her shit together more than most married people do. She's one I'll truly miss." Abby gave the contents of the skillet a stir, and then squeezed a wedge of lime onto the vegetables. "And I have a bone to pick with you, Mister."

Hayden took another drink from his glass. "Oh shit. What'd I do now?"

"You told me this used to be an old school."

Hayden shook his head. "And?"

Reaching for her own glass of sangria from the island, Abby raised it and pointed at him. "*Not* an old school. An old hospital called Harper's Grove." She glanced at the simmering skillets and then turned back to Hayden. "It's where they used to put mentally handicapped children, or kids with deformities."

Hayden cocked his head and gave her an expression of disbelief. "You're bullshitting me."

"Apparently not, according to the locals. One of them was even kind enough to give me a link to a video of a Ouija board session that got out of hand. Supposedly, some girl ended up getting attacked by an… *unseen entity* or something." Abby pursed her lips and raised her eyebrows, waiting for Hayden's response.

"Ouija board? What're we, at summer camp?"

Abby smiled at hearing him react the same way she had.

Hayden put his glass down, patted his pants pockets, and leaned forward on the couch. "Shit, that reminds me, I have to go."

"Wait, what?" Abby glanced at the frying skillet. "Why?"

"I have an exorcism scheduled at seven o'clock with Father Karras and—"

"Yeah, okay, okay, smartass." Abby pulled two plates from a cabinet and set them down on the kitchen counter. "But this building *wasn't* an old school."

"Maybe not, but that's what I was told. Besides, are you really freaked out by something the locals brewed up to scare teenagers?" Hayden stood from the couch.

Turning the stove dials to OFF, Abby began plating the fajitas. "I'm freaked out by the rats in Philadelphia. But this…" She looked out over the apartment, once again amazed at how beautiful the place actually was. "No, not really. I'm sure the video looks like some low-budget horror flick anyway."

"You didn't watch it?"

Abby turned back. "No thanks. I have a certain quota for hoax videos and I get that quota filled by Bigfoot sighting footage."

"You believe in Bigfoot?"

"Definitely. Easter Bunny, too."

Hayden snickered. "Glad to hear you have my same taste in believing the… unbelievable, because…" He stuffed a hand into his jeans pocket and pulled out a slip of paper and grinned like a child full of mischief. "I have a little adventure for us after dinner. One based in real life creepy, if you're up for it, that is."

"What's that?" Abby walked with two steaming plates and set them onto the dining room table.

"The address of the crazy guy." Hayden's smile grew into a grin.

"The one that showed—"

"That one."

Abby's mouth fell open in surprise. "Shut up! Really?"

"Really."

Popping the microwave door open, Abby pulled free a basket of flour tortillas. "I'm truly impressed by whoever's skills you employed to—"

"What makes you think I didn't find it?"

Abby stared at him as she walked the tortillas and a bowl of shredded cheese to the table.

"Okay, okay, I didn't do it, but still, you could give me the benefit of the doubt and all—"

Abby stepped closer and crossed her arms, though she smiled at him. "What'd it cost you?"

Hayden sighed and gave a small shrug. "A couple o' joints."

"That's what I thought." Abby slapped his shoulder. "C'mon. Let's eat."

On his first bite of fajita, Hayden's eyebrows raised and he gave Abby a glance.

"What? You don't like them?"

Shaking his head, Hayden wiped his mouth with a napkin. "No, no. They're amazing, just didn't expect you to like spicy so much."

Abby leaned back from her plate. "Oh, girls can't like hot and spicy—"

"No, *nooooo*. That's not what I said, so calm your girl parts a second." Hayden took a swallow of wine. "It's just that it seems to *me*, that hot peppers have more male fans than women."

Abby broke into a smile. "Just bustin' your balls, Hayseed."

"You do it well."

"I'm aware."

"Shouldn't shock me that you like hot peppers, hell spawn that you are." Hayden took another bite from the stuffed tortilla. "By the way, I blessed your shower earlier. It's holy water now, so good luck not bursting into flames an' shit later."

Abby smiled at him as she chewed a mouthful of shrimp and sautéed vegetables. It felt good to be in her own place like this, cooking a meal instead of eating take out. She sighed and swallowed and rested her elbows on the table. "So, is there a plan or anything to this adventure? Or are we just showing up on the front doorstep like we're taking donations? We setting brown bags of dog poo on fire or anything?"

Shaking his head, Hayden cleared his throat and drank more sangria. "*Naaaah,* that's so two decades ago. Besides, it's too close. Get caught as a kid and the worst you might get is an ass-beating. Get caught as an adult and it's all sorts of stupid shit they charge you with."

"Personally familiar with this, are you?"

Hayden waved her question away and cleared his throat again. "I brought a drone with me in the car."

Abby paused with her glass of wine in mid-air. She nodded at him. "Okay, first, that's awesome. But second, why do you have a drone in the first place?"

"I used to have a neighbor who was into nude sunbathing."

"Wouldn't binoculars be easier?"

"Binoculars don't come with high-def video." Hayden shrugged, a smirk on his face, and finished the last bite of his fajita. "Besides, she knew what was going on. Even waved to the drone camera a couple times. Did this thing with suntan oil once—"

"Stop talking. Just...stop talking." Abby closed her eyes and shook her head, though a soft smile rested on her face. "Were you this perverted in high school?"

"*Ummm, duh.* Yeah." Hayden sipped from his glass and gave her a nod. "And so were you."

"No way."

Hayden's expression changed to mock surprise. "Do you remember spray-painting a penis on the Marlboro Man billboard out on Route—"

"That was not my idea!" Abby spoke through laughter.

"It was your artistry. You also gave a guy blue-balls, because he stood you up on a date *two years* before that."

Abby's eyes narrowed. "Bart Wal—"

"Walder, yes. Bart Walder." Hayden raised his glass in a toast and drank.

"How do you...no, *why* do you remember shit like this?"

"Because he was talking shit about it in the locker room the day after and..." Hayden let his words fade and he cleared his throat.

"You're the one who punched him?" Abby leaned forward, her gaze locked on him. "That's when you got suspended in eleventh grade and you never told me why."

Hayden let out a slow exhale, not meeting her eyes.

"You were standing up for me?" Abby noted the blush in Hayden's face and grinned. She clutched her hands together in front of her heart. "My hero."

"Yeah, yeah, whatever." Hayden gave a sarcastic nod and changed the subject. "So back to this crazy old guy."

"I have to say, he kinda freaked me out. The drone's a good idea, but what're we going to do, spy on him through his windows?"

Hayden wiped his mouth again and pushed the napkin aside. "I figure we'll do a little recon with the drone first, and maybe I'll knock on the door and make sure he's okay, y' know? Call it a wellness check."

"*Iiii* might stay in the car while you do that."

"Fine by me."

Abby drank the last of her sangria and gently rested her glass on the table, thinking about what Hayden had said. The old man was probably suffering from PTSD or something. Flashbacks from Vietnam.

Then why the hell was he here, looking scared to death at the building?

She rose from her chair and brought the plates to the counter, rinsing them in the sink. The pleasant, sweet smell of sautéed vegetables still hung in the air.

"Do you…" Hayden turned his chair toward Abby and took a sip from his glass. "Do you remember that party at Robbie Noble's house? One where his parents were away in… Cabo or some shit?"

"The pool party?"

"That's the one. We all ended up in the basement and Eddie Steele puked on their new pool table."

Abby made a face and leaned against the kitchen island. "Blackberry brandy. Yeah, I remember it, alright."

Hayden stared at his glass with a smile on his face. "They all wanted to play seven minutes in heaven and—"

"Me and Preston got blindfolded and picked to go in the closet first." Abby shook her head and glanced at the ceiling. "That guy was a total jerk but *damn* he could kiss when—"

"Yeah, about that. You dated Preston for, what, two whole days afterward?"

"Seriously, how the *hell* do you remember that?" Abby picked up her sangria and laughed as she pointed at him. "Wait... how do you even *know* that? I didn't even tell anyone!"

Hayden shrugged, grinning. "It was easy to know who you were dating. I just looked for the douchebags and—"

"Easy to be judgmental when you're still a virgin."

"*Owwwww.*" Hayden put a hand over his heart. "Right out of the gate, gotta go for the *you're-a-virgin* card." He winced in mock pain. "I mean, *technically,* I'm not really a virgin, but thank you for making me try to justify my childhood trauma in relationship to my accepted sexual status in society. That's really kind of—"

"Oh shit, Hayseed. I'm—"

"No, no, it's fine. Years of therapy gone to hell with a few sentences. It's okay, really. I'll just—"

"*Allllllllright.*" Abby set her glass down and stepped closer to Hayden. "Laying it on a little thick, but I'm sorry, I really am. I'll make it up to you."

"Yeah?" Hayden feigned wiping away tears and looked up at her with a sad expression.

Abby played along, wiping his imaginary tear-stained face, and then kissed Hayden's cheek.

Color rose to Hayden's face. "What's that for?"

She watched him a moment without saying a word, and then smiled. "C'mon. Let's go on an adventure."

"Yeah?"

Abby nodded and swallowed the last of her wine.

"*Sweeeeeeet.*" Hayden tilted his glass as well and set the empty on the kitchen island. "I *may* or *may not* have also brought walkie-talkies."

Chapter Twelve

"I'M THE NAVIGATOR and *you're* the driver, did you forget how this works?" Abby studied the map on the screen of her phone.

"I don't trust those things."

"Is this why you're not on social media? Don't trust the technology?"

"I'm not on social media because I don't need Big Brother watching me."

"I wish you were. It's just easier to post something for family and friends to see rather than emails and phone calls."

Hayden glanced at her and grinned. "Easier to avoid talking to your mother."

"Don't change the subject, besides, what about Big Brother? Got something to hide?"

Hayden smirked. "Porn. A *lottttt* of porn."

"Probably tentacle porn."

"*Ewwwwwwww,* that stuff's disgusting!" Hayden gave Abby another quick glance. "A friend told me."

"I truly have no idea what I'm going to do with you."

"Well you keep telling me those directions, you're gonna make me drive into a cornfield or some shit."

"Am not." Abby pointed ahead. "Up here on the right. Hartmann Road."

Hayden slowed down and made a right-hand turn. On the left side of the road there was a baseball field and two tall rows of bleachers beside concrete block clubhouses for the players. Playground equipment was nestled into raised beds of mulch close to a row of picnic tables and a small gravel parking lot.

"His address is 430 Hartmann, *soooo...*" Abby stared out the window at the mailbox of the house on the right. "That's 426, so two more houses down."

Hayden cut a hard left into the gravel lot and stopped the car. "This'll give us a little distance."

The man's house was a forgettable dull gray rock in a dismal line of single-family homes with little more than a car's length separating them. While some had faded cement siding in sun-bleached yellow and Robin's-egg blue, the house at 430 Hartmann was weathered wooden siding the worn condition and gray color of a farmer's hay barn.

The shingled roof bowed along its peak and the tin flashing by the chimney had peeled away from the bricks on one side in an angry twist of metal. Beneath the eaves of the roof, Abby saw windows absent of curtains, while on the first floor, the windows all had curtains—drawn, dingy and drab as they were.

"Okay, I'm going to go set up over there at that picnic table." Hayden pointed to the third farthest table in the park. "Here." He thumbed a power switch on a small black walkie-talkie, and handed it to Abby.

"Are these really necess—"

"Yes," Hayden nodded. "Yes, they are." He got out of the driver's side and then retrieved the drone and its controller from the back seat. He peered in at Abby. "Time for some recon."

"Okay, Jason Bourne."

Hayden used his hip to bump the rear door closed and made his way to the table.

Abby watched him set down the walkie-talkie and then push some buttons on the drone controller. A few seconds later, she saw the machine rise from the table, hovering a few feet away from Hayden's smiling face. He picked up his walkie-talkie and looked in her direction. "Woodchuck to Gray Squirrel, Woodchuck to Gray Squirrel, mission has been initiated. Over."

She pushed the TALK button. "Woodchuck works for you, but I'm Gray Squirrel? You saying I look old?"

"Focus on the mission, Gray Squirrel." Hayden set his walkie down and turned his attention toward the drone, maneuvering it high overhead and forward.

Abby popped the handle on the passenger side door and quietly got out. The drone whirred by the treetops until it cut a hard right-angle into the space between the houses. She stepped onto the grass and walked toward the table where Hayden sat. The display screen of the controller showed the drone's point of view, and Abby watched as it hovered outside one of the upstairs windows. It was dark inside the room and Hayden steered the drone further to the rear of the house, flying above a backyard overgrown with weeds.

She saw another darkened window, though a soft glow as if from a hallway, was at the rear of the room. Hayden positioned the drone outside a third window, and Abby saw the interior of the room was lit with dim light from a ceiling lamp. On the left side of Hayden's video screen, Abby saw the edge of a bed mattress, and on the right side sat an antique-looking roll-top desk. The walls of the room were yellowed and unadorned except for a crack in the plaster, curling from the ceiling and over a doorframe.

Hayden let the drone hover in place and he reached for the walkie-talkie. "Woodchuck to Gray Squirrel, we have—"

"I'm right here."

"Holy fucking—" Hayden yelled and jumped on the picnic bench, and then put his head down with a heavy breath. "What is *wrong* with... you can't use the talkie if you go walkie, you get that, right?"

"Figured it would be easier than—"

"You are a thief of joy." Hayden set his walkie-talkie on the picnic table. "A murderer of happiness, you know that, right?"

"Would you forget about the walkie-talkies?" She whispered and gave a nod toward the screen. "Pretty depressing bedroom."

"Cotton Mather would be right at home in—" Hayden stopped talking as the video screen showed the man walking into the room and taking a seat at the desk. He flipped open a book and stared at the contents, turning the pages slowly.

"Family album?" Hayden's attention never left the screen as he spoke to Abby.

"Old war buddies, maybe?"

The man closed his eyes and leaned his head down, chin almost resting against his chest, reached out and closed the book. He remained that way, and Hayden kept the drone hovering in place.

"He fell asleep on—"

With a snap of his neck, the man raised his head and turned with his cataract eyes to stare through the bedroom window, directly into the camera of the drone. Lean and gaunt, the man's face held an expression of pain and misery Abby had never seen before in her life.

"Not asleep." Abby whispered, and the hair on her arms rose with a chill.

"Abort, abort!" Hayden thumbed the controller and the drone zoomed away from the window, slicing through the air back toward the street, and directly into the branch of an oak tree. It careened downward with an angry buzz saw noise, and bounced off the withered front lawn.

"Shit!" Hayden rose from the bench of the picnic table and broke into a run toward the house.

"Hayseed!" Abby whisper-yelled after him, but he was making a beeline for his downed drone. It took him three bounding steps into the man's yard before Abby saw the front porch lights go on and watched as the man stepped outside.

His hands were crossed behind him, body language that of a detective about to reveal the cause of a mystery, and he stepped slowly to the edge of the porch and glared at Hayden.

"Why have you come here?" His voice was strained and raw, the sound cut with anguish.

Hayden put his hands out in front of him, palms out. "I was just... I got a new toy and I thought—"

"They're back again, aren't they?" The man climbed down one step and his voice dropped to a rough whisper. "You've gone and woke 'em up."

He rocked on the heels of his feet. To Abby, *now* he looked like someone jonesing for a fix.

"Mister, I'm sorry. We saw you, y' know, I saw you in town and I just wanted to make sure you're—"

"What *have you DONNNNE*?" The man jerked his right hand in front of him, and Abby watched as he put the barrel of a pistol into his mouth and pulled the trigger.

The sound was a sharp crack against the silence of the quiet street, and the ceiling of the porch suddenly had a narrow splash of red on its sagging wooden slats. He fell backward, and his body hit the stoop with a dull thump. Abby watched the man's feet twitch several times and then go still.

Chapter Thirteen

YOU'RE JACK'S SON, aren't ya?"

"Nephew actually." Hayden watched two uniformed men lift the stretcher with the sheet-covered body and carry it toward the ambulance parked in the driveway.

The cop nodded. "Right, right. Studying to be a pastor or something."

"Priest, but yeah, something like—"

"Detective Dave Simmons, I'm a member of the Moose Lodge with Jack." The man reached out and shook Hayden's hand. "Your uncle's a good guy. Crazy as a shithouse rat, but a good guy. Haven't seen him in—"

"He is." Hayden smiled, and nodded. "And... he is. He's been back in Florida for a while now."

Reaching into his suit jacket, Simmons withdrew a small notebook and pen. "So, what's the story? You know this old man?"

Hayden's expression drew a blank. "Actually, no, I was, uh…"

"Wellness check." Abby stepped beside Hayden and crossed her arms. Simmons' gaze flitted from Hayden to her.

"Wellness check?"

"Yeah, it's part of Hayden's community outreach course at college." She smiled. "You know those helpful priests and... stuff."

Hayden cleared his throat. "Uh... yeah, that's... I'd seen the guy around town a few times and—"

"He wasn't exactly acting...*normal.*" Abby interjected as the cop jotted notes and then he paused and looked up at her.

"How do you mean?"

"Seemed pretty upset about something, but wouldn't say what. Ran off both times without answering why he was so upset."

Simmons looked from Abby to Hayden and back again. "Ran off from where?"

"The Lofts. I just moved in."

"The Lofts..." The detective nodded slowly. "The new..." he nodded faster then, as recognition seemed to arrive. "Harper's Grove. Gotcha."

He shook his head and sighed before glancing at Hayden. "Glad your uncle's finally doing something good with that place."

Hayden caught Abby's eyes and then focused back to the officer. "You know about it? I mean, about what that place was?"

Simmons gave a light shrug. "Only what my mom told me when I was a kid. Hellhole of a place. Awful goddamn things—"

"Simmons, you gotta come in here." A young officer called to him from the front porch.

Abby looked at the patch of bloody ceiling. Someone had turned on the porch light and the spatters on the bulb steamed slightly in the low light. She called after Simmons as he began to walk away. "The book!"

The officer turned back to her. "What book?"

"We saw him messing with a book inside the house, like a... a photo album kind of thing."

Simmons took a step back. "You were inside the house?"

"No, no." Abby pointed to the upstairs windows. "He was holding the book when we walked up to the house. Upstairs."

Turning his head to look at the darkened panes of glass, Simmons looked back at Abby. "You saw him holding a book from down here?" His expression shifted to skepticism, but Simmons nodded and continued toward the house.

Hayden put his hands in his pockets and whispered sideways to Abby. "Those helpful priests and... stuff? Really?"

"It was the best I could do on the spot, alright, Woodchuck?" Abby whispered in response.

"You stuffed the drone in the back seat?"

"Beneath that ratty blanket, yeah." Abby watched the silhouettes move behind the windows inside the house. "Hayseed, you think... I mean, did we push this guy over the edge by being here or—"

"Absolutely not." Hayden turned and put his hands on her shoulders. "This guy had issues. This isn't our fault, Abs."

Simmons came walking out of the house, carrying a thick scrapbook in his hands. "Found the book but..." He shrugged and flipped it open so Hayden and Abby could see.

Yellowed newspaper clippings lined the pages, all a similar theme in the headlines:

HARPER'S GROVE INVESTIGATION

FAILURE OF OVERSIGHT AT HARPER'S GROVE

HORRENDOUS CONDITIONS AT HARPER'S GROVE FACILITY

Flipping another page, Simmons paused to lift a loose Polaroid photo between the pages. A thin man in a teal-colored workman's outfit held a mop in one hand and a cigarette in the other. Simmons stared at the photo and then waved it in his fingers. "That's him."

Abby studied the shot and saw it as well. "He worked there."

Simmons nodded, an expression of disgust on his face. "And that's not all." He thumbed toward the house. "You're Jack's kid, *uh...* nephew, same thing, so I'll tell you this, but don't go running your mouth all over town."

"Of course not, no."

Simmons nodded. "Cases of candy in the guy's living room. I mean, goddamn cartons of it almost to the ceiling."

"Candy?" Abby glanced toward the front door but couldn't see past several officers crowded at the entrance.

"Hard candies, buttermints, peppermints... looks like a goddamn penny-candy shop in there. Something's off, that's for damned sure." Simmons turned and waved at the young officer standing on the porch. "Blevins, run a list for me of any reports over the last year or so involving an old Chevy Nova and a guy offering candy to kids."

"Hey kid, here's some candy, get in the car? *Seriously?*" Hayden crossed his arms.

"I wish to hell I was joking, but it's a shit world we live in at times." Simmons shook his head. "I've got your numbers and information, so if you two want to head home, go on ahead. Tell Jack I said hello next time you talk to him, and…" He reached into his suit jacket and withdrew a business card, handing it over. "Put my cell number in your phone."

Simmons headed back inside the house, pausing to look up at the red splotch. He sidestepped, and moved on through the entrance.

From the yard, Abby noticed the splatter was still dripping to the floorboards below.

Chapter Fourteen

"WANT ME TO stay?"

Abby unbuckled her seatbelt and considered Hayden's question, before shaking her head. "I'll be okay. I need to email a few clients back and pretty sure I'm going to collapse into a coma."

"Same. All that adrenaline leaving makes me feel like a dying battery." Hayden stared through the windshield. "That wasn't some shitty horror movie on the SyFy Channel. That actually…"

Abby put a hand on his shoulder and gave a gentle squeeze. "Are *you* okay?"

The silence hung in the interior of the car a moment, and Hayden nodded. "Yeah, yeah, I'm good." He turned toward her and Abby slid her arms around him in a hug.

Hayden felt warm against her, and Abby closed her eyes and nuzzled her cheek against his. A soft smile rose on her face and she whispered. "You smell good."

"Good to know." He whispered back and tightened his embrace. "I almost smelled way worse because I damned near shit my pants when—"

Abby pulled back and pressed a finger to his lips. "*Shhhh.* I know." She tilted her head closer, kissed his cheek, and then opened the passenger door. "See you tomorrow?"

"Absolutely. Good night, Abs."

"Night, Hayseed."

She shut the door and heard Hayden's car pull away only after she had typed in her keycode and opened the front door. That made her smile, him waiting like that. Making sure she was safe.

Abby walked down the hallway, hearing her feet scuff against the grit of drywall dust and construction dirt. She went inside her apartment, poured herself a tall glass of sangria from a pitcher in the fridge, and sat at the dining room table. A few hours ago, she and Hayden had been laughing over dinner, and then a man blew his brains out in front of them.

Tears came like a hard and fast storm, rolling in out of nowhere. Abby put a hand over her face and released a few sobbing cries before shaking her head side to side and forcing it away.

It's not like I actually knew *the guy or anything.*

But he was in pain. The kind of pain that drives a person to take their own life. You know that pain, don't ya, Abs? Up close and in your face?

Abby slid the sweater sleeve higher on her left arm and stared at the faint white lines on her wrist. They had faded with time, but they were still there, like the matching scars on her thighs and her lower stomach. She traced the reminders on her wrist before letting let the cloth fall back in place. It had never been serious, not really, but it had been a release of sorts, a way to feel and not feel at the same time.

Taking a deep inhale and then exhaling slowly, Abby rose from the wooden chair and picked up the cold glass of sangria. She turned to the mannequin by the window and raised the wine in a toast. "Marilyn, never forget to live in the *right now*." Abby took a sip of the fruity mixture and savored the taste of the citrus flavors.

She stared at the mannequin, took a step closer, and whispered to herself. "Well shit."

Along the left side of the figure's face, Abby saw a thin lightning bolt crack running from temple to neck. She ran her fingers along the jagged line, and sighed. "I'll fix you up love, don't worry."

She glanced at her laptop and decided the emails could wait until morning. The door of the apartment was still wide open and Abby looked through the frame into the hall beyond. An idea bloomed, and she smiled to herself and gave a nod. After topping off her glass with more wine, Abby stepped into the hallway and walked down the long corridor until she reached the end. There were several other open thresholds, and from the looks of the spaces beyond, they were going to be storage closets or utility rooms of some kind.

Abby turned left and walked another short hallway until she reached double-doors of frosted glass with modern aluminum pull handles on them. Shifting her sangria to her left hand, Abby pulled the handle on one of the doors and stopped as she stared at the room before her.

The ceiling reached at least fifty feet overhead and the roof was a wide stretching mural of fierce looking angels among massive clouds. Four skylights broke the image of the mural, but the moonlight shining through the panes of moisture-beaded glass only added to the religious tones, making it appear as if angelic light was beaming down straight from heaven.

To the left side of the room was an empty swimming pool the size of which would be easily welcomed by athletes training for the Olympics. It was finished in bright white tile with thin ribbons of blue intersecting each one. The room smelled slightly of bleach and fresh paint.

Abby's gaze scanned the pool and then she turned to the right side of the room and paused. "Oh *helllll* yes."

It took her a few moments to locate the proper controls in the recessed wall panels, but Abby began filling the hot tub with water. The splashing sound was soothing and she sat down on the steps that descended into the tub, letting her feet rest just above the water level. Two tiled columns bookended the stairs and Abby leaned against one and took a drink of wine, enjoying the light buzz starting to flow through her body. She worked the muscles in her neck, twisting her head side to side, and let out a long sigh.

"Wanna go for an adventure?"

Abby looked up to see Hayden, grinning at her and holding the drone's controller in both hands. "Hayseed? What... what're you—"

"You've woken them up again, haven't you?" The gray-haired man stood at the edge of the empty swimming pool. His expression was lost and hollow. He raised a bony hand, pointed at her with a single shaking finger, and spoke in a low trembling voice. "What have you done?"

Abby pushed with her feet, pressing herself against the wall.

"Wanna go for an adventure?" Hayden swiveled a thumb against one of the controller switches and a drone buzzed by overhead, circling and then hovering inches away from the old man's head.

Abby saw he had a pistol clenched in his right hand. He raised the barrel and pushed it past his pale, thin lips and aimed at the roof of his mouth.

"Look!" Hayden, still grinning, sat down beside her, tilting the video screen so Abby could watch.

The gunshot echoed off the walls of the large room and Abby watched the man's brains explode from the back of his skull in high definition. Blood arced through the air and landed against the bone white tiles of the pool, a red explanation point, wet and stretched.

Abby screamed out loud and tried to push herself through the wall as she kicked her feet.

Hayden laughed and rewound the footage, playing it again in slow motion.

The old man's right arm fell limp at his side and he walked closer until he stood at Abby's feet. Blood poured from his mouth, dribbling lines of red-stained drool at first, and then faster, gathering mass in a liquid puddle at his feet.

Abby jerked her feet away, pulling her knees tight to her chest, but the puddle kept growing larger, tracing the lines between the tiles and then overtaking them in her direction. The blood reached her toes first, and then ran beneath the soles of her feet.

"Wanna go for an adventure?" Hayden thumbed a switch and the drone zoomed around the room.

Strands of graying hair had become a bloody nimbus at the rear of the man's head. Dark circles bruised beneath his eyes and he pointed at her again, screaming in a wet, garbling voice. *"What have you DONNNNNNNE?"*

Abby jolted awake and yanked her legs away from the rising hot tub water. Her heart raced in her chest and she reached out to the tile column to steady herself. The splashing sound of running water had stopped when it hit a certain level, but the water kept flowing in, reaching Abby's knees as she sat on the stairs.

"I'll hold off until tomorrow for the hot tub." She stood from the stairs and let out a long breath as she stepped to the wall panel and turned the water valve off. As she tightened the valve, a quiet noise came from near the glass doors of the room, as if a handful of metallic objects had been tossed to the tile floor.

It's just old water pipes, Abby thought, and picked up her glass from the tile column.

Steam rose from the hot water and swirled through the moonlight beams from the skylights.

Some sleep, Abby thought. *Definitely sleep, and this hot tub is in my future tomorrow. Maybe with a good book and more sangria.*

She reached the double glass doors and as she pulled the handle, Abby heard that metallic noise again, a gentle tinkling sound, but closer. She paused and strained to hear as the door whispered closed behind her.

There it was again—a tinny crumbling noise falling against

cement. Abby walked farther down the hall and stopped at the intersection where the main hallway led toward her apartment.

Tink, tink.

The sound came from the hall and Abby took a step. The overhead lights hummed. In the spaces between the reach of the lights, the darkness seemed to swirl.

Abby strained her eyes, trying to focus, and as she looked, the showering metallic sound rained down loudly behind her, and she spun around.

Nothing. There was nothing.

Abby broke into a run down the hallway, reached her apartment door and lunged inside. She spun around, closed the door, and twisted the lock.

She stepped away and stood in the living room, staring at the door and the silence beyond. The wet sensation on her left arm made her look down and realize she held an empty glass in her hand. The sleeve of her sweater was soaked with sangria and she walked to the sink to set the glass down, running some tap water inside it. She put her hands on the sink and lowered her head, forcing herself to take slow deep inhales and exhales.

It's just the day. The fucking day, that's all. You're spooking yourself, Abby.

Shrugging off her sweater, she looked over the sleeve again, considered rinsing it with water, but since the fabric was black, she decided it didn't really matter. She draped it over a dining room chair and thought about calling Hayden.

No. He needs the sleep as much as I do.

Abby sat on the couch and turned on the TV for the background noise, clicking the remote until she found an old episode of *The Office*. She pulled the throw blanket around her, curled her legs up close, and rested her head against the armrest. At some point, Abby slipped into a gossamer-thin sleep.

Chapter Fifteen

BS?"

The sound of Hayden's voice from the hallway made Abby pause and check the clock at the top of her laptop screen. It was past six o'clock. *"Holy shitttttt,"* she whispered to herself. The workday had been a busy one and she'd lost track of time.

There was a knock at her door and she uncurled herself from the couch, wincing at the jab of pain in her back from sitting in the same position for so long. "Just a sec, Hayseed!"

As she opened the door, he gave her a wide smile and held up plastic grocery store bags. "You never replied so I decided."

"Replied to what?" Abby pulled her phone from her jeans pocket and saw a string of text messages from Hayden and a missed call from her mother. She had been so in the zone of work, she hadn't registered any of them.

"Dinner." Hayden marched through the living room and put the bags on the kitchen island.

"Didn't you live off Twinkies and mac 'n cheese in high school?"

"I had very selective culinary tastes back then. I've expanded since." He shrugged and pulled items from a bag. "But hey, if you don't want me to make you crab-stuffed portabella mushrooms, it's cool. I'll just—"

"*Whoa, whoa, whoa.*" Abby reached forward, her palms out. "Hold on, big guy. Run that by me again?"

Hayden smirked and made an act out of inspecting the contents of the bag he held. "You heard me. Crab stuffed mushrooms. Some…" He peeked into another bag on the island top. "Gruyere cheese and heavy cream for the *most amazing* scalloped potatoes you will *ever* have in—"

"Okay, alright." Abby leaned against the counter and smiled at him. "Bring it on, Gordon Ramsey. I'm intrigued." She gave a nod toward a third bag on the counter. "And that?"

His smirk broadened into a smile and he reached into the bag, withdrawing a large plastic bottle of margarita sour mix. "I mean…"

"Perfect!" Abby broke into a laugh and nodded. "I'm gonna grab a quick shower, so try not to burn the place down."

"Yeah, yeah. Go do you. I'll be out here creating culinary perfection." Hayden turned and continued pulling items from the bags and setting them on the counter. "Slaving to please you."

Abby shook her head as she walked toward her bedroom and eased the door shut. A few days ago, the ground of her life seemed to be lined with eggshells to avoid, but now it felt like life was supposed to feel.

Almost.

She smiled, turned the shower on, and undressed in front of the sink mirror. Even the purple half-moon beneath her eye didn't make the good feeling inside Abby fade away.

The hot water felt amazing, washing away the hectic day, and Abby let it cascade over her skin. She went through her normal routine, and when she rinsed the conditioner from her hair, she turned and enjoyed the waterfall over her face.

Ding. Ding-ding. Ding-ding-ding-ding-ding.

Abby stepped clear of the spray and wiped her eyes. Beyond the mottled glass shower doors, she saw nothing, but the high-pitched noise continued. "Hayseed?"

She rinsed her hair through the shower spray one last time, turned the water off, and slid the glass door open. Abby cautiously peeked her head out, and then stepped onto the soft gray rug on the floor. Through the warm steam of the shower, she felt an ice cube brush against her left thigh, and she yelped, flinching and looking down at her body, but the sensation was gone.

What the hell?

Abby shook her head, toweled off, and walked into the bedroom.

Has to be old waterpipes. Has to be. Something stupid like that.

Abby kept glancing at the bathroom as she pulled on a clean pair of faded jeans, and grabbed the top T-shirt from a folded stack in her clothes dresser. She held it out by the collar and let it fall open on its own.

"Nice." Pearl Jam's stick-figure graphic was emblazoned across the front of the shirt and she grinned as she pulled it over her head.

The moment she opened her bedroom door, the smell of the food captured her attention—sweet and aromatic and complex. Hayden had his back to her as he stood at the counter, a kitchen towel over his right shoulder, and was swaying to the sound of Van Morrison belting out *Brown Eyed Girl*.

Standing in the living room, her arms crossed, Abby watched him dance and sing along to the lyrics. Hayden's arms moved with a rhythm, and Abby heard sounds of something getting sliced. He stopped and stepped back, nodded to himself, and then turned toward the island with a handful of lime wedges in his hand. His gaze flitted to Abby and Hayden jolted in place, sending several slices flying into the air.

"*Holy Christ*, Abby!"

She burst out laughing at Hayden's reaction, as he leaned against the kitchen island, breathing heavily and clutching a hand over his chest.

"I didn't mean to scare you! I was just enjoying the entertainment."

"Holy shit. Wear some bells on your ankles or something." Hayden exhaled a sigh of relief and shook his head. He straightened and fitted a wedge of lime onto the rim of one glass and then another. The margarita itself came next, and Hayden filled two tall glasses before handing one to Abby. "Cheers."

"Cheers right back to you." She raised the glass and took a drink, relishing the sour flavor and the swirl of tequila. "Dinner smells incredible, by the way."

"*Thannnnk* you." He set his glass down and turned back to the oven, flipping the light on to look inside. "We've got a little while before the potatoes are done. Want to turn on a movie or something while we wait? Comedy, maybe? I think we could both use it."

"Solid plan." Abby brought her margarita with her to the couch, sat down and turned on the TV. She scanned through the streaming services she had set up, and settled on *Waiting* starring Ryan Reynolds.

Hayden glanced at the screen. "Oh, hell yeah! Love this movie. The goat!" He stifled a laugh, put the kitchen towel on the island, and brought his glass to sit by Abby on the couch.

"Of course, you'd mention that part. Why do men play with their genitals so much?"

"Usually it's because girls won't." Hayden sipped from his drink.

"Fair point." She leaned against him and felt his warmth. It made her smile and though Hayden's attention was on the TV screen, she saw the corners of his mouth turn up in a slight smile.

They watched the movie, sipped from their glasses, and laughed at Reynolds' delivery of his character's sarcasm-soaked dialogue. A timer on Hayden's phone went off and he set his drink down on the coffee table and hurried to the kitchen.

Abby picked up the remote and hit the pause button as he withdrew the potatoes from the oven, and then a baking sheet with four portabella mushroom caps heaped with crab meat. He set the food on the stovetop and stacked the potholders he was using to the side.

Watching Hayden plate the food and sprinkle fresh chives on top of the scalloped potatoes, Abby had to admit he had done an amazing job with dinner. She refilled their glasses with margarita and sat down at the dining room table.

The first bite of the mushroom was in silence, and when she put a forkful of the scalloped potatoes in her mouth, Abby actually closed her eyes to focus on the flavor. She swallowed, put her fork down, and slowly turned to look at Hayden. "So… you're becoming a chef instead of a priest?"

"I did okay?"

"Okay?" She picked up her fork again to gather another portion of the crab and mushroom. "It's not just *okay*. Hayden, this is seriously incredible."

"Glad you approve." Hayden watched as she took another bite of potatoes, and smiled as he dug into his own food.

"Oh hey." Abby wiped her mouth with a napkin. "Can you ask your uncle if there's something going on with the pipes in the building?"

"What about 'em?"

"I hear this sound once in a while, this dinging kind of noise." Abby reached for her margarita and took a drink. The mild buzz of the drink made her feel relaxed inside.

"Yeah, sure, I'll ask. I think a lot of it is new pipes now, but a building this big, hard to tell."

"Are you sure Uncle Jack doesn't want to, you know, meet me in person or anything? I'm living in one of his properties. I could be a serial killer or some—"

Hayden shook his head and took the last bite of potatoes from his plate. "I'm sure he feels like he already knows you. He's heard me talk about you for years."

"Oh really?" Abby sipped again.

"Shut up."

"For *years?*" Abby smiled and blinked at Hayden like a cartoon princess.

Hayden chewed and picked up his napkin to wipe his mouth. He glanced down the hallway toward Abby's bedroom. "Oh hey, did the holy water in the shower burn earlier?"

"It was a little warm, yeah." Laughing, Abby stood and started clearing the table. "Hey, do you remember that girl Marcy in high school?"

"She the one that ate glue all the time?"

"No no, that was Shannon… something or other. Marcy had the black and pink hair and loved skater punk music."

"Oh yeah, I remember." Hayden nodded as he drank. "What about her?"

"I saw on Facebook she got married." Abby began to clear the table, taking the plates to the kitchen counter. She glanced over her shoulder as she rinsed the dishes, and then loaded them into the dishwasher. "To Todd Kitterling."

"Get. Out!" Hayden stood from the table and walked closer to see Abby's face. "Kitterling? Mr *I'm-gonna-direct-porn-films-after-I-graduate* Kitterling?"

"One and the same."

"And what'd he end up doing?" Hayden leaned against the counter.

"Porn." Abby smirked as she saw the surprised expression on Hayden's face, and they both busted out laughing. "Not even kidding."

Wiping at the corners of his eyes, Hayden exhaled the satisfied breath only hard laughter brings with it. He nodded at Abby's glass. "Need a refill?"

"Fill me up, Buttercup." She dried her hands on the kitchen towel, shut the door on the dishwasher, and pressed the start button. Taking her glass from Hayden, she stepped toward the couch again and stared at the TV screen on pause. "How many times have you seen this movie?"

"I don't know. *Mmmmm...* a dozen or twenty."

Abby turned toward him and gave him a visual onceover. Hayden caught her gaze and looked himself up and down. "What? I spill something on me?"

Shaking her head, Abby gave him a smile and a soft nod. "Boxers or briefs?"

"Taking a survey?"

"No," Abby pressed the power button on the remote, turning the TV off. "But I have a much better idea."

"WHY DO I feel like my parents went out of town, and I'm alone with a girl for the first time?"

Abby snickered. "Latent guilt of frequent masturbation in your adolescent years and knowing God's been watching you the entire time, including now."

"Thanks." Hayden stared at her and slow blinked. "Thank you, yes. I appreciate the breakdown, Abs."

"Come on." Abby set two towels on the tile column at the edge of the hot tub and stepped down, wading into the steaming water. She had searched through the clothes dresser until she found her only bikini, and put it on before they left her apartment. Now she paused, pulled off her Pearl Jam T-shirt and tossed it to a dry spot of tile. Taking her margarita with her, Abby waded to the far side of the tub and sat down in the bubbling water. She leaned her head back and looked at Hayden, standing in his boxers at the edge. *"Ahhhhhhhhh."*

"Yeah, okay." He took the first two steps, water up to his shins, and nodded to himself. "Oh man, I get it now. Okay." Hayden walked in slowly and eased himself down, looking over the frothy surface. "No wonder people love these things." He took a drink from his glass of margarita, and set it down on the tiled landing.

"So, if not a priest, then what?"

Hayden sighed and closed his eyes, letting himself slide lower into the water. "I guess after I finish school, maybe I'll teach. Theology or something, I suppose. I don't know. I'll figure it out." He opened his eyes and turned toward her. "What about *you*, anyway? Didn't think *online brand management* is what you wanted to do in life either."

"Not exactly, but I sort of fell into it. I'm good at it."

"Yeah, well… just because you're good at something doesn't mean you enjoy it."

Abby considered his words. "You're right, but for now it pays well until I figure things out." She reached for her drink and then turned to Hayden, who had a faraway look on his face. "Whatcha thinkin' about, Hayseed?"

"Marcy."

Hayden ran his wet hands over his face and an expression of realization washed over him. He spoke more to himself than Abby. "Marcy was at the pool party."

"She was?"

Hayden nodded slowly, as if he was dredging up the memory. *"Ohhhhh* yeah. She was there, alright."

Abby tilted her head and grinned at him. "Did you have a thing for her back then?"

An abrupt laugh escaped Hayden and he shook his head as he reached for his drink.

"Okay, what was that? How come you remember her there?" Abby smiled and nudged Hayden's arm with her elbow.

He took a drink from his glass, returned her smile, and then his expression grew serious enough Abby thought she saw some sadness there. Hayden gave her a nod. "Do you remember when you got blindfolded for seven minutes in heaven?"

"Yeah, somebody led me and Preston into—"

"No." Hayden put his glass back onto the tile landing. "That wasn't Preston."

His eyes looked into hers, and Abby felt a sudden flutter in her stomach. She glanced away and then back to Hayden. He reached out and gently took her glass, setting it beside his on the tile.

Abby thought back to the night long ago. "But… Preston acted like he kissed—"

"They put him and Lisa Koyce in the downstairs bathroom. He kissed someone, yeah… just wasn't you."

The beating moth wings in her stomach grew stronger and Abby stared at Hayden's. He put his hand out against the side of her face, and brushed her steam-damp hair away with his thumb. Hayden leaned closer, gently pulled her toward him, and then his lips were on hers.

Abby's hands reached on their own, finding homes at Hayden's waist and back. She felt her mouth open against his attention, the warmth of his tongue against hers. The sour but sweet flavor of margarita. He pulled away slightly, and looked into her eyes.

"Hayseed…" Her words came out in a whispered quick breath. "That was…"

He smiled and began to say something, but Abby pulled him close and kissed him again. In her life, Abby had felt tender kisses, loving and passionate ones, kisses full of hunger and desire and raw animal lust. This was all of them and none of them at the same time—something else entirely. Heat coursed through her body as she felt Hayden's hand on her waist beneath the bubbling water. She felt her breath quicken with each feel of his lips on hers.

"Wait." Abby felt her body trembling as she pulled back and stared at him. "*Wait, wait, wait…* are you… I don't want to be the reason you…" She took a deep breath. "Am I the reason you're not going to be a priest?"

The corners of Hayden's eyes tightened as he smiled at her and shook his head slightly. His voice was soft in tone, as gently as his touch. "No, Abs. You're not the reason, but if you were," he rose from the water and Abby stood with him, her arms still around his neck. "You'd be more than a good enough reason."

He kissed her again as they stood, hands lightly exploring along each other's warm skin, speckled with water. Abby felt her breath, ragged and fast, as she kissed him back.

Hayden pulled away and looked at her. "This isn't because of the alcohol, is it?"

Abby smiled and trailed the fingertips of her right hand along his collarbone, down over his chest, and then slid it up around the back of Hayden's neck. "It's not because of the alcohol."

Both of his hands went to her waist, and Abby felt Hayden lift her from the hot tub and gently set her down on the surrounding platform. Hayden kissed her and folded his left hand, tenderly brushing the backs of his fingers along her cheek. He looked into her eyes and Abby noticed his gaze landing on the dark bruise beneath her eye. A brief wince of empathy crossed his face and he leaned closer, kissing her there, before moving back to stare at her again. He whispered to her. "When's the last time you felt treasured? Worshipped?"

Something inside Abby collided with desire, and she suddenly felt tears spring to her eyes. She gave Hayden a slight shake of her head and shrugged. "It's uh… it's been a long time."

Hayden kissed her again, softly, as he moved closer, standing between her parted legs, his hands at her hips again. Then his mouth was on her neck, tasting her, her pulse beating in time to the feel of his lips on her skin. Abby felt her hands tighten and grip his back, and she closed her eyes as Hayden planted a trail of kisses along her collarbone and then her chest.

A breath escaped her and she tilted her head back, running her fingers through Hayden's hair with one hand, her other reaching to untie her bikini top. She heard the quick intake from him before his mouth moved to the nipple of her left breast first, and then her right. Taking his time, giving attention to her as he moved.

Abby felt her nipples harden beneath the caress of his mouth and then the touch of his left hand. She groaned and felt a hand behind her back, easing her to lie down against the wet tiles. Overhead, beams of silver moonlight shone through the skylights, and Abby felt her eyelids flutter.

Soft kisses along her left ribs, across her stomach, and then her right side, slowly circling along her hips. A shudder of pleasure rippled through Abby's body and she felt heat bloom at her very core as Hayden's kisses grew closer.

She felt the tie string on her bikini bottom being drawn free. Abby bit her lower lip and her body arched off the tiles beneath her. Hayden kissed the soft, tender skin of her thighs and she felt him slide the fabric away, exposing her to the open air.

Hayden's lips moved against her body, tasting her excitement. He traced her with his tongue, teased, grazed against her skin and made fresh waves of heat rush through her.

Abby's body ached with need and she felt herself open for him. She felt how wet she was for him and bit her bottom lip harder. She ran her hands through his hair, urging him on. When he licked her clit, her body tightened and she gasped.

Hayden traced the wet divide of her parted lips with a fingertip. His mouth returned and remained.

Abby felt his tongue swirl against her. *"Ohhhh goddd."*

He groaned against her and pulled back slightly. "The god talk really gets me—"

"Holy shit." Her words came out in a whispered rush as his finger explored her.

"That's it, yes. More god and holy—"

She couldn't help herself and her laughter cut his words off, and Abby felt the *moment*. It was one of those rare, completely vulnerable moments during sex where you feel free enough to laugh with your partner. Breathless, she glanced down at him and smiled. "How do you know how to—"

"I read a lot."

His fingertips brushed against her and Abby felt all of the muscles in her thighs tighten with pleasure. She put her head back against the tile. "I fucking *love* literature."

The sensation of his mouth and finger made the tension inside Abby build and grow like a wave. The trembling inside her was rising, increasing with his every movement. *"Yes,"* she whispered to him. *"Don't stop."*

He groaned against her and the vibrations from that alone almost sent Abby over the edge. She arched her back and stared up at the skylights.

Something moved beyond the panes of glass, stretched across the surface and blocked the beam of moonlight. Abby felt Hayden's finger inside her, moving in a curling motion, and she released a deep moan and clutched at him. The figure above the window shifted again, and Abby strained to focus. "What the fuck..."

The skylight overhead shattered into a glistening hailstorm of glass.

Chapter Sixteen

"TWICE IN THE same week with you two and a dead body." Detective Simmons raised an eyebrow and looked from Abby to Hayden. "People in town are gonna start talking."

He stared up at the broken glass of the skylight and then at the broken, bloody corpse on the tiled floor. Simmons released a heavy exhale. "Alright, so what happened?"

"We were in the hot tub and—"

"You two were in the hot tub?" Simmons glanced at the still water and his gaze lingered on the two glasses sitting there. He turned to Hayden. "Studying to be a priest, huh?"

Hayden's face flushed with color.

"He's going to be a professor. Theology teacher." Abby stepped in, saving Hayden from his fish out of water expression.

Simmons eyed Hayden up a moment, and then gave a slight nod. "Well, I guess anyone who can teach other people not to be assholes is okay in my book. Either of you know the guy?"

Hayden cleared his throat and nodded. "His first name's Dennis, but everyone called him Denny. I used to see him at the soup kitchen two or three times a month."

"Probably crawled up there somehow." Simmons studied the busted skylight again, "Overdosed or something."

"I don't think so, Detective. Denny didn't use. He drank once in a while, but never messed with drugs. His wife died years back and he just... y' know, wasn't able to keep it together. Been homeless for quite a while." Hayden stared at the sheet-covered body. A pool of blood had spread around where the man's head lay. "I got the feeling the ol' guy just wanted to be left alone. He was a veteran. Army, I think."

"Yeah, I saw an Infantry patch on his field jacket." Simmons released a tired exhale.

Abby's attention drifted to the bloody sheet. "What, uh... what happened to his face?"

She'd seen the man's body on the tile floor after he fell, after the blur of screams and running back to her apartment to call 9-1-1. The way his limbs were twisted at odd angles, the cracked and broken skull, but Abby had also seen the condition of his face—it looked as if the flesh had been peeled away like a section of orange rind.

Simmons shook his head and winced. "If I had to guess, he's been up there a few days. Could've been birds, hell, could've been feral cats. It happens. Animals don't have a conscience."

Feral cats.

Abby felt her stomach roil inside as she thought of the kitten sounds she'd heard.

Simmons cleared his throat. "I'll see if he touched base at the men's shelter or the Veterans Association. Maybe they have some useful information." The detective took a step toward the body, where an officer stood by a man in a jacket with CORONER across the back, and then Simmons stopped and turned back. "Look, Hayden… I know you're Jack's nephew, and you're studying to be a prie— *uhhh*, professor and all that. But I have to ask, any connection with you and these two dead guys?"

"None that I know of, no." Hayden put his hands into his jeans pockets.

"Alright, then. They're going to do an autopsy as standard procedure. Hell, maybe the poor bastard got up there and had a heart attack or something." Simmons resumed walking toward the coroner. "We've got your contact information if we have any other questions."

Abby watched the detective walk away and then her gaze once again landed on the sheet covering the dead body. A chill ran through her and she turned to Hayden, resting a hand on his back. "Let's go, Hayseed. They don't need us here."

ABBY WATCHED HAYDEN settle onto the couch, pull the throw blanket over him, and start to stretch his legs out on the cushions. "What're you doing?"

"I'm gonna crash. I thought you—"

"Get off the couch, stupid." Abby took his hand in hers as he stood, and led him down the hallway toward her bedroom.

"Abs, I'm not sure after all that, I can—"

"*Shhhhh*. Don't get any ideas about continuing things from earlier right now. That's not what this is." Abby stood on her tiptoes to give Hayden a quick peck on the lips. She took her sweater off, and hung it on the back of her closet door, and then pulled her phone from her pocket and set it on the nightstand. Abby slid her jeans off, and left the Pearl Jam shirt on. She pulled the covers back on her side of the bed and sat down, staring at Hayden, who stood there unmoving. "Are you..."

"Yeah, um... I was in my boxers in the hot tub, so right now, I'm going—"

"Commando." Abby nodded, and smiled. "Got it."

Her gaze lingered on him a moment, and then Abby turned off the light on her nightstand and slid her legs beneath the covers. She watched Hayden's darkened silhouette as he walked around to the other side of the bed and removed his jeans. He pulled the covers back and lay down.

She curled against him, putting an arm across his chest, and they lay there in silence for a moment before Abby whispered to him. "You still believe in God?"

Hayden adjusted his pillow and was quiet a moment. "Yeah. Well, I... I believe in *something*. Call it whatever you want, I guess, but God works."

"Do you think God, or *whatever*, does everything for a reason? Like everything happens according to some sort of pre-determined plan?" Abby turned on her side and propped her head on her hand to face him.

"I haven't quite worked that one out yet, the whole God has a plan versus man's free will thing. Why?"

Abby ran her hand over Hayden's chest. She lowered her voice to a whisper. "Because if that's true, if everything happens to some kind of holy *plan*... then God is the biggest cockblock that ever existed."

There was a beat of silence, and then she heard Hayden snicker in the dark. Then another.

And then they both laughed out loud, shaking against the mattress. Abby fell to the mattress, and tears spilled down her cheeks. Her stomach ached as she curled up and laughed harder.

As the two of them calmed, she leaned forward and put her forehead against Hayden's shoulder, and then moved closer still, feeling him lift his arm and put it around her as she lay her head against his chest.

She watched his arm move in the shadows, his hand wiping his face, and Abby smiled as he brushed his other hand along her back.

"Hey Abs?"

Abby turned her face up toward his, and he kissed her, soft and tender. He put his hand along the side of her face as she lay it back down against his chest. "I never should have let you go back then."

She smiled in the darkness and gave a quick kiss to his chest before sliding her arm around him. "You're naked, so you're little spoon tonight."

"There is no spoon." Hayden whispered back in a way Abby could hear he was smiling.

She snickered and kissed his chest once more and they fell into a slow rhythm of breathing.

She woke a little before six in the morning, to the buzzing sound of her phone.

Chapter Seventeen

"ABS, CAN YOU meet me later?"

"What... where are you, Hayseed? What time is it?"

"I left a couple hours ago, I'm sorry, I had to... look, this is... it's important. Come meet me at the college at eight o'clock, okay?"

"Mmmmhmmm." Abby felt her grip on the phone loosen as her mind tried to let her slide back to sleep.

"Abs!" Hayden yelled on the phone and Abby's eyes snapped open.

"Okay, alright! Shit, man. I'm awake." Abby sat up in bed and took a deep breath. "Meet you at the college at eight, yep." She ran a hand over her face. "Are you okay?"

There was a pause on the other end of the line and she heard him release a heavy breath. "I really don't know, Abs. I'll see you later."

"Okay, well—" Abby heard a dead silence on the other end, and pulled the phone away to see Hayden had ended the call. She scooted backward and leaned against the headboard. Almost immediately, Abby's eyelids closed, and she flinched and sat up with a sharp inhale. "Okay, yeah. Coffee. There needs to be coffee."

By her second mug, Abby had turned her attention to her laptop and email replies. She found herself repeatedly glancing at the door, but the only sound was her fingers tapping on the keyboard and The Rolling Stones playing softly from her speakers.

She typed up a press release for a start-up company focused on cleaning the oceans of floating garbage, and sent it to their team for approval. Next was input on tagline options for a California jewelry company, and after that, Abby edited two blog posts and sent them back to a New York model hellbent on being one of the next Victoria's Secret girls.

Changing quickly into fresh jeans and a blouse, Abby slipped on a pair of sandals, grabbed her purse, and rushed toward the door. She paused as her fingers pinched the lock, and then she put her ear against the door and listened. Nothing but silence. She shook her head, inwardly admonishing herself.

No shadows morphed into existence. No dead kittens meowing in the darkness. No strange noises like a rain of pocket change falling to cement.

"Spooking yourself over nothing." Abby whispered to herself, hurried down the hallway, and walked from the building to her car.

IT TOOK LESS than fifteen minutes to drive to the college— The Divine Covenant Seminary—and Abby pulled into the visitor's parking lot. There was no sign of Hayden, so she got out and walked to the main entrance. It was a tall gothic building, decorated with ornate cement cornices of fleur-de-lis. A metal-roofed portico extended from the entrance, and shaded several benches.

Abby stood next to a support column and watched the parking lot for Hayden's old Buick to pull in.

"Good morning."

She turned to see a man with a salt and pepper beard and gray hair pulled back into a ponytail. He wore dark sunglasses, and a short-sleeved black shirt and priest's collar, but had faded blue jeans and flip-flops. Abby had the startling feeling she was looking at the real-life man *The Big Lebowski* was based on, but she returned the smile. "Good morning."

"I'm Father Walker." He shifted the strap of a laptop bag on his shoulder, and stuck his hand out. Abby shook it and introduced himself.

He lifted his Ray-Bans to rest on top of his head, and the similarity of *The Dude* only became more cemented in Abby's mind. "Father, has anyone ever told you—"

"I know, I know." He put his hands up to stop her. "It's like Jeff Bridges joined the priesthood."

Abby smiled wider. "It's... *uncanny.*"

"I was in the Philippines last year and people didn't believe me when I said I wasn't him. I signed his autograph about thirty times and took a few dozen photographs with people and they all left me alone after that."

He let his arms rest at his sides and Abby noticed the beaded bracelet wrapped around his right wrist, nestled beside a tied loop of red yarn.

"I'm guessing you're not here to join the right hands of God, so you must be here to meet Hayden."

"I… yes, I am, but how did you—"

"Come sit with me while we wait. I've trekked halfway around the world and I rest my knees whenever I can." Father Walker stepped away and sat down on the closest bench. He leaned back and crossed his legs and leaned into the backrest as Abby joined him. "Hayden called me early this morning. Wouldn't talk much about it, but something was really upsetting him."

"Sounds like the call I got."

Father Walker sighed. "Hayden's a good kid, he really is. But I'm not sure his journey is going to include being a priest. He raised an eyebrow at Abby. "Don't worry, I won't try and press you for information. Sometimes our paths in life aren't what we expected them to be."

The priest reached his hand into his pocket and withdrew a thin joint and a mini-lighter. He nodded sharply, snapping his sunglasses back down into place, lit the joint and took two rapid puffs.

Abby smirked at his actions, shocked, but amused at the same time. "Does *everyone* smoke down here?"

"Hey, God makes it this way. Besides that, most priests are wound up tighter than a frog's ass. The nuns? Don't even get me started." Father Walker shook his head as he took another puff and then stubbed out the end of the joint. "A lifetime of sexual frustration with God? *Pleeeeease.* Each and every one of them would benefit from a few puffs of the Devil's Lettuce once in a while. Besides, I have to write a sermon and this always helps a little."

"If I knew a priest like you when I was younger, I'd probably have never stopped going." Abby grinned.

"Never too late." He smiled and crossed his arms. "What did make you stop? Church, that is." The tone of his voice was soft and caring, not only making small talk, but truly interested.

"My dad died." Abby turned toward him.

"That'll do it," Father Walker nodded. "Crisis of faith *or* the birth of it is usually because of one of the three D's." He counted off on his right hand, one finger at a time, emphasizing his words. "Death, disease, divorce."

"My father was a good man. I've never understood how God could take someone as sweet a person as him." A shallow wave of hurt washed through Abby, and she supposed the grief never would truly leave.

"*Ohhhh*, well, painful as it is, if God didn't take people like that, Heaven would be full of assholes, don't you think?" He tilted his head away, appearing to be searching for what to say, and then he uncrossed his legs and leaned forward, his bent elbows on his knees. "I have faith. I love God and I know he loves me. It's like a… sort of like a marriage. I sing his praises and tell people if they'd *only* listen…"

Father Walker motioned with his hands and straightened up again. "Even so, I have good and bad days as well. I read the news and see horrible, *terrible* things. The confessions I hear, the weight people bear for their sins. Everyone's screwing someone else or *wants* to. Sins of lust. Greed. Sloth. Have you been to Walmart lately? It's the very house of sloth."

He turned to face her better. "Point is, even *I* have days where my faith waivers, but at the end of it all, I still love my savior. For me, it's the one shining light that will never dim. It's a long war, and he chooses his battles."

"I choose my battles too. All of them."

The priest and Abby both turned to the voice of Hayden as he walked toward them.

Father Walker smiled at him. "And *that*, my friend, is why you're meant for something amazing in his life."

"Mornin', Hayseed." She gave him a nod and a smile to hide the worry she felt. Hayden looked like he'd been awake all night, and she suddenly felt a sinking feeling in her stomach she was somehow responsible for it. She wondered if Hayden was feeling some sort of religious guilt over what happened between them.

"Mornin' Abs." He looked at her and the corners of his mouth turned up slightly, and then his expression turned serious again as he turned to the priest.

"Father Walker, thank you for meeting. I uh…" Hayden put his hands into his jeans pockets and sighed.

"Hayden, your call this morning—"

"I know, Father… I *know* how I sounded, but I honestly didn't know who else to talk to."

Abby stepped closer, studying his face and asked in a soft voice. "What's going on, Hayseed? What's so—"

"You'll see. It's… I don't want to mislead you." He withdrew his right hand from his jeans pocket and held out a thumb drive toward the priest.

Father Walker took it with a puzzled expression. "Mislead us? About what?"

Hayden shifted in place, his face pale. He shook his head slightly. "I'm not sure how to answer that, actually."

Chapter Eighteen

THE THREE OF them walked down a long hallway with a polished floor until they reached a pair of massive double-doors. A brass plaque with CHAMBERS HALL was secured to the wall above the entrance. Hayden opened the door for Father Walker, and waited for Abby to enter, his hand at the small of her back, into a large, sloping lecture hall.

At the front of the room, on a small platform stage, rested a wooden podium and a large silver movie screen. The closer they got to the stage, the paler Hayden seemed to get.

Abby saw the worry there, the fear. She whispered, "Hayseed?"

He gave her a nervous glance and watched Father Walker as he plugged his laptop into the projector sitting on the podium. "Pull up the video clip and tell me what you see."

In a moment, video filled the large screen on stage, and Abby watched the footage from Hayden's drone as it zoomed around the old man's house and hovered outside his bedroom window. Hayden released a slow, controlled breath, and took a step backward as he watched.

The man entered the bedroom, sat down at his desk, and turned the pages of the album. Father Walker turned to Hayden. "What am I looking at here?"

"Just watch a moment longer." Hayden chewed his bottom lip and appeared as if he didn't really want to watch the video so large and looming in front of him. "Get ready to pause."

On the screen, the man suddenly turned his head and stared through his window directly at the drone. The man's hopeless expression, lost and forlorn, hit Abby all over again. The misery there. She crossed her arms and continued watching.

He stood from his desk, heading toward the hallway, and the moment before he left the room and Hayden steered the drone away, is when it happened.

A chipped rind of ice grew along Abby's spine, spread along the back of her neck and the length of her arms. A harsh exhale escaped her and her legs felt weak.

Father Walker cleared his throat and paused the video, rewound it a few seconds, and then tapped the right arrow on his laptop, taking it forward frame by frame. The man on screen, rising from his chair, standing, and turning away from the camera. One step, two steps, toward the hallway, his head turning toward the right as he crossed the threshold of the bedroom.

Father Walker stopped and stared at the screen, then tapped the forward arrow again.

Frame by frame, in the hallway outside the man's bedroom, a shape took form quickly, a black shadow growing in density. The figure seemed to be crawling on the wall itself, arms reaching forward in the direction the man had walked. It moved fully into sight through the frame of the doorway, and the bulbous shape where a head would be, turned toward the drone camera, hesitated, and then continued to the right, out of frame.

Abby put a hand out on the podium to steady herself. Her heart thumped in her chest, but she couldn't turn away from the screen.

Father Walker tapped his laptop to rewind several frames, stopping where the figure stared at the drone. He stepped toward the screen and stared quietly for a long moment before he turned to Hayden again and gave a curt nod. "Unless you're pranking a man of the cloth, this is…" He glanced back at the screen and then to Hayden again. "Quite something."

"It's real, Father."

The priest studied Hayden's expression, and coughed, clearing his throat. "Let's uh…" He closed his laptop and unplugged it from the projector, gathering the computer beneath his arm. "Let's head to my office and talk for a moment."

Hayden and Abby followed the priest from the lecture hall, the sound of the man's flip-flops echoing off the walls. Midway down the hall, Father Walker paused by a wooden door with a frosted glass panel on the upper half. He opened it and held his arm out in front of him. "Please, come in."

He closed the office door behind him as Hayden and Abby sat down in the worn but comfortable leather chairs in front of a wide desk. Bookshelves lined the walls, along with framed photographs.

A tall window was behind the desk, its wide sill home to a row of potted cactus and other succulent plants.

Father Walker put his laptop on the desk and paused, his hand resting on the computer. "Yes, well." He sat down and opened a desk drawer, pulled a bottle of Jameson whiskey and a short glass tumbler. "And yes, I'm aware how early it is, but uh…" He shook his head as he uncapped the liquor and poured a finger's worth into the glass. "There's paper cups at the water cooler behind you, if either of you…"

The lines of the man's face appeared to have deepened over the last ten minutes. He took his sunglasses off the top of his head and set them aside on his desk, sipped from his glass and seemed lost in thought. Another drink, and Father Walker's attention landed on Hayden. "This morning, you mentioned this man committed suicide?"

Hayden gave a slight nod and the priest leaned back in his chair with a heavy exhale. "People in a depressive state, the sort where taking your own life is a real consideration… I've always felt they attract predators." He leaned forward and picked up his glass again. "Much like the calls of a sick or weak animal in the wild."

"Predators?" Abby still felt the chill inside her, kept her arms crossed to feel what little warmth she could.

"The *spiritual* kind." Father Walker flicked his tongue out over his lips. "They've been called different names. Demons, obviously. Ancient Babylonians called them *those that lay in wait*. The Djinn. Evil spirits. They all uh…" The priest let his sentence fade as he stared at his glass and then looked back at Hayden. "What else do you know about the man?"

"Not much. He was pretty upset about something, but not sure what, exactly." Hayden shifted in the chair.

"He showed up a couple of times standing outside my apartment building, but didn't explain why." Abby rubbed her arms and pulled her sweater up close around the back of her neck. "Screaming and asking what we'd done."

"What you've done?" Father Walker shook his head. "What does that mean? Where do you live?"

"The man, he uh…" Hayden chewed his bottom lip. "He used to work at Harper's Grove. It's the site of the—"

"Goddamn that place," the priest whispered the words. His expression sharpened, lips pursed tightly together. His eyes took on a weary, tired look. He glanced at his empty glass, toward the Jameson bottle, and then propped his elbows on the desk.

"What happened there?" Abby's voice sounded quiet, timid, as if she was telling a secret in church.

The priest flicked his tongue out over his lips again to moisten them, and then reached for the whiskey. "The worst kind of hell there is."

Chapter Nineteen

HAYDEN, WHY DID you want me to see this?" Father Walker stood with his back turned, staring out his office window to the manicured college grounds. "For some sort of validation or—"

"I didn't know who else to talk to about it. Plus your..." Hayden glanced at Abby and then continued. "Your studies, I thought maybe—"

"That's something else entirely, Hayden." He turned to face the two of them, and then addressed Abby directly. "For years, I've read about and studied serial killers, Bundy, Ramirez, Gacey, all the greatest hits, so to speak. But also, the lesser-known events. Places where terrible things might have happened, or small-town killers, the ones that don't end up turned into some kind of sick celebrity."

"You should see his collection." Hayden muttered.

Abby turned to Hayden. "Collection?"

"Drawings from Manson, a John Wayne Gacey painting, and—"

"You make me sound like I'm making a skin suit in my basement." Father Walker raised an eyebrow at him, and continued speaking to Abby. "There are auctions that take place, oddities, different things with bad history attached."

"A little... morbid, but why?" Abby shifted in her chair.

The priest shrugged. "I guess I'm trying to understand what makes a person do these kinds of horrible things. Is evil itself a traveling thing, jumping from person to person? Or are these people, these killers, are they only a product of poor nurturing and circumstance?"

"I also thought maybe..." Hayden said, "you've been in town for, what, thirty years or so? I thought you'd know something, maybe even know the man."

The priest shook his head slightly, sighed, and turned back to stare out the window silently. He swirled the liquor around in his glass, took another sip, and cleared his throat. "When I was a young man, I spent some time in Haiti, must have been '78. Missionary work, the kind of *save the world* grunt work only young priests are prone to do." He put his drink on the windowsill and leaned against it, crossing his arms. "I was in this little rural town, north of Hinche, helping build a well for the village.

"I was digging right along with the other local men, and we hit this... this *pocket* underground. Was a cave, I suppose, though not much of one." Father Walker uncrossed his arms and motioned with his hands. "Barely big enough for two men to stand side by side, but we exposed it and the man closest saw the entrance had been sealed off with a stone wall.

"He pushed the end of his shovel inside the busted wall and all of us heard a breaking sound inside. Men scrambled closer and pulled the stones loose until we could see inside."

Hayden leaned forward. "What was it?"

"A clay vessel," he reached for the bottle of Jameson and held it up. "About this size, little smaller maybe." Father Walker set the bottle down on the desk again. "It'd been sealed up in there, but it looked brand new, except for the broken shard from the man's shovel. Could still see dried splashes of blood on the thing. Black feathers and bones tied around it with a woven cord tying the lid shut and wrapped 'round and 'round it, like a post on a boat dock."

The man's voice was calming to Abby, smooth and even-tempered, but there was something in his words that made her anxious as well. She pulled the sleeves of her sweater down lower on her arms.

"That man, the first one, he staggered against the sides of the hole and his eyes rolled back in his head. Started talking gibberish, a language no one could understand." Father Walker looked at his desk and he continued. "Hell, I thought he was having a stroke or something right there, but no, he came back out of it a minute or two later. Somebody gave him cool water to drink and he seemed fine the rest of the day."

"But?" Hayden asked.

The priest coughed and cleared his throat, turned away from them and studied the campus grounds again. "He went home and murdered his entire family. Both of his daughters and his two-year old son, his wife, and his mother-in-law. They weren't... easy deaths. He used the blade of a spade shovel."

"My God." Abby whispered and put a hand to her mouth.

Father Walker nodded slightly. "I saw that man the next day when they dragged him through town in ropes. Saw him when the other villagers… they took care of law themselves. He didn't have any fear in his expression, no *remorse* in his eyes. The man I knew was long gone. Whatever had hold of him wasn't afraid of dying, it was… *amused.*

He leveled his gaze at Hayden. "I've seen evil in my life. I know what it *is*, and what it *isn't*. That thing, Hayden, what you showed me on the video footage, that is real darkness."

The priest stood still, his attention falling away from Hayden as he seemed to mull something over, and then he sat down in his office chair. "Would you two excuse me a moment? There's someone I need to call privately."

"Of course, Father." Hayden stood up, and Abby followed as they walked out of the office and stood in the hallway. Closing the door, Hayden turned toward her. "You okay?"

"Not so much, no." Hearing him ask, the shaking feeling inside Abby threatened to bubble free.

"It's a lot, I know." He put a hand on her shoulder, and gently rubbed the outside of her arm. "I couldn't explain it over—"

"I get it." Abby's throat constricted her words and she tried to swallow. She felt herself drawn into Hayden's embrace and he held her there, patting her back softly.

From beyond the frosted glass of the office door, even though she couldn't make out the words, Abby heard the priest's voice raise slightly, and then return to an even calm tone. She pulled back slightly and turned her head, whispering. "Will you come over tonight? Please?"

"Yeah, of course." Hayden rested his chin on top of her head and squeezed her close.

"Come back in, please." Father Walker called from his office.

He was writing on a sheet of notepaper when they walked in, and he handed it to Hayden. "Cora Jean Myers. That's her phone number and address." The priest put his hands flat on the top of his desk. "She had a chemotherapy session today, so in *her* words, she's not worth a pinch of shit the rest of the day, but she's agreed to meet with you tomorrow. Any time after nine in the morning."

Hayden glanced at the paper and nodded. "Who is she?"

"She's the last person alive who used to work at Harper's Grove."

BOOK TWO

Chapter Twenty

ORA JEAN'S HAND shook as she filled the coffeemaker with water to the halfway mark.

She returned the glass pot to its nesting place on the metal heating plate and flicked the switch to ON. The soft burbles and burps of the coffeemaker began to sound out in the small kitchen, and Cora Jean reached for her pack of Virginia Slims and the lighter beside it.

A practiced flick of her thumb on the lighter, and the thin cigarette caught fire at the tip. She inhaled and then slowly exhaled, watching the smoke curl into the air. The doctors had told her to quit smoking.

At your age, we insist, they said. *You've been lucky so far.*

But it's not their life to live, is it? And what the hell do they know about luck?

Raising the cigarette to her lips, Cora Jean took a long drag. Her stomach was an empty canyon, but she knew the moment she put so much as a bite of oatmeal in her belly, she'd throw it right back up again. The nausea was worse on treatment days, though by the next morning, it eased off. A little.

"Chickenshit!"

She turned her head in the direction the voice had come from. After putting her cigarette in the ashtray on the kitchen table, she walked into the living room to look through the window. The morning sunlight made her wince, but Cora Jean narrowed her eyes and saw three boys straddling their bicycles out on the sidewalk. She studied them, guessing the boy in the middle, with his baseball hat flipped backwards, was about twelve years old. The other two were shorter, lankier, a year or two younger at most.

"See, Wiley?" The kid with the baseball hat turned to the boy closest to him. "I *told* you he was gonna puss out."

"Am not!" The third boy spoke in a raised voice, and with a swipe of his foot, flipped the kickstand out to park his bike on the cement. He swung his right leg off the seat and stood still, his right hand a balled-up fist. "Besides, I think *you're* the one who's chickenshit, or else *you'd* do it."

"Whatever you say." Baseball Hat snickered, shook his head, and turned to the other boy. "C'mon Wiley. He's not gonna—"

"I *am*, okay? I'll go get one of the stupid things!" The boy being accused of pussing out turned his back on the two others and started walking the cracked cement sidewalk toward the front porch. His pace was quick to start, fueled by anger and the unique sort of peer pressure only kids can conjure up for other kids, but the closer he got, the slower his gait became.

Cora Jean knew why they were here. It happened from time to time, but no real harm was ever done, and if she lived out the rest of her life being the scary crazy lady in the neighborhood, that was fine with her. Let the rumor mill fly.

I'm half past give a shit, Cora thought, as she walked to the closed front door and rested her hand on the knob. She gently twisted the knob on the auxiliary lock to the open position, and then turned the doorknob in her hands far enough to feel the lock give way.

Cora Jean waited and listened at the door. She heard the soft rustle of sneakers against weeds at the edge of her porch and then a cautious footstep on one stair tread, the boy's stealth betrayed by the creak of wood. There was an extended moment of silence, and then she heard another step, and the familiar groan of the floorboards on the front porch itself.

One little shit, two little shits, three little shits.

She swung the front door open in a full arc and lunged out onto the porch, an expression of rage on her pale, gaunt face, downy tufts of her chemo-hair splayed out in matted spikes. The boy standing on her porch drained of color like a time-lapse of sun bleaching driftwood. His eyes widened as quickly as his mouth, and he screamed as he jumped from the porch, stumbled into the grass, and then regained his feet.

Raising one shaking, bony finger at the boys frozen on the sidewalk, Cora Jean screamed out at them. "You stay away from them, y' hear?"

She put her index finger at the bottom of her chin and slid it slowly across her throat. "Lest your little heads becomes one of 'em!" The three of them fumbled to make their feet push their bike pedals, and as they regained motor function, Cora Jean gave her best impersonation of a wicked witch's laugh.

Their high-pitched screams continued as they raced away, and Cora Jean smiled, pleased with herself. She glanced at the row of plastic baby dolls hanging from the edge of the porch roof. Some were old, and some were new, the majority purchased at yard sales and thrift shops. A light breeze blew in and she watched as their plastic bodies turned in the air. A few had missing arms or legs. Most of their eyes were sun-faded, turning their irises a blind cornflower blue.

A chill rippled through Cora Jean and she pursed her lips, the humorous feeling inside her quickly shifted into something else. She watched the pink plastic figures sway in unison, and then she shuffled back inside the house and closed the door. After locking the door, she walked through the shadows of the living room, following the smell of freshly brewed coffee.

The clock on the wall over the kitchen sink showed it was almost nine o'clock.

Won't be much longer 'fore them people Father Walker told me about will show up.

She frowned as she poured a mug of coffee and added a splash of vanilla creamer. For a moment, she watched the mixture, swirling in light and shadow in the confines of her mug.

She took a sip of hot coffee and held it in her mouth a moment, savoring it, and then swallowed it quickly before her mind had time to realize her stomach had fuel to toss back up.

"These people have seen something," the old priest spoke in that stern priestly tone of voice. *"Cora Jean,* the father said, *"you are the only one left. It would be a sin to not help if you can."*

And Charlie Heath committed suicide.

And so, she had agreed, albeit reluctantly. Partly because the priest was right, but mostly because he'd been a good friend to her over the years, *hippie priest pot smoker* that he was.

Her stomach roiled and, for a second, she thought maybe asking Father Walker for a puff of weed to help her through the sickness might not be a bad idea. Cora Jean walked to the sink and rested both hands on the counter, holding herself steady, waiting to see if her stomach would accept the sweetened coffee. A flash of heat rolled through her and she closed her eyes, but her stomach held.

From outside, she heard the sound of two car doors closing and she sighed and nodded. Cora Jean picked up her cigarette and re-lit the end, took a drag, and walked toward the front door again, uncertain if she was ready to revisit the past.

She paused and took a pink handkerchief from a coat hook to the right of the door, took the time to drape and tie it over her head.

No use in them seeing what chemo is doing to my once beautiful hair.

She opened the door, as the sound of footsteps made the boards of the porch creak, and saw a woman and a man standing there.

The girl is pretty, a hair's breadth shy of beautiful, Cora Jean thought. *And the man looks a little like that actor, the one in all those funny movies, only he's thinner and his beard is a lot shorter.*

"Cora Jean?" The woman spoke, the tone of her voice soft, the expression on her face one of friendly concern.

She glanced at the girl and then turned back to the man. There was something unsettled in his eyes and he looked pale.

"You two the ones that gone and woke 'em up?"

Chapter Twenty-One

WHO'S THE DAMNED fool that decided to turn the place into apartments?"

"Uh, my... my uncle." The man, Hayden, looked sheepish as he answered. He crossed his arms and leaned against the porch railing.

Cora Jean shook her head and flicked her cigarette, watching the ash float down to the boards of the porch. "I'd say he's responsible, but that ain't the truth, not really." She sighed, walked toward a folding lawn chair set to the left of her front door and eased herself onto it.

"What can you tell us about Harper's Grove?" The girl leaned forward from her seat on the porch swing. "What did you mean when you asked if we woke—"

"Young man? Do me a favor." Cora Jean nodded toward the entrance to the house. "Walk on into my kitchen and you'll see a bottle of Southern Comfort on top of the fridge. In the cupboard to the right of the sink are some little cartoon glasses. Bugs Bunny or Elmer Fudd will do me just fine. Bring the glass *and* the bottle out here for me, please."

Hayden nodded and started toward the door, but paused. "Ice?" She shook her head.

He took another step, his hand on the doorknob, and paused again, his gaze on the small sign by the threshold. "Beware of dog?"

Cora Jean snickered. "Just there to scare away kids and salesmen. I don't own so much as a goldfish."

"No cats?"

"Why, 'cause I'm a crazy ol' lady? I should have cats?" She arched an eyebrow and stared at him, watched the color in his cheeks deepen, and then she snickered. "I'm just givin' you hell, Boy."

An image in her mind hit her hard and fast, as they always did.

The girl, Flower, holding that wriggling white tidbit in her fingers and stuffing it in her mouth.

Cora Jean shook her head. "No, Son, no cats. Never much wanted one." She watched him head inside and saw the girl staring at the line-up of hanging dolls. "It helps keep them away. One of them at least."

"Who?"

A tinge of pain squirreled its way through her chest, but it was only a flash, one of those odd, no-explanation things that arrives with age. Cora Jean raised the cigarette to her lips, took the last drag and stubbed it out on the arm of her chair until she saw no more fire in it. She let the dead cigarette butt fall to the porch boards.

"Geraldo Rivera tried to interview me once, tracked me down in 1971, I think." She withdrew her lighter and pack of Virginia Slims from her sweater pocket. She pulled a cigarette free of the pack and held it. "Son of a bitch just showed up one day with a camera man and some assistants. No phone call, no nothing."

"What'd you do?"

Cora Jean glanced at Abby and smirked. "Told him and his greasy mustache to piss off and slammed the door in his face." She put the cigarette between her lips, lit it, and then spoke through an exhale of smoke. "I decided to move a couple days after though. Had an unlisted phone number and a PO Box with no forwarding address. He either decided I wasn't worth the trouble, or couldn't find me, and he went on to report about the Willowbrook State School up in Staten Island. That place..." she shook her head. "Luxury resort compared to Harper's Grove."

Hayden stepped onto the porch and handed Cora Jean a glass with Bugs Bunny's smiling face on the side. He took the cap off the bottle of liquor and poured for her. "Say when."

Cora Jean watched until the glass was filled halfway and she put a hand up. "Thank you."

He put the cap back on the bottle, set it down next to her chair, and went back to leaning against the porch railing.

She took a small sip, swirling the tingling liquid around her mouth, and then swallowed, enjoying the warm sensation.

Stomach doesn't have a problem with this, huh?

Looking out at the front yard, Cora Jean felt a hint of amusement at scaring the boys earlier. They weren't the first, and they wouldn't be the last. She took a drag from her cigarette, tasting the tobacco mixed with the sweet alcohol in her mouth.

"I asked about waking 'em up because they showed up here about six months ago, give or take a few days. Dead kittens on my doorstep. Sound of something crawling down my hallways at night—like something that'd fallen and was dragging itself along." She flicked ash to the porch again and took another sip from her glass.

"And that goddamn noise with the glasses. Ringing out in broad daylight, middle of the night..." Cora Jean crossed her legs and shifted into the chair. She looked up at the girl's face. "My parents had me when they was young. Momma was nineteen and my father was barely twenty. He got called off to Vietnam and didn't come home. It was hard and Momma struggled. She tried but with her, my little brother and I...

"I was three months shy of graduating high school when I had to drop out and get a job to help Momma make ends meet. Later on, I went and got my G.E.D., but it wasn't the same. *Wantin'* to quit school, and being *forced* to quit are very different things. Does somethin' to you as a person, not having a choice."

She watched the curls of smoke rise from her cigarette, the glowing tip. "I started at Harper's Grove in the spring of 1964, few weeks after I turned seventeen, and worked there until it was shut down, couple months later. I'd heard it was bad, but... what you hear and what you see are often very different things."

Tears sprung to her eyes, surprising her. Cora Jean blinked them away and drank from her glass. "My first day there, Dr. Roy Dobsen, he ran the place, assigned me to the third floor C-Corridor.

Some people called it the Cake Walk, but I can assure you, it was anything but."

Cora Jean flicked her cigarette without thinking, gray flecks sifting down to the porch. "Dead Pennies is what they called them."

"Called who?" Abby whispered. She leaned forward on the swing. "Cora Jean, what happened?"

Chapter Twenty-Two

1964

"AIN'T YOU GONNA eat breakfast, too?"

"Don't say *ain't,* Henry."

"But ain—*aren't* you gonna eat breakfast?" Henry dropped his bookbag on the floor as he slid onto a chair at the kitchen table and then propped his chin on the palms of his hands.

Cora Jean used a spatula to push the single scrambled egg from the skillet onto a small plate beside two small strips of bacon. "Not this morning, no." She grabbed a clean fork from the dish drainer and set the utensil and plate in front of her little brother.

"Feels nice outside this morning, but you know how it's been, sunny to start and flurries to end. Make sure and take a jacket with you to school. You might need it at recess." Cora Jean felt her insides churn at speaking the word *school,* but steered her mind away from it.

Henry's expression fell slightly, even as he crunched on a strip of bacon. "You're not going to school today?"

"I'm... I'll get there." She poured a small glass of milk and set it beside his plate. "Don't dillydally now." Cora Jean turned away from him as her eyes got hot and glassy. She busied herself washing the butter grease off of the skillet and then set it in the drainer to dry. By then, Henry had finished his breakfast and she turned back to him with a nod. "Brush your teeth quick, you've got to get going."

He rushed upstairs and she heard the sound of the bathroom faucet, the enthusiastic scrubbing sound as Henry brushed his teeth, and then the water getting cut off. A moment later, he bounded down the stairs, jumping off the third from the bottom, and landing on both feet with a smile.

Cora Jean shook her head at him, and couldn't help but smile at Henry's attitude. "Come here and let me check you over."

He walked closer, stopped in front of her, and she glanced over his combed hair, mouth absent of breakfast remnants, and shirt free of wrinkles. She gave him a nod and leaned down for a hug. "Good job, now get ya butt going!"

Henry grinned and grabbed his bookbag from the floor as he beelined it for the front door.

"Jacket!" Cora Jean called, and watched him swipe his jacket from the coat rack and rush outside. She closed the door behind him as he headed to school and it all hit her then, the raw and brash reality of it all. Tears flooded her eyes. She walked upstairs to her bedroom and quietly eased the door shut.

A stack of books rested on a shabby wooden desk in the corner of her bedroom and Cora Jean went to stand beside them. She picked the one off the top and read the title: GEOMETRY FUNDAMENTALS. Next was: THE STUDY OF EARTH SCIENCE.

Cora Jean let the two thick textbooks fall into a wastebasket beside the desk and looked at the next book on the stack. Tears spilled from her eyes and ran down her cheeks.

She ran her fingertips over the title lettering on the cover: EXCELLENCE IN ENGLISH LITERATURE. Cora Jean opened the cover and flipped through the pages, reading bits and pieces. She closed the book, traced the title again with her fingers, and as she blinked, more tears escaped the dam. She sniffled, shook her head, and then tossed the book into the wastebasket with the other two.

"Cora Jean!"

She cleared her throat and yelled back a reply. "Yes, Momma!"

"Don't be late on your first day, now."

Cora Jean heard the sound of her mother's wheelchair maneuvering through the rooms downstairs. She looked at herself in the mirror, wiped her eyes with her fingers and then wiped those on her skirt. Taking a deep breath, Cora Jean let it out slowly, left her room, and walked downstairs. Momma was in her wheelchair, sitting in the living room.

"Momma, want me to make you breakfast 'fore I leave?"

"No, you ain't got time. 'Sides, I'll be fine." Momma was staring, her weary expression strung across her face like dull tinsel. "It's only for a little while, Cora Jean. I'll get better, you'll see."

She glanced at her mother, faked a smile and nodded. There'd been enough tears for one day already. "I know, Momma." Cora Jean planted a soft kiss on top of her mother's head and then grabbed a sweater off the coat rack. "Love you and I'll see you after work."

"I love you, too." The tired expression, the look of absolute weariness, on her mother's face was almost too much.

I'm glad she doesn't come out for Henry to see before he goes to school.

Cora Jean pulled the front door closed behind her and stood on the cement stoop.

Momma's diabetes was something neither of them spoke about, but was always present. Time and again, buying insulin was ignored in favor of having food in the house, or keeping the electric on. She wore doubled up men's white cotton socks on her left foot most of the time, but when she didn't, Cora Jean had noticed the blue-black-yellow color on the toes.

It was only a matter of time before doctors decided to amputate, and though neither of them mentioned it, they both knew the fact as surely as their own names.

School can wait. Family is the important thing.

Cora Jean pulled the sides of her sweater and buttoned three holes along the seam. It was time to start her first day at Harper's Grove.

Chapter Twenty-Three

1964

YOU'RE EXPECTED TO be prompt and do the duties assigned to you." Dr. Ray Dobsen had shaken Cora Jean's hand and made eye contact when he introduced himself, and hadn't looked at her since. His attention was on a clipboard he held in front of him, flipping pages and pausing occasionally to read. He was tall and lean, hair combed back from his face, which was home to dark, narrow eyes behind silver-rimmed glasses. Dr. Dobsen acted like a man who needed to be somewhere else, but Cora Jean couldn't decide whether his behavior was from being incredibly busy with other duties or because he was annoyed with what was in front of him.

He paused with papers in his hand, and she noticed a thick ring on his hand, gold with a large faux ruby set in place, the kind of ring she'd seen some military men wear.

"You'll be paid every Thursday. If you are able, I allow two fifteen-minute…" He curled another paper over the top of the clipboard. "Breaks. One at nine-thirty and another at three o'clock. A half hour lunch is…" He put the papers back in place and met her eyes again as he gave a slight shrug. "Whenever you can take it."

He rapped his ring on the desk in the lobby and a woman sitting behind the desk looked up from paperwork as Dr. Dobsen continued to speak. "Diane, make sure Cora Jean signs all the IRS forms by tomorrow at the latest."

Diane nodded and went back to jotting notes on her papers.

He pointed down a corridor behind Cora Jean and she turned to look.

"Any questions, my office is at the end of the hall, down there on the left. I hope you have a good first day."

The doctor was walking at a brisk pace down the hallway when Diane called out. "Dr. Dobsen, where is she assigned?"

He stopped walking and turned back, slowly. "C3. Miss Myers could use the help."

Diane glanced at her, and as the footsteps of the man receded down the hallway, Cora Jean noticed the worried expression on the woman's face. When the sound of an office door closing carried back to them, Diane put her pen down on her desk and leaned back in her chair. "How old are you?"

"Seventeen." Cora Jean felt on display, inspected.

"Mmmmmhmm." Diane crossed her arms. "Couldn't get a job at the Tasty Freeze or the rollerskatin' rink?"

Cora Jean shifted in place and flicked her tongue over dry lips. "My momma, she… I need a full-time job is all."

Diane's expression softened and she broke eye contact, looking at her desk. She nodded and sighed, pushed her wheeled office chair away from the desk and stood. "Alright then, come with me." She walked from behind the desk, heading toward a wide, impressive flight of steps leading upward. "Elevator's broken, hell, it's *been* broken for a couple months now, and my guess is it'll be a while before it gets fixed, so you'll be getting your exercise." She slid her hand along the thick wooden stair railing as she climbed.

The two of them reached the first landing on the stairs and Cora Jean paused at the sound of crying beyond a set of double doors.

"This is C2, the corridor where the youngest stay." Diane pulled one of the doors open and waved Cora Jean through the entrance.

It was the smell that hit her first, the humid odor of urine and feces that reminded her of the goat barn at the county fair. She wrinkled her nose and Diane nodded without speaking.

The left side of the hallway had a row of windows revealing a room beyond, and Cora Jean stared at what lay before her. Two nurses moved inside, walking the rows with clipboards in hand and checking things off.

A large room was filled with a grid of bassinets. Small pale bodies moved in some of them, and were still in others. Bare arms and legs, pale and twisted like driftwood. Misshapen faces. Cleft palates. From newborns swaddled in cheap blankets, to what appeared to be several toddlers, their legs drawn and curled against their bodies to fit in the bassinets. Stains of brown and yellow smudged the cloth diapers. A sharp wail pierced the air and Cora Jean flinched. The two nurses inside the room were unfazed and continued on with their clipboards.

Cora Jean's stomach shifted inside, and a sick heat flashed through her.

"It's a lot to take in, I know." Diane crossed her arms and peered through the windows. One of the women looked up and gave Diane a little wave, which she returned.

Two nurses, Cora Jean thought. *Two nurses to take care of about sixty children.*

"Come on. Time to get you to Miss Myers." Diane headed back for the double-doors and the stairs, and Cora Jean followed her onto the landing.

"Look, Cora…" Diane paused, turning her head slightly as if she was listening for sounds downstairs, but it was quiet. "This place can be… *difficult.* Things here take a while to get used to and maybe they're things you *shouldn't* get used to. Maybe nobody should."

"I can do it," Cora Jean replied, though her voice sounded shaky and weak.

Diane's gaze remained on her a moment more. "C3 is what most people here call the Cake Walk." She pointed at the double doors they'd walked through. "That? That's a nursery, no matter how you look at it. Feed and change diapers." Diane pointed above them. "The Cake Walk is something else entirely."

"Why do they call—"

From the flight of stairs above them, sounds of people yelling broke the silence, and Diane broke into a run up the steps with Cora

Jean behind her. Reaching the set of doors, Diane grabbed a handle and flung it open.

"Grab her goddamn arm!"

It was a woman's voice, and as Diane rushed in, Cora Jean took several steps and stopped at the sight. A young girl thrashed on the floor, screamed through vocal chords of broken glass. The noises were an animal in agony, shrieking anger and fear and pain. Her head twisted from the tangle of blonde, shoulder-length hair, and Cora Jean saw her mouth and chin were bloody.

"Hold her, Carl!" The yelling woman was crouched, holding the left wrist of the girl in one hand, and trying to put her knee on the girl's stomach.

The man she was referring to was kneeling on the opposite side of the girl, and as Diane reached them, the man gripped the wrist of the girl's flailing right arm.

She kicked out with two knobby-kneed legs, almost catching Diane in the ankle, but the woman dodged the kick and dropped to the floor. With both hands, Diane grabbed the girl's kneecap and pressed it to the floor. The girl bucked her hips and as she thrashed out, almost kicked Carl in the face. She stretched her neck, trying to get her mouth on his hands and he twisted away, wrenching her elbow joint.

Another piercing scream burst from the girl's throat.

The nurse snapped her head up at Cora Jean. "Get over here and help! Hold her goddamn leg down!"

Cora Jean broke free of her paralysis and bolted toward the other three people. She moved back from the girl's kicking leg and then pounced down, grabbing the girl at her protruding kneecap and laying down on it, pinning her to the floor.

The man produced a syringe from somewhere and Cora Jean watched as he jabbed it into the girl's upper arm and pressed the plunger. Almost immediately, the girl's head lolled back toward the dull tile floor and the sounds emanating from her throat dropped to a soft whine. Her arms and legs stopped thrashing, and then she was still against the floor.

Carl released her arm and stood up first, followed by Diane and then the other woman. Cora Jean was the last one to let go, and adrenaline coursed through her veins, making her feel like a live electrical wire, as she stood on her feet again.

"That little bitch."

Cora Jean turned to the sound of the voice and saw a woman walk out of a small room to her left. Her face was blanched of color, but tight and constrained, holding back rage.

"I... am fucking... *done*." The woman held her left arm, wrapped in sheets of brown paper towels, out away from her body. Red blossoms bled through the paper. The woman spoke in a low, even, but angry tone. "I'm going to the Infirmary to get this patched up, and *then* I'm walking the *fuck* out of here."

"Anna—"

The woman turned with a glare and then headed out the double doors, leaving a liquid trail of burnt cherry droplets in her wake.

"*Shiiiiiiiit.*" The nurse whispered under her breath and snorted, shook her head in disgust, and then turned to Carl. "Put her on a gurney and strap her ass down, wrists *and* ankle cuffs."

The man walked into a room with an open door to his right, emerging seconds later pushing a hospital gurney in front of him. The nurse released a heavy exhale and walked toward a desk near the double doors. She slid into the chair behind it, and lifted a phone receiver from its cradle. A thin wooden plaque sitting on the desk read MISS MYERS.

Diane caught Cora Jean's attention and then she looked down at the girl on the floor, splayed out and unconscious. She stared at the girl for a few moments and turned to Cora Jean again, mouthed the words, "good luck, today." And with that, Diane walked past her and through the double doors. The sound of her receding footsteps faded as the doors closed.

"That's correct." Miss Myers nodded at the voice on the other end of the phone. "This is the third... yes, exactly." She slid a clipboard on the desktop in front of her. "Alright then, thank you, Doctor." She hung up the receiver and her gaze landed on Carl as he finished strapping in the girl's wrists to the gurney.

"Carl? Dobsen's orders. Third time's a charm for her. Today was the last."

The man gave a silent, curt nod, buckled the girl's ankles into thick leather cuffs secured to the gurney's metal frame, and pushed it toward the rear of the large room.

Cora Jean watched as he paused to open a door, and then wheeled the gurney inside, closing the door behind him. "Where... what's going to—"

"You work this job, on *this* floor, you *have* to react quickly." Miss Myers leveled her gaze at Cora Jean and stood from the desk chair. "I know it's your first day and it's... it's a lot." She walked from around her desk to stand in front of it. "From now on, if I or anyone else yells at you to help, you do it and you do it immediately. Around here, hesitating gets people hurt, or worse."

Cora Jean felt that flush of heat through her veins again. "They're *children*."

"*Uh huh*, children who don't know any better." Miss Myers's expression grew stern. She pointed to the doorway Carl and the girl had gone through. "That girl, that... *child*... attacked a nurse a few months ago. Less than a week on the job, and that *child* used the metal clip of a pen to peel that woman's face off in less time than it takes to brew a pot of coffee."

Cora Jean's stomach twisted into a wet knot of rope.

"Don't turn your back on them. Don't *ever* let your guard down." Miss Myers nodded toward the trail of blood drops leading toward the double doors.

"Use nicknames instead of their real name. It helps." A soft whimpering sound came from beyond the doorway of the room Carl had taken the girl. Miss Myers didn't even so much as glance in the direction. "Don't get attached to *them*, and don't dare let them get attached to *you*."

"Attached?" Cora Jean silently scolded herself for how weak her voice sounded.

"You don't *really* want them to like you. If they do, you'll be the *sole* focus of their attention, and trust me when I tell you..." Miss Myers took a step closer and her strict tone eased, if only slightly. "That's the last thing in the world you want to happen."

Chapter Twenty-Four

1964

YOU CAN FEED Milk his breakfast. Normally, at any mealtime, we need to make sure Flower, the girl from this morning, and Milk are separated. He won't give you any trouble and you won't have to worry about Flower for…" Miss Myers glanced at the room Carl had taken the girl into. "A few hours at least."

Cora Jean stirred a bowl of steaming creamed wheat, set the spoon down, and continued on with helping. With the elevator broken, Miss Myers had said the food was made right here in the corridor, but it was all easy enough. Cora Jean had helped prepare bowls of creamed wheat and oatmeal, paper cups of sliced cantaloupe, and bananas, slices of toast. Simple. Childlike. "Why do you separate them?"

"Ten, eleven, twelve." Miss Myers whispered to herself as she counted paper cups of cubed cantaloupe and then put them on a

wheeled cart she'd pulled from a storage room. She looked up at Cora Jean. "Flower's been here for about seven years now. She had problems before she was even born, but life didn't get any better. When she was four years old, her daddy tried to burn the house down, with Flower still in it. Somehow, she made it out alive, but just barely. Her parents died instead."

Diane was right, Cora Jean thought. *A lot to get used to, and maybe things no one ever should get used to.*

"I... I noticed her burn scars."

"Third degree burns on over three-quarters of her body." Miss Myers's voice lowered. "It's a terrible thing to say out loud, but I wonder if she'd have been better off going with her parents instead."

Miss Myers's attention was elsewhere as she studied the food cart, and then she looked up at Cora Jean once more. "Flower's taken Milk under her wing as some kind of... she babies him, mothers him. We tried to put a stop to it, but gave up. She's not really hurtin' anything, fussin' and fawnin' over him. We'll find Milk sitting in his wheelchair or in his cot, some sort of cloth wrapped around him like a diaper. She'll try to rock him to sleep, hums songs to him at night, that sort of thing." She nodded at the row of creamed wheat and oatmeal bowls. "Stir."

Cora Jean went down the line, stirring the contents of each with the one spoon she'd been given, watching steam escape from the surfaces.

"Flower wants to hug everyone, unless she thinks Milk's getting hurt." Miss Myers pulled a keyring from a pocket in her nurse's uniform, and unlocked a lower drawer on her desk. She withdrew two sections of chain about the length of a large man's belt, and a steel spoon with a slot drilled out of the handle, and then set them both on the desktop. "This morning, Flower took a bite out of Nurse Anna's arm because the woman took a stuffed animal off of Milk's lap."

The swarm of angry bees in Cora Jean's stomach made fresh waves of heat rush through her. Children or not, she'd have to be careful.

"We have to separate them at meal times or else you won't get a damned thing done. She'll try to help you shovel food into his mouth the entire time, and if you don't let her help, she'll lose her goddamn mind."

Cora Jean looked over the bowls of breakfast on the cart. "How many children are here in C3-Corridor?"

Miss Myers continued prepping and spoke without looking up. "There are thirty-seven residents on the Cake Walk and four of… well, after this morning, *three of us,* to take care of them all."

Cora Jean did the arithmetic in her head. Twelve children per caregiver seemed impossible.

It is *impossible. To do it correctly at least.*

"Okay, come here Cora." Miss Myers took the length of chain, the links about the thickness of what someone would use for a collar on a small dog, and looped it behind Cora Jean's waist, bringing it around to the front. She reached to the desktop, picked up the spoon, and brought it in line with one end of the chain.

Cora Jean watched the woman thread the chain through the hole in the end of the spoon handle, and then clip the chain belt closed with the snap hook on the other end. Miss Myers spun it to the side and let the spoon dangle from the short remaining length of chain, and then met Cora Jean's eyes. "Some of them here, they get hold of a metal spoon like this and it's deadly as a butcher knife. We don't take any chances."

Miss Myers lifted a bowl of creamed wheat from the food cart, handed Cora Jean a white hand towel, and then pointed at an open doorway at the far end of the room. "Go feed Milk his breakfast. It'll most likely be the easiest thing you do all day."

She had taken several steps when a sound broke behind her, a high-pitched crystal noise, and Cora Jean turned back.

Ding-ding-ding-ding-ding-ding.

Standing at her desk, Miss Myers was using a ballpoint pen to tap against a glass of water. Most of the children moved around the corridor, standing at their doorways or at the very least, focusing directly on Miss Myers.

Like Pavlov's dogs, Cora Jean thought.

The spoon swung against Cora Jean's hip as she walked toward the doorway at the end of the room. She could feel eyes on her as she walked with the steaming bowl of creamed wheat, the attention of hungry children on her, and heard the moist smacking sounds of lips and grunts of excitement.

As she got closer, Cora Jean could see part of an open window through the entrance to the room, and sunlight spilled through. Steam had stopped rising from the creamed wheat, but the bowl felt warm against the palms of her hands. Heat, however, wasn't what almost made her drop the bowl as she stepped inside.

That's not real.

Her legs felt like dry reeds in late fall, swaying and ready to snap in high wind, but Cora Jean held her breath and tightened up inside.

The boy, *Milk,* sat in a wheelchair parked beside the window. One spindly arm stretched along the rest of the chair, the other was bent at the elbow and tight against his bare chest, the hand atrophied and twisted at the wrist, forcing his thumb and first two fingers to extend in a grotesque sideways peace sign.

One of his eyes was pinched almost shut, the iris behind the wrinkled folds of his eyelid like a figure pacing behind a half-pulled window blind. Milk's other eye was open wide, and a bright crystal blue, the color of an icicle against a clear cyan sky.

That can't be real.

His nose and mouth appeared smaller than they should, but otherwise normal. But what made Cora Jean's pulse race in her chest was Milk's head, swelled and stretching behind him into an impossible distortion the size of a bed pillow. It was bald and riddled with lightning bolts of blue veins beneath the skin, stretched taught and shiny. Cora Jean watched the muscles flex in the boy's slender neck, noted the way his chin pointed higher than it should as the weight of his skull pulled him back.

Milk's good eye swiveled in its socket and his gaze landed on Cora Jean. He blinked at her and then began to rock slightly against the chair. Noise gurgled from his mouth, the sound wet and garbled, but the tone a recognizable one.

He's excited, Cora Jean thought.

She forced herself to take a step forward, and then another. Milk's parted mouth revealed his lower lip, glassy and lacquered with fresh spittle. He slapped the palm of his outstretched hand against the armrest again and again.

Cora Jean walked to the window and set the bowl down on the sill with shaking hands. She leaned against the wall, stared out the window, and released the heavy breath she'd been holding. Her next inhale included the smell of urine and the yeasty scent of unwashed skin. She closed her eyes and straightened her back.

The wheelchair creaked as Milk rocked back and forth.

She took another breath and then opened her eyes, lifted the bowl of creamed wheat, and raised the spoon from her chain belt. Gathering a bite of the warm cereal, Cora Jean brought it to Milk, his mouth gaping open like a baby bird. He shook, his head bobbing slightly as his lips found the spoon.

He raised his unafflicted arm from the chair and wrapped his damp hand around Cora Jean's wrist. She fed another spoon into his gulping mouth and felt his small fingers begin to knead her flesh.

Again, and again, she returned the spoon to the bowl and scooped another bite. Each time, Milk rocked back and forth during the wait, anxious for more, and issued excited snaps and pops from his throat.

Cora Jean swirled the spoon in the bowl, scooping up the last of it, and showed him the utensil. Her voice was the gentle sing-song tone of someone speaking to a toddler. "This is the last bite, okay? All done."

Milk's hand tightened slightly around her wrist as Cora Jean brought the spoon to his fluttering mouth, turned the utensil on its side, and slid the warm cereal against his tongue. For a moment, she thought he wouldn't let go. She could feel the wiry strength in his functioning hand. That one blue eye swiveled on her, and Milk released her arm.

Cora Jean set the empty bowl on the windowsill and used the hand towel to wipe off the spoon. She folded the towel in half and wiped Milk's chin and the corners of his mouth.

"Good boy." She offered him a small smile.

She picked up the empty bowl as movement two doors down caught her attention. Inside one of the rooms, through the slight gap of an open door, Cora Jean saw a figure standing there, watching her. The room beyond was dark and the shape stepped back from the doorframe.

After a moment, the figure shifted back and forth as it stood in place. In that moment, Cora Jean felt studied, as if she was being *judged*.

Chapter Twenty-Five

1964

WANT ONE?"

Cora Jean stared at the pack of cigarettes Diane held out toward her. Shaking her head, Cora Jean leaned against the brick wall of the building and closed her eyes. "Thank you, but no. I don't smoke."

"Might wanna take it up," Diane said, and Cora Jean heard the sound of the woman lighting a cigarette and taking a drag. "You're too young to buy liquor, and ya need something to help deal with working here."

It was her lunch break, and though there hadn't been much food at home to pack, Cora Jean had no appetite anyway.

"I can't say it gets easier." Diane shifted and bits of gravel crunched beneath her feet.

"Why do they call it the cake walk?" Raising her head, Cora Jean opened her eyes and met the other woman's gaze.

Diane turned and leaned a shoulder against the wall. "It changes from time to time, depending on the residents, but it's the nicknames. Flower, Milk, and Sugar. Dark humor of any kind sometimes helps. Oh, and candy. Do yourself a favor, get some candy."

"For what?"

"Peppermints, butterscotch, even those cheap little butter mints like fancy restaurants give out sometimes. Keep 'em in your pockets and give them like treats for being good or to help calm them down when you need to. And *trust* me, there'll come a point when you need to." Diane flicked ash from her cigarette.

"The girl, Flower... what did Miss Myers mean when she told Carl *third time's a charm?*"

"Look..." Diane took another drag and spoke through her exhale. "Harper's Grove is *badly* understaffed, okay? We—*some of us*—do the best they can, but..." Diane shook her head and looked down at the cement.

"Flower bit people three separate times, and today was the third. They can't have that shit. They just can't. So, they prevent it from happening again." She took a quick hard inhale from her cigarette. "Ever."

The meaning of the woman's words didn't fully register in Cora Jean's mind.

Diane studied her silently for a moment, and then continued speaking, clarifying. "They get their teeth pulled. Upper front, about ten to twelve of them usually. Most of them can't even break skin after that, let alone take a chunk out of someone's arm."

Cora Jean's knees weakened and she forced them to lock in place. She put her palms against the rough brick wall and eased herself down to crouch on one knee.

"I know it's a lot. There's a mix here, children who were born that way, others made that way, some abused like animals, even some failed abortions that fought their way to be born."

Her stomach rolled yet again, and Cora Jean felt as if a current flowed through her veins. She looked up at Diane, who raised an eyebrow questioningly.

"You meet Sugar yet?"

Cora Jean shook her head.

Another fast and angry inhale from her cigarette, and then Diane dropped the butt to the cement and ground it beneath one crepe-soled shoe. "You will, Cora Jean. You will."

Chapter Twenty-Six

1964

IT'S LIKE THE monkey exhibit at the zoo."

Cora Jean heard Carl's snickering words but didn't acknowledge them. She'd given him the benefit of the doubt as she did most people, but had eventually arrived at the conclusion she didn't like the man. The image in her mind of him pulling out Flower's teeth wouldn't fade, and whenever he was close by, Cora Jean felt uneasy in the pit of her stomach.

As the warm, clear days of mid-May arrived, Tuesday and Thursday afternoons were set aside for outdoor recess. The yard was the size of a basketball court and bordered by a tall chain link fence. Though the grass was kept trimmed, the four corners remained untouched by the radius of a mower blade and deemed unimportant enough to warrant clearing the waist-high weeds by hand.

Miss Myers always stayed behind in the corridor as Carl and Cora Jean rotated the residents, six at a time, outside in the sunshine for half an hour. At some point, a repairman had fixed the elevator, and that made things easier, but the cramped ride three floors down filled Cora Jean with dread each time. That many people in the same small space reminded her of the odor of a recently rinsed garbage can.

Flower gave Milk a quick hug and then she ran through the grass to stand at the chain link fence. She put her burn-scarred fingers on the thick wire mesh and stared at the fields stretching beyond. Cora Jean saw the girl smile, noting the new, sunken profile of her upper lips, absent of teeth.

"Got yourself a man?" Carl's scratchy low tone.

"I'm still in high…" Cora Jean began, but clipped her sentence and shook her head slightly, still avoiding eye contact with him. "Don't want one. Life's too busy right now."

From the corner of her eye, she saw him give a soft shrug.

"Right man could make life a lot less busy."

Cora Jean released a soft exhale, feeling the angry heat rising inside her. She watched some of the other residents she'd come to know over the past few weeks. Some sat and picked at blades of grass or took their slippers off and walked barefoot, laughing as the weeds tickled soles. Others ran or spun around and then looked up at the sky, laughing their skewed laughs as they fell to the ground.

Milk sat in his wheelchair, his good hand tapping the armrest. A thin blanket was draped around his shoulders and over his thin chest down to his diapered bottom. His sapphire eye shifted to the sky, the yard, Flower. She had moved away from the fence and lay on her stomach in the grass, staring at a cluster of weeds in the corner of the yard.

Telling ladybugs little secrets, Cora Jean thought, and smiled at a phrase her mother used to say.

A squeal from a boy on the left side of the yard drew her attention, and Cora Jean started to head in his direction but paused. He was holding up his left hand and staring at it, releasing his high-pitched squeals and slapping his right leg with his hand.

"Goddamn caterpillar." Carl snorted and shook his head. "You'd think he found a treasure chest or somethin'."

"To *him*, it is." She turned to look Carl in his eyes. "Come on, it's time to go."

Cora Jean stood behind Milk, raised her hands overhead, and clapped three times. "Time to go inside everyone."

"You know they don't understand what you're sayin', right? May as well tell them it's time to go play in traffic or somethin'." Carl took the arm of a girl with wide, almond eyes close to him.

Flower ran over and stood beside Milk's wheelchair. A dark-haired boy hobbled closer and stood still, waiting. Cora Jean turned to Carl. "I think they understand a lot more than most give them credit for."

The group walked back to the rear entrance of the building, and Flower pulled the handle of the heavy door to open it for Cora Jean to push Milk's wheelchair inside. Carl pushed two boys ahead of him, and marched inside, still holding onto the girl's arm.

In the elevator ride up to C3, Flower stood with her arms crossed around her middle. Her head was down, hair covering most of her face, but she rocked back and forth, softly humming. Cora Jean smiled as she saw Milk tapping his palm in time to Flower's tune.

MISS MYERS WAS the first to notice the change in Flower's behavior.

At mealtime, the girl still seemed happy enough, joyfully eating and not causing problems, but she stopped fawning over Milk during her every waking moment. She started spending time quietly in her bedroom rather than in the common area.

It took less than a week for Cora Jean to find the reason why. The smell of rot hung in the air of the corridor, syrupy and heavy.

"Carl, you set out rat poison again?" Miss Myers raised an eyebrow as she questioned.

"Not since last October." Carl stared at the ceiling as if it were made of glass and ready to reveal a mystery. "Might be a squirrel died up there or somethin'."

"Well it stinks to high heaven. Spray some of that orange cleanser around."

Carl went to a supply closet, and then started pacing the common area with a spray bottle, misting the air. The citrus scent didn't so much *dull* the stench as *added* to it, and the combination was worse than before, a stomach-turning odor of decay and fresh orange. He went around the room, and one by one, unlatched the windows and tilted the upper panels outward to get some fresh air circulating.

By lunchtime, the corridor smelled of flower blossoms, orange sanitizer spray, and death.

Cora Jean had finished feeding Milk a bowl of butter noodles for lunch, and she walked toward the food cart to swap the empty dish for a full one to feed the next resident. She passed by Flower's room and the rotting stench seemed to rupture from the girl's partially open door.

Wincing, Cora Jean stopped and gently pushed the door open. There, on her cot, Flower was laying down, her legs drawn toward her chest. Her thin blanket was bundled in front of her, and Flower was humming a soft tune. The girl paused her song, reached a hand into the folds of her blanket, and withdrew something pinched in her thumb and forefinger. Cora Jean watched as Flower brought it to her mouth and put it inside, and after a moment, she continued her melody.

"Flower, what're you eating?"

At the sound of Cora Jean's voice, Flower snapped her head up, and sat straight on her cot. She didn't make eye contact, like a child caught stealing a cookie, and she began picking at the cloth of her gown.

"Flower?" Cora Jean stepped farther into the room and the stink was a thick cloud of death. She reached for the blanket, and Flower snatched the cloth and pulled it closer.

"What do you have in there?" Crouching to one knee, and speaking softly, Cora Jean slowly reached out toward the girl's blanket. "I only want to see, that's all."

Flower's mouth carried the softest of frowns, and her focus remained on the blanket in her hands. *"Beebeeee."*

It was a rare thing, but Cora Jean had sometimes heard Flower talk. It was the speech of a toddler, unpracticed and sometimes garbled, but if you listened closely enough, it was easy to get the gist. "You have a baby?"

Flower nodded and the corners of her mouth turned up into a soft smile.

"I only want to see, alright? That's all." Cora Jean eased the folds of the blanket and peeled the fabric apart. The last of the cloth fell open and the smell of rot uncoiled.

Cora Jean screamed and stumbled back.

The remains of a dead kitten lay on the blanket, tufts of fur, matted with fluids of rot, splayed out in different directions from its tiny head. The eye sockets were void of the eyes themselves, replaced with small writhing clusters of maggots. Thin spikes of teeth were visible in the open, frozen mouth, and a rug of larvae wriggled where the kitten's tongue should be.

"*Beebeeeee!*" Flower's burn-scarred face held a disapproving expression, and she grabbed the dead kitten and cradled it protectively to her chest.

The sound of Miss Myers running to the doorway made Cora Jean's head turn. She watched the woman's face wash over with disgust as she comprehended the scene. "Carl! Bring a hypo and get in here, now!"

The next moments were a frenzied blur. Flower, kicking and thrashing at Carl as he approached her with a syringe. Miss Myers, trying to use the blanket to wrap the dead kitten and take it away from the girl. Cora Jean trying to hold Flower's feet as the girl kicked and fought, trying to keep them from stealing her baby. Cora Jean was certain Flower knew her fight was futile, but it didn't stop the girl from screaming on breath that stank of the dead.

Chapter Twenty-Seven

MY HANDS DON'T work so well anymore, Dear, could you..." Cora Jean tilted her empty glass back and forth.

"Yes, ma'am." Hayden stepped forward and picked up the bottle of Southern Comfort. He uncapped it and poured into her glass until she motioned her hand to stop.

Cora Jean sighed and lit another cigarette. "After we took that away from Flower... oh, she went back to motherin' Milk with an outright vengeance. Huggin' and kissin' on him all the time, tryin' to change his diaper." She paused and pointed her hand holding the cigarette toward Abby. "She's the one that woke him up."

"What do you mean?"

"Sexually." Cora Jean sipped from her glass. "Most of 'em, they didn't have the wherewithal to know about their... you know. Unless someone else drew attention to it, their privates were same as a finger or an elbow, just another part of their body.

"Before that, he was innocent. *Naive.* But Flower, her messin' around with Milk's diapers and all, and I..." She took a drag off her

Virginia Slim and looked out at the yard. "I think… I know, there was abuse goin' on at Harper's Grove. Girls, of course, but boys too.

Carl, in Flower's room. The screams of that little girl going quiet.

"If I had to put a guess, Flower had learned, *been exposed* to some things she ought not have been." Cora Jean pulled the edges of her sweater closer together. The morning breeze was developing teeth, turning the afternoon air chilly.

She took another pull from her cigarette and continued through her exhale. "Milk tried to kiss my hand when I was feedin' him. At first, I figured maybe he was just bein' sweet, tryin' to mimic Flower kissin' his cheek maybe. But then he got worse. He'd try to lick your hand or arm if you got close enough. Try to slide his hand up beneath my skirt when I had a bowl in one hand and a spoon in the other. He was repeating what he'd learned from Flower, alright. Between what had been happenin' to her, and all her motherin' of Milk, girl was bound to get things all confused…

"When Milk learned about that, he was almost unbearable. Only good thing about it was he was stuck in that wheelchair." She flicked ash away and rested her arm on the chair again.

"At first, I'd slip him a buttermint or some candy from my pocket, something to distract him away from me, but that didn't last very long. Got to the point I had to start slapping him away, his tiny hand on that spindly branch of an arm. Not hard, mind you, but enough so he'd know he was getting scolded." Cora Jean pointed at Abby again with her cigarette hand. "Had to watch it though. Yell at Milk when Flower was within eyesight and she'd charge like a lion, ready to protect her cub."

Carl, pulling a filled hypodermic from his pocket, dragging the girl kicking and screaming into her room. Smiling as he closed the door.

"The ones that can't bite can't fight." Cora Jean stared at the yard again. Birds chirped in the distance. She brought the glass of liquor to her lips and then pulled it away without taking a drink. "He wasn't long like that though, not really. Milk died on a Monday when I wasn't at work. Had to take off that day, drive Momma to the doctors and... well."

Hayden stepped away from the porch railing to sit beside Abby. He leaned back and Cora Jean noticed how the girl leaned against him, *into* him. She smiled at the observation, but her mind was elsewhere.

"I'll never know what happened for sure, only what I was told, but I have ideas on it. Diane told me she was up there on C3 at the time, and she swore up and down that somehow, Flower knew he'd died before anyone else did. Somehow, that girl..." Cora Jean shook her head. "Flower threw a fit to beat all hell. Wailin' and cryin' and screamin' about her *dead beebeee*. Diane said Miss Myers had to give the girl a double-dose to calm her down."

Cora Jean took a drink of the alcohol and felt the sweet burn against her lips and mouth. She was starting to feel a lovely detachment inside, that warm floating sensation.

"Dobsen was up there on C3 when it happened too, from what I heard. Maybe he had somethin' to do with it, I don't know. All of the residents was scared of him, him and that goddamn ring of his. I watched him turn that thing over, ruby side down, and slap the back of heads more than a few times. Sometimes it was as a harsh warning for something they did, other times, I think that son of a bitch did it just to hear the crack against their skull. Brought blood and the need for stitches more than once. Behind closed doors, who knows what he…" Cora Jean cleared her throat and stared off at nothing for a moment, then she blinked and took a drag from her cigarette.

"Point is, I'm not sure whether Milk's death was natural or not, but either way, he was dead. Flower, she went on like that for a few days, almost from the second she woke up, wailin' and grievin', cryin' up a storm." Cora Jean turned her attention to the line of dolls strung along the porch. "Until I had the bright idea to cheer her up."

She took another drink and felt the heat on her fingers from her cigarette. Cora Jean dropped it to the porch and reached for a fresh one to light in its place. "That's one goddamn decision I've regretted ever since."

Chapter Twenty-Eight

1964

"SHE'S SOILED HERSELF already this morning." Miss Myers informed Cora Jean as she came through the doors to C3. "She'll have to learn that throwing a fit like that won't get her anywhere, so Carl made her wait for an hour before he cleaned her up."

"Is she sedated?"

"No. She hasn't started *screaming* yet." Miss Myers's expression was already agitated and the day had only begun. She turned back to paperwork on her desk.

Cora Jean glanced around the common area but didn't see Flower—she was probably in her unlit room, curled up on her cot. Pushing a wheeled mop bucket, Carl walked through a doorway at the far end of the room with a look of disgust on his face.

Lifting the paper bag in her hands, Cora Jean lowered her voice to the older woman. "Well, I might have something to help, with *uh,* your permission of course." She uncurled the top of the bag, reached inside, and Cora Jean withdrew the baby doll.

Miss Myers looked at the plastic doll and then at Cora Jean's face. "The baby Jesus?"

"Okay, yeah, it's the baby Jesus, but don't mind that. I got it at Kresky's for a quarter because they couldn't sell it last Christmas."

She held it out a little further for the woman to see better. It was the length of a fresh loaf of bread, its legs and arms drawn close to its body. The eyes were painted on, and even the hair was molded plastic in a light brown. No moveable parts at all, only a simple one-piece plastic doll. Nothing to tear apart, swallow or choke on, or use to hurt anyone, including herself.

That realization seemed to wash over Miss Myers's face, but her expression was still pulled taut. She took the doll from Cora Jean and turned it over, inspecting it from all sides before she handed it back to her. "Go on, then. I suppose it can't hurt, and if it works, it's a hell of a lot better than sticking her with a hypodermic two or three times a day. Supplies are running low, anyway."

Cora Jean smiled, as she crumpled the bag and tucked it beneath her arm, and then walked toward Flower's room. She nudged the door open with her foot and saw the interior was washed in the blue hues of early morning light. The girl was curled up tight on her cot, her blanket in twists of cloth. She whimpered softly and sniffled.

"Flower?" Cora Jean spoke in a low gentle voice and took another step into the room. "Hey, Flower, I brought you something. A present."

Flower's sniffling paused. She opened her red-rimmed eyes and turned to look at Cora Jean. The girl focused on Cora Jean's face, and then down to the doll in her hands. Flower's eyes widened and her mouth opened in surprise. She sat up, holding herself with one arm, and an excited smile broke on her face—a child's face on Christmas morning.

"Beebeee." Flower whispered.

"That's right, a baby." Cora Jean replied softly, and smiled as she crouched down on one knee and held the doll out for Flower. "Go on, you can have it. I brought it for you."

The girl's eyes flickered from the baby doll to Cora Jean's face, and she reached out tenderly to take the doll. Flower held it close to her chest, cradling its plastic form. She kissed the top of the doll's head and brushed a hand over it gently.

Flower began humming and softly rocking on the cot. Cora Jean reached into her pocket and withdrew a butterscotch candy, unwrapped it, and handed it out to Flower, who took it with a smile and popped it into her mouth.

She's happy, Cora Jean thought. *That might be the first time I've ever seen her truly happy.*

Cora Jean stood up and took slow easy steps backward from the room. She was still smiling to herself as she walked out into the common room, and saw Miss Myers at her desk, staring in her direction.

"If things go south over that doll, it's *your* responsibility."

"Absolutely." Cora Jean nodded and walked toward the food cart. The old shrew's cold temperament wasn't going to cast a raincloud over how this made her feel inside.

Carl was standing at a window, staring at something outside, and though being close to the man still made her feel like a goose walked over her grave, Cora Jean stepped closer to see what held his attention.

Beyond the recess yard and to the left of the open field, there was a copse of tall oak and locust trees around a mowed plot of land. A short wall of stacked stone framed the plot, and though Cora Jean hadn't noticed the area from ground level, from up here, it was easy to see. And strange.

A man stood in the patch of grass and used the blade of a spade shovel to tamp a rectangle of fresh dirt in front of him. Several other dirt patches, smaller ones, lined up in a row to the left.

"What's he—"

"You *know* what he's doin'." Carl gave her a sideways glance.

"But that's not even..." Cora Jean watched the man put his shovel into an empty wheelbarrow, and then he wiped his forehead with the sleeve of his shirt. Her stomach twirled inside. "Is that hallowed ground?"

"They won't know the difference, honey." Carl snickered and turned from the scene outside to stare at her. "Besides, who's gonna pay for that kind o' burial, you? With the budget cuts this place is gettin' shoved up its ass, it's a wonder..." He pointed through the glass. "Speakin' of, there's this week's fundraiser, right on time."

A panel van drove up the long drive and kept going past the main entrance, pulling around to the side of the building and slowing to a stop near the wide double-doors. A man got out of the driver's seat and walked around to the rear of the vehicle. Cora Jean saw Dr. Dobsen open one of the doors and hold it open as the man carried what looked like a heavy sack inside. A moment later he emerged and slung a second bag over his shoulder and took that into the building as well.

"What's he delivering?" She lowered her voice.

"Dead pennies."

Cora Jean shook her head slightly, confused.

Carl snorted and shook his head. "Little girl, you've been here two months and still don't know shit from shit, do you?" He nodded at the delivery truck. "That's from Dobsen's brother, works in a division of the Treasury Department. Ain't exactly on the up and up, but helps keep the lights on around here."

"What do you—"

"If you two are done lollygagging, it's time to serve breakfast." Miss Myers stood with her arms crossed, standing behind the food cart.

Cora Jean and Carl walked like scolded children, and began the morning routine.

Even with his change in behavior the last few weeks of his life, seeing Milk's room, dark and empty inside, made Cora Jean a bit sad. She picked up a bowl of oatmeal and headed toward Flower's room, the frame of the door reminding her of the fresh grave outside.

A pale hand made of twisted vines gripped the doorframe, and Sugar stepped into the opening. She glanced up at Cora Jean and kept moving, offering a quick flash of her dead shark eyes from beneath her long bangs.

Cora Jean flinched and tightened her grip on the bowl in her hand.

Sugar moved fast, her right hip jolting forward like the stubborn, jerky motion of a rusted hinge. Her left leg snapped forward to lean weight on it, before she quickly took a step with her right leg.

That curling fear of a sudden scare was fading as quickly as it had come, and Cora Jean watched Sugar return to the entrance of her own room. The girl glanced back before she receded inside, and Cora Jean turned away.

Those eyes look like there's no soul behind them.

Flower sat on her cot, gently rocking her doll. Her head was tilted down as if she was staring at the baby Jesus, and it made Cora Jean smile.

"Do you like your baby?"

Flower nodded and her head rose slightly. Her bottom lip was puckered out, and Cora Jean bent to one knee to see the girl's face. She brushed Flower's hair from her forehead and tucked the longer strands behind the girl's left ear. A glistening swell of tears held in the girl's lower eyelids.

"*Heyyyy,* what's wrong?"

The girl remained quiet and Cora Jean decided to distract her with food and not to press her for more. "Let's eat a little bit, okay?"

Flower remained motionless for a moment and then with a slight nod of her head, she turned her attention toward the warm oatmeal and accepted every spoonful. When she was finished, Cora Jean wiped her mouth with a hand towel, and then wiped the spoon. "Maybe your baby needs a nap. Why don't you sing a little song, Flower?"

A soft melody came from the girl as she cradled her doll, and Cora Jean smiled and walked out of the room quietly. It crossed her mind that maybe it was the first kind thing anyone had done for Flower in a long time, maybe even the only one the girl could remember.

It was Thursday, normally a day for going outside, but the gray clouds threatened rain, and Miss Myers cancelled outdoor recess before Carl and Cora Jean began ushering residents downstairs. Maybe it was because of the dismal sky outside, but the afternoon remained mostly quiet on the corridor. A few sat by themselves in the common area, but most remained in their rooms. Of course, there were always diapers to be changed, bodies to wash, and the time passed quickly.

Cora Jean put her last empty dinner bowl onto the food cart and unclipped the chained spoon from around her waist. She handed it to Miss Myers, who immediately unlocked her desk drawer and returned it to the plastic tray inside.

"Have a good night, Miss Myers." Cora Jean nodded and headed toward the stairwell. A flash of movement came from her right, and she saw Flower, running at full speed from her room, directly toward her.

Cora Jean barely had time to raise her hands and brace for the attack, but Flower stopped, wrapped her arms around Cora Jean's waist and hugged her tightly.

"Ankoooo." The garbled *thank you* was heard by Cora Jean as much as felt, with the girl's face nuzzled against her.

An exhale of relief escaped Cora Jean's lungs. She rested a hand on the girl's head and gave it a gentle pat. "You're welcome, Flower." She brushed her hand over the back of the girl's head, softly. "You're welcome."

Flower released her then and ran back to her room as quickly as she'd come from it.

"Looks like you've got a new friend." Miss Myers stood at her desk and Cora Jean noticed the woman held an uncapped hypodermic in her hand. "Good luck."

Chapter Twenty-Nine

"**S**ON, DO ME a favor? There's a shawl draped over the back of my sofa, would you get it for me?" Cora Jean rubbed her thin hands against her arms. "My old bones can't take the slightest chill these days."

Hayden went inside without a word, and Cora Jean took a drink of liquor. The warmth sliding down her throat didn't seem to catch spark in her stomach, and she supposed it had less to do with the temperature outside and more to do with the cold memories she was digging up.

"Doctors took my mother's leg off at the knee not long after Harper's Grove shut its doors. The other got amputated about a year later. She lived on for another, *ohhhh…*" Cora Jean tried to think of the timeline, but the memory was blurred in her mind. "Another five years or so, and then it was just Henry and I. We got on alright, I suppose. He was a smart student, but he had to work hard for it. I think he knew he had to."

"Does he still live around—"

"No." Cora Jean smiled at Abby. An ache streaked across the inside of her chest. "Henry was an attorney up in Baltimore, worked on domestic violence cases." She shook her head and lit another Virginia Slim. "Terrible things sometimes."

"Was?" Abby leaned back and rocked slightly in the porch swing.

"Guess he pissed off the wrong husband. Man came to Henry's office and shot him six times in the chest."

"Oh, I'm… I'm so sorry."

Cora Jean gave a soft nod. "Been about fifteen years now. Henry was a good man."

Hayden came back outside and instead of simply handing the shawl to the woman, he walked behind her chair and spread it out over her shoulders. She looked up at him and smiled.

"No children of your own?" Abby asked.

"Me? Oh… oh no. No, after Harper's Grove, I…" Cora Jean shook her head, took a drag from her cigarette and stared at the front yard.

"Wasn't until the last few weeks when I truly saw the place for what it was. The abuse and neglect. Dobsen was… well, at first, I thought he was a cold, clinical sort of man. Sometimes men like that, they're not pleasant to be around, but sometimes those type of men are what's needed to do things a kinder heart can't." Cora Jean flicked her Virginia Slim and glanced at the small pile of ash on the porch. "But I was wrong. Dr. Dobsen… the residents, those *children*, they weren't living things in his eyes. They were numbers, nothing but dollar signs, and when funding started to get cut…"

She coughed a harsh laugh absent of humor. "The corridor on the second floor, one with the youngest children, that was down to a single nurse for day and another for night. There was simply no way *any one person* could take care of them all. Not properly. The smell hit you as soon as you stepped through the building's entrance." Cora Jean waved her cigarette. "I don't know how Diane could stand the stink of it being right there at the front desk all day."

Hayden cleared his throat and spoke in a soft voice. "You said Milk was buried there, out in that patch of ground."

"*Mmmmhmm,* him and others, at least half a dozen or so while I was there. Before me…" Cora Jean shrugged her thin shoulders. "Hard to say how many. I'm sure their deaths weren't reported, buried out there in that potter's field."

"Why's that?"

He's handsome, but not the sharpest tack, Cora Jean thought.

"Funding for Harper's Grove was based on the number of residents. As it was, toward the end, they barely had enough money and supplies to care for the ones they had. That's how they got their nickname from…" Cora Jean took a long drag from her Virginia Slim as memories flashed through her mind. "Dead Pennies."

Cora Jean rested her hand with the cigarette against the armrest of the chair and sighed. She sipped from her glass.

"That delivery man, one that come all sneaky like, hauling those heavy sacks into the building, they were bags of pennies. They used to be collected at a place Dobsen's brother worked at, part of the Treasury."

Cora felt a shiver trickle along her spine and she shifted in her chair. "Every week, he'd put aside several bags, steal 'em that is, and bring 'em to Harper's Grove to give to Dobsen. He'd take 'em to the basement, melt the pennies down, and sell the copper for the money." She took a pull on her cigarette and exhaled slowly, watching the smoke curl in the air.

"Dead pennies was in them sacks. Kind that's been set on a train track and run over, stretched out like paper-thin brown taffy. Ones that's been bent or nicked badly, defaced. Unfit for public circulation." Cora waved her hand slightly as she spoke. "That's how the residents of Harper's Grove were viewed. Shameful. An embarrassing secret to hide. Little unimportant dead pennies."

Chapter Thirty

1964

GOOD MORNING, DOCT–"

"Morning." Dr. Dobsen passed Cora Jean in a brisk walk down the hallway toward his office. His face was flushed and the edge of his hairline damp with sweat.

Cora Jean ignored his curt response and paused at the front desk. Diane was sitting down, pulling things from the drawers and sitting them on top of the desk by her purse. The woman glanced up and then glared at the back of the walking doctor. Diane leaned forward, an expression of distaste on her face. She lowered her voice as she questioned Cora Jean. "You know the Aeromark plant? Over on the other side of town?"

"Near the canning factory? Yeah, I know it, why?"

Diane glanced down the hall and then turned back. "Pay's about the same, but a hell of a lot better than here. You go on down there and ask for Gibson Withers, that's my brother-in-law, and you tell him I sent you."

"Wait... are you leaving?" Cora Jean felt a swirl in her stomach. Diane had always been friendly to her.

"Mmmmhmmmm." Diane stuffed a pack of cheese crackers into her purse, and tossed a half-empty pack of gum in the trash pail beside her. *"Everyone* is pretty soon. Just now on my lunchbreak, I tried to give my two-weeks notice to Doctor Dickhead, and he told me to finish today and *not bother* coming in tomorrow." She put a handful of pens and pencils into her purse, lifted it as she stood up, and pulled the strap over her shoulder. "He's gonna cop an attitude like that, *I'm* not gonna bother with the rest of today."

Diane adjusted her purse strap and let out a heavy sigh as she looked at Cora Jean. "This place is closing, there's no buts about it, but I'm guessin' your momma needs your check more than you need me complaining in a huff."

A twist of fear ran through Cora Jean's stomach, the thought of no longer getting a paycheck to help out at home. Diane stepped closer and gave her a warm hug.

"You stay 'til you can't if that's what you need, but you come over and see Gibson when you're ready and I'll make *sure* you get a job, you hear me?"

Cora Jean nodded and swallowed hard. "Thank you, I..."

"It'll be alright. You're a good girl, Cora." The woman's expression softened and she rested a hand on Cora Jean's shoulder and gave a gentle squeeze. "Go see Gibson, and soon."

Cora Jean watched as Diane marched out the front door and

the bright sunlight flooded the foyer. The heavy door swung closed behind Diane, and for a moment, Cora Jean stood in the quiet. She took a deep breath, let it out slowly, and then headed toward the elevator to go upstairs.

It's to help Momma and Henry. Diane might be right about a new job, but nothing's for certain until it is.

She reached the third-floor and took another deep breath before walking into the corridor. The usual patchwork of sounds greeted her first, residents crying, others laughing, and then she saw Miss Myers, her expression flat and irritated, standing with her hands on her hips as she glared at Carl.

"I asked you *yesterday* afternoon to restock it, and now here we are." Miss Myers turned at Cora Jean's approach. "Since Carl seems to be too busy to do essentials, you'll do." She went to her desk, tore a sheet from a notepad and handed it to Cora Jean. "Go down to the supply room and bring those back. You'll need to take a cart with you."

Cora Jean looked at the list, seeing diapers and linens and bedpans among the list. She shook her head. "I don't even know where the downstairs supply room is."

The older woman shifted her stance and set her jaw. "How is it possible you've never restocked before?"

"Just lucky, I guess." Cora Jean gave a slight shrug.

"Well luck's run out. First floor, and turn left. Walk to the end of the hallway and you'll find it."

With even this minimal direction, Cora Jean was sure she'd figure out where the room was, and if nothing else, it was a reason to be away from this floor and Miss Myers, even if only for a little while. She walked to one of the rooms at the rear of the corridor and rolled an empty cart into the elevator.

Watching the doors close off the sight of the corridor filled her with calm, and Cora Jean released a long breath. The elevator car shimmied and gave a groan as it began to descend. She held onto the handle of the wheeled cart and waited until the elevator jolted to a stop on the ground floor. There was another shimmying motion of the elevator and the doors groaned open. She rolled the cart out and turned left down the hallway.

Seeing Diane's empty desk made a swirl in Cora Jean's stomach at the uncertainty ahead of her, but she trusted the woman when she said a job was hers for the asking. The manufacturing plant would be a hard job, but it was all in how you looked at things, and a paycheck was a paycheck.

Cora Jean pushed the empty cart down the long stretch of hallway, the rattling wheels the only sound. Several unmarked doors greeted her as she reached the end of the hall, and Cora Jean parked the cart.

The first door opened on a closet lined with empty, plain wooden shelves and a box of rat poison on the floor. The second door Cora Jean opened was an area about the size of a small bathroom, with shelves on all three sides. Stacks of linens and thin blankets filled the shelves, though judging from the coating of dust, they hadn't been disturbed for quite some time.

A scuffling noise farther down the hallway made Cora Jean step from the closet and she saw Dr. Dobsen walking away in the direction of his office. The door he'd just used clicked shut, and Cora Jean waited, watching the man's back as he reached the foyer.

She waited a moment longer, standing in the quiet of the hallway, and then she marched toward the doorway. It was unlocked, and when she opened it, Cora Jean was a bit surprised to see the stairs leading down to a darkened basement level. On her right, she noticed a light switch mounted on the wall. She leaned out from behind the door to check the hallway—still empty—and then she flicked the light on and walked downstairs.

From the size of the area, she could tell this was only a small section beneath the building. The floor was gritty beneath her feet and the air felt moist, the smell was like an old paperback left outside during a rainy day. She took a few steps and heard a low murmuring growl to her left, beyond a closed door. There was a hiss and the pipes overhead began to emit a soft whine.

What were you doing down here?

Cora Jean walked to the door, opened it slowly, and saw a large boiler, steel tentacle pipes snaking from behind it to thread through the ceiling. Several jet-black molds lay on the floor by the boiler, all of them roughly the shape and size of a brick. Bits of copper lay on the dirty cement beside a canvas sack and she reached down to spread the fabric open at the top.

The cloth bag was partially filled with coins, each of them twisted or damaged or with gouges and grooves across their surfaces.

Dead pennies.

Cora Jean reached inside and lifted a handful, stared at them a moment, and then let them sift from her palm back to the rest.

Tink-tink-tink.

Her attention turned to a group of cardboard boxes resting on the floor and she stepped closer to see. File folders. Stacks and stacks of manila folders, stuffed with reports and notes and photographs. Residents. Notes on how they had ended up at Harper's Grove. Medication records. Photographs at various ages.

She flipped through several of the folders, set them aside, and then pulled another. A black and white photograph was paperclipped to papers and Cora Jean stared, unable to avert her eyes.

The boy, perhaps two years old at most, was stretched out on a dirty mattress pad. His body was thin and skeletal. A loose-fitting pair of pajamas draped over his bony frame. His head rested sideways against a pillow, the skull elongated and freakishly bloated.

Her breath caught in Cora Jean's chest and she threw the file back on top of the others.

Milk.

She turned to look at the cast iron smile of the grate on the boiler.

Dobsen. He's burning these files. Getting rid of them all.

Cora Jean stepped away from the boxes, moved away and then ran up the stairs. Out in the hallway, she glanced to make sure she was alone and then quietly pushed the door closed.

She leaned her back against the door and then took several uneasy steps toward the cart. Cora Jean put a hand against the wall to steady herself, and took a breath.

A single closed door was on the wall on the other side of the cart, and Cora Jean forced herself to move forward. The room was stocked with metal shelving units and supplies, though many of the shelves were empty. With shaking hands, Cora Jean looked at the list Miss Myers had given to her. She collected the items, placed them all on the cart, and went inside the supply room again after the list was complete.

She closed her eyes and breathed, thought of Henry's smile, and then Momma, with the lines of worry deepening on her face with each passing week.

Finish today, Cora Jean. The rest of the day, and that's it. You never have to come back ever, ever again.

Just the rest of the day.

Cora Jean let herself take three more slow, deep breaths and then she gave herself a nod of encouragement. The cart was much heavier now, and even though the wheels whined much louder than they had before, it still moved easily enough after getting it started with a hard push.

The bulk of the loaded cart forced Cora to press herself up against the corner of the elevator by the button panel, and she pushed the number three. The doors closed shakily and the sudden difference of being in the small elevator compared to the large open area of the foyer made her feel closed in and cornered.

There was a jolt as the cable took hold and the elevator car began to rise. Cora Jean leaned against the wall and stared at the panel of buttons. A cold sensation swirled around her left leg and she flinched and looked down. Even in the dim, closed-in light of the elevator, there seemed to be a darkness swelling on the floor, a *heaviness* to the air.

Cora Jean took a step backward to stare at the filthy floor, and the icy feeling curled around her calf muscle. A moist, frosted tongue licked the soft skin at the back of her knee, and she screamed. The sound was loud and piercing in the confined area, and she kicked her left leg out, running both hands down along her leg, frantically slapping at the cloth.

Ding.

The elevator doors rumbled and when they slid open, Cora Jean half-stumbled, half-leaped out onto the corridor. She turned to stare at the loaded cart and the space beneath the bottom rack, but there was nothing there.

"Cora?"

She didn't turn to the sound of Carl's voice, and when the doors began to close, Cora Jean made no move to stop them.

"You going to bring the supplies onto the floor or let them have a joyride back down—"

A long and terrible shriek sliced the corridor in half. Cora Jean spun around and saw Dr. Dobsen and Miss Myers standing by her desk, both of their heads turned toward Flower's room. The scream ended with a deep gasp for breath, fueling for another wail, and Cora Jean ran toward the girl's opened bedroom.

Flower was kneeling on the floor, cradling the doll tight to her chest. She filled her lungs with air and threw her head back as she unleashed another agony-filled scream.

"Christ Almighty, do something about that, will you?" Dobsen yelled across the space.

Cora Jean ignored Dobsen's voice, and she crouched down beside the girl, putting a hand gently on her shoulder. The girl's face immediately snapped in her direction, and Flower's expression crumpled on itself. She heaved with great wracking sobs, held out her baby doll, and tried to stammer out words.

The doll's face had been completely cut out.

No, Cora Jean thought, *not cut out. Chewed.*

Flower's chest lurched with effort as she cried and presented the doll, showing a jagged edge encircling the hollowed face, reaching from forehead to below the chin. Tears streamed down the girl's reddened cheeks and her mouth was slimed with spittle.

A loud crash came from beyond Flower's bedroom in the common area, and Cora Jean stood to her feet and stepped past the threshold.

Sugar hunched over on all fours, scrambled from her bedroom. She held up one arm, her hand holding the plastic doll's face over her own, and she spoke in low, wet syllables. *"I'm jusht lyke youuu… jusht lyke youuuu."*

Miss Myers uttered a clipped bark of surprise as Sugar ran, fast as mercury, toward Dr. Dobsen, who stumbled backward and dropped the file folders in his hands. He wasn't quick enough, and Sugar rose to her feet and climbed the man, her weight throwing him off balance. The doctor slammed to the floor and the girl was on him.

Sugar clawed at Dobsen's eyes with her free hand, all the time growling her mantra *"I'm jusht lyke youuu,"* and holding that painted plastic over her own face.

The doctor brought his hands up to defend himself, and Sugar moved the mask away and clamped her mouth onto the edge of his right hand, biting down so hard her eyes squeezed shut with the effort. Blood burst from the girl's mouth as Dobsen screamed and hit her with his other hand.

Carl dropped the mop he was holding and ran toward them, pulling a capped hypodermic from his trouser pocket mid-stride. He fell to his knees and slid a needle into the side of Sugar's neck. Her body jolted in place but she didn't release her hold, only shook her head like a dog with a new toy. Dobsen raised his free hand in a clenched fist and punched the left side of Sugar's face. Her head snapped to the side, dropped the plastic doll face, and her ebony eyes fluttered, refocused, and then she glared at the man beneath her.

Rivulets of blood ran down her chin. Sugar, still clenching down, pulled back her lips in a sneer and smiled at him.

She's amused, Cora Jean thought, *my God, she's amused.*

It was the first time she had clearly seen Sugar's face, free of the long hair that usually covered most of it. One nasal cavity was exposed on the right side of her face, and the flesh of the lower half of her face appeared to be made of melted wax. The jagged, half-rotted legion of her teeth were slicked bright red, the blade of a tree saw thick with fresh sap. The girl ground her lower jaw, tightening against the doctor's hand.

"Get her the *fuck* off me!" He swung at her face again and Sugar snapped her head to the side, yanking his hand with her, but dodging his blow.

Carl produced a second syringe from his pocket, pulled the cap off with his teeth, and jammed the needle into Sugar's arm. The girl's eyes flickered, and she released Dobsen's hand.

The doctor pulled away, and Carl grabbed the girl's shoulders and slung her to the side. She groaned and her hands scrabbled against the smooth floor. Her chin and throat and the edge of her gown along her collarbone were soaked in blood. The plastic doll face lay beside her, its painted eyes staring vacantly at the ceiling. She whispered again, blood bubbles popping along from between her lips. *"I'm jusht lyke youuu…"*

Dobsen pushed himself to his feet, leaving a bloody handprint against the tile. He shook with anger and gritted his teeth, reached one hand to the other and spun his ring around on his hand. Dobsen raised and swung his hand down fast and hard, the sound as he hit the back of Sugar's head loud as the crack of a bullwhip in the room.

He growled at Carl. "Give her another."

"A third?"

"You fucking heard me." Dobsen leaned forward, rage lining his face as he glared at the other man. He nodded toward Sugar, stretched on the floor. "Act like a goddamn animal, we'll treat you like one."

Carl glanced at the girl, back to the doctor, and then withdrew a third syringe from his pants pocket. He pulled the cap and injected Sugar's arm. Her obsidian eyes rolled back beneath her eyelids and Sugar's hands stopped moving. She released a soft groan and went quiet.

Dr. Dobsen watched her for a moment, seemed to remember his hand was injured, and then lifted it across his chest, cradling it. He glanced down at the file folders scattered on the floor, and then turned to Miss Myers. "I'm heading to the goddamn infirmary. Gather these files and bring them to my office."

Carl grabbed Sugar by her wrists and dragged her toward her room, while Miss Myers collected the paperwork on the floor into a stack. As she picked up the last folder, she turned to stare at Cora Jean. The woman's voice was filled with razorblades. "I warned you when you gave that doll to her…" Her head snapped toward the noises of sobbing from Flower's room. "Clean up your goddamn mess."

Cora Jean watched Miss Myers march through the double-doors to the stairwell. The dotted path of Dobsen's blood trailed back across the floor and met up with the spilled blood where Sugar's body had been.

A thumping sound drew Cora Jean's attention and through the open door of Sugar's room, she watched Carl sling the girl's body across her cot like a ragdoll. She was quiet, and her arms had stopped moving, but the black stones of her eyes still rolled in their sockets.

Cora Jean stared for a moment longer. Though Carl's focus was on the girl, he stepped into view. He rested his hand on his belt buckle before he shut the filthy door, and the remainder of the scene was hidden from view.

A sickness bubbled in Cora Jean's stomach as she stared at the closed door. Flower's ongoing sobs pulled her away, and she went to sit by the girl. She put an arm around Flower's shoulders and another across her front, holding her close. Cora Jean rested her chin against the back of Flower's head and rocked her, and then softly started humming.

A soft mewling sound came from beyond Flower's bedroom. A rhythmic sound, muffled and repetitive, turning the sharp whine into a stutter. Cora Jean closed her eyes and continued her melody a little louder.

After a while, Flower's crying slowed and then stopped altogether. Cora Jean smiled to herself as she heard the rhythm of the girl's breathing deepen and slow. She continued to rock the girl for a little while longer, and then eased her down to the floor where they sat. A thin blanket was balled up on the cot and Cora Jean pulled it down and draped it over the girl. She waited, saw Flower flick her tongue out to lick her lips, and give one last shivering cry, and then the girl drifted completely to sleep.

Cora Jean waited a solid minute, counting off the seconds, and then carefully eased the doll away from Flower's body. The girl's sticky hands clung to the faceless doll for a second, and then fell to her side.

As she stepped from the room, Cora Jean looked at Sugar's closed bedroom door.

The thumping sound and the pained mewling had stopped.

Chapter Thirty-One

1964

"WHY IN THE good goddamn is there blood still on the floor?"

Cora Jean turned to Miss Myers as she walked through the doors onto the ward.

The door to Sugar's room opened and Carl stepped through, paused, and his gaze flitted from Cora Jean to Miss Myers. He had color to his face and slowly eased the door shut behind him.

"A mop and bucket. *Now!*" Miss Myers's face was simmering with anger. She glared at Carl as he hurriedly walked toward the supply closet at the rear of the common area, and then she turned her attention to Cora Jean. The woman's focus remained on Cora Jean's face, and then down to the doll. "Get that thing out of here."

Miss Myers nodded at the chewed-off face on the floor. "That too. Don't even put it in the trash can or else she'll sniff it out like a goddamn sewer rat."

Nodding, Cora Jean bent to pick up the doll face. Blood was sprayed out on the floor around it and the visual made her stomach clench. The corridor felt tight and the thought of taking the elevator made her knees weak. Cora Jean concentrated on her footsteps one at a time as she headed toward the stairwell. She paused outside the double doors, put a hand on the railing to steady herself, and then focused on one step at a time as she made her way down.

Cora Jean reached the marble-floored foyer and glanced at the empty desk, thinking again of Diane's advice to go to the plant. A loud squall echoed from overhead and the sound of the doors banging from the walls followed.

"Goddamn it!" Miss Myers's voice, yelling from the upstairs corridor, and the sound of running footsteps.

The screaming continued and Cora Jean looked upward at the slapping sound of bare feet on the stairs. And then she saw Flower as the girl tumbled down the stairs and battered into the wall at the top of the first section of stairs. Flower fell onto her side and she lifted her head, catching sight of Cora Jean.

Flower unleashed another feral cry and tried to scramble to her feet but got tangled in her gown. She reached for the railing and missed, and that mishap was all it took. Flower tumbled down the stairs like a dandelion seed in the wind. The bones in the girl's right forearm snapped and burst through the skin. Her right ankle landed on the edge of a stair tread and buckled to the side with the sound of breaking celery. Down, down, down in a twisting whirl until Flower's body slammed onto the marble floor at Cora Jean's feet.

Both of Flower's legs were bent unnaturally, one arm curled beneath her body, the other outstretched, her hand clenching at air. Flower's neck was twisted at an impossible angle. Her mouth opened and closed like a fish on land. She blinked her eyes.

"Flower!" Cora Jean screamed and dropped the doll parts as she ran to the girl. She knelt beside her and took the girl's hand in her own. The sound of approaching footsteps made her glance up and Cora Jean saw Carl, running down to the foyer.

Flower was murmuring something and Cora Jean squeezed the girl's hand and bent down and put her ear close to listen. Her words were a slushy whisper of accusation. *"Eww ook mah beebeeee."*

You took my baby.

Cora Jean stared at the girl's expression. The anger there. The absolute rage.

"Eww ook... mah beebeeee..." Flower's breath faded, drawing out her last word in a parchment dry whisper.

Carl came to stand by the girl's feet. He put his hands on his hips and shook his head with a look of disgust.

"Fate did her a favor."

Cora turned toward the voice and saw Doctor Dobsen standing at the edge of the hallway. He had one hand bandaged heavily and held a short stack of folders in his other.

"I'm..." Cora Jean trembled inside but she pushed herself to her feet. Swirls of disgust and shame and anger collided inside her. She felt tears of frustration building. "A favor?"

Dr. Dobsen stepped closer as he took a deep inhale through his nose. His gaze focused on the dead girl on the floor. "If the government won't fund a shithole like this place, where do you think she was going to end up next when the doors close?" He sucked air between his lips and front teeth and looked at Carl. "Clean it up."

Turning from the scene, Dr. Dobsen walked down the hallway toward the supply rooms and the boiler.

Erasing more children. Cora Jean gritted her teeth, that shaking feeling inside her grew.

Carl headed toward the elevator, leaving Cora Jean standing there, staring at the young girl's broken corpse. The tears that had been threatening to burst free, streamed down her face now that she was alone, and Cora Jean knelt beside Flower. She saw her through blurred vision, but reached out and brushed the girl's hair from her forehead. "I'm sorry... I'm so sorry."

She sat there, stroking the girl's hair, until she heard the elevator rumble, coming back down from C3, and then Cora Jean rose to her feet. Lingering a moment more, she looked into Flower's dead eyes and found the hatred-filled expression still resting there, blaming her even in death.

Chapter Thirty-Two

PRESENT

I LEFT HARPER'S GROVE right then and there, 'course it only saved me a little bit of hell. They closed the doors a few weeks later." Cora Jean took a drag from her Virginia Slim. "Families, if they had one, had been notified. Some made arrangements to transfer residents to other facilities. Others…" She waved the rest of her sentence away and gave a soft shrug.

"These days, a woman has a male doctor and he's gotta have a nurse there for everything, you know? Watching, making sure no funny business goes on. Back then, especially with the Dead Pennies, wasn't nothing for a male attendant to look after females. Do what they wanted… not only on C3 but other corridors too."

Cora Jean turned away from Abby to look out at the street. So long ago, but she felt the tears wanting to well up inside her. "No one there to watch and see. And even if someone did, what was a woman gonna say back then? I wasn't much more than a kid that needed money."

"Cora, you can't—" Abby began, her tone soft, but Cora Jean motioned her hand to stop her.

"Blame myself, yeah, I know what you're going to say, but it still don't make it right." She shook her head. "I knew Carl was messing with her, probably others. I'd seen the way he looked at the girls sometimes. I've tried to cover up that rotten truth in my mind for years, but I *knew*. Wasn't unusual for residents to scream in their rooms. Happened all the time over something as trivial as their blanket fell off their cot, or shadows on the wall scared them. But Sugar, that day... she almost looked numb. Even drugged up, she knew what he was going to do. It hadn't been the first time."

Cora Jean shook her head and bit down on her emotions. "When Father Walker told me Carl killed himself, I can't say I was happy about it. Carl... he was a bad man, yeah. But a bullet of his own hand? No, that son of a bitch deserved way worse for the things he's done."

The three of them remained silent for a moment, and then Cora Jean cleared her throat. "Miss Myers, well, she was up in her years back then. I'm sure she's passed on one way or another by now. And Dobsen... was two, maybe three years after Harper's Grove closed its doors, I heard Dobsen hung himself in a truck stop motel out by the Interstate."

Hayden stood up from the porch swing and walked to lean against the railing. His eyes glanced over the row of hanging dolls. "What happened to Sugar?"

"She had no family to have a say in where she stayed, so I don't... I don't know if she lived or died after I left." Cora Jean took one last puff from her cigarette and let it fall into the sliver of remaining liquor in her glass. She put the glass down on the porch and leaned forward, pulling the shawl around her tighter.

"You listen to me now, the both of you. I've told you all I can and that's all there is. But if you've... if they've woken up again, you steer clear. You can't reason with them. If they get a taste, a liking for something new, they'll hunger for it. You don't want them mad at you." Cora Jean's face sharpened as she continued.

"Get them mad and they'll come for you then, but more than that, if they take a liking to you, well you really don't want that. They take a liking to you, they'll never let you be. Either way..."

A breeze curled in from the direction of the front lawn and rattled the plastic figures hanging above. Cora Jean watched them a moment until they stilled. "You two go on now. Go on, I'm tired."

"Can I, can we get you anything, Cora?" Abby stood from the porch swing and went by Hayden's side.

"Just peace, but I don't think that's something you can provide." Cora Jean gave a nod toward both of them and watched as Hayden put his hand out for the girl as she stepped from the porch onto the walk.

Sweet of him, Cora Jean thought. *Gentlemanly.*

The Southern Comfort wasn't taking hold and giving warmth as it normally did, and Cora Jean thought of lying down on the sofa, her throw blanket drawn around her. She watched as Hayden started the car, and the girl watched her back as they drove away.

She gripped the armrests and pushed herself to stand, ignoring her glass on the porch. A fleeting thought of what she would have for dinner crossed Cora Jean's mind, but it didn't matter much anymore. Everything tasted bland and absent of flavor lately, especially on treatment days. She went inside, locked the door, and sat down on the sofa. Cora Jean used the remote to turn on the TV, flipped through several channels, and then turned it off again. She pulled the throw blanket from the back of the sofa and pulled it around her chest as she stretched out on the cushions.

Another flush of wind kicked up outside and made the dolls rattle against each other. Cora Jean looked through the window as the figures twisted and turned. She squinted her eyes, trying to focus on a doll hanging near the porch stairs as it swung in the wind. The plastic figure shifted and rocked and then twisted back again.

A fist-sized area, where the doll's face had been, was now a gaping empty hole.

Cora Jean swallowed hard as she stared at the figure. The blanket offered little comfort and she sat up on the sofa. From the hallway, she heard the soft cracking noise of the floorboards. She swallowed again and stiffened. "Hello?"

A biting chill began at the base of her spine and clawed its way upward to the back of her neck. She glanced toward the kitchen and then back to the threshold of the darkened hall. Another gentle cracking.

Cora Jean stood up from the couch and took a step toward the hallway. Her hands tingled as she balled them into fists and she felt her heart thump against her thin ribs. She took another step forward to peer down the hallway.

Liquid onyx moved within the shadows. A twist of limbs formed on the wall, crawling forward, insect-like, in her direction. *"Eww ook mah beebeeee…"*

The sound was the frigid blade of a February wind and it sliced Cora Jean to the bone. Her stomach roiled and threatened to purge its meager contents. Her legs trembled and refused to move. Along the outer edge of her left wrist, Cora Jean felt the sensation of an icy tongue lick her skin. She jolted in place and jerked her arms, crossing them in front of her body.

"Leave me alone!" She screamed into the darkness as another figure of blackest mercury moved in a series of fits and jerks along the hallway floor.

"I'm jusht lyke youuu…"

Cora Jean felt a lightning bolt race through her left arm and her heart lurched inside. She clenched her teeth and fell to her knees on the living room floor. Thin fingers curled around the doorframe and she watched the burn-scarred face peek around the edge. Eyes, white as bleached bone, glared at her.

The other figure moved crablike on the hallway floor, snapping its gaze toward Cora Jean. Dead shark eyes, void of humanity, staring in her direction.

Another arc of electricity, and a sledgehammer hit her chest. Cora fell, catching herself on the floor with the palm of her right hand. She held herself there for only a moment, and then collapsed to the carpet.

The cloak of death was upon her, that much Cora Jean was aware of, but as her heart labored in her chest, the wraiths descended, and she realized death wouldn't arrive quickly enough to save her.

Chapter Thirty-Three

BUT YOU *SAW* the video footage from the drone, Abby! That is some truly messed up shit on there. And you think it's—"

"I *know*, okay? I know, it was creepy as hell, but what if it was just the shadow from the drone? Or what if the old guy had a cat or something?"

Hayden gripped the steering wheel and gave Abby a glance. "Unless the cat can climb the goddamn walls, I—"

"Look, Hayseed." Abby let out a slow breath. "My dad was an engineer. Logical thinker and skeptic and all that. And if he—"

"Didn't your dad believe the government was keeping aliens hostage under Area—"

"Yeah, okay, but no. He believed in aliens but not in Roswell. Mathematically, there's no way the only intelligent life exists on Earth. There's just..." She shook her head. "We're getting off topic. What I'm saying is, outside of this, have you ever experienced anything supernatural at *all?* Ever?"

Hayden drove in silence, staring ahead. After a moment, he sighed. "No, not really, no."

"Neither have I." Abby rolled the passenger window down slightly to get some fresh air. "Yeah, the place is strange, and there's the creepy ass drone footage. But Carl had mental issues going on, probably racked with guilt in his old age over all the bad things he'd done years ago. And Cora Jean—"

"It's some messed up shit, Abby."

"It *is*, okay? I agree with you, but... I haven't seen anything strange happening there."

Keep telling yourself that, Abs.

"You mean besides a homeless man falling through the skylight?"

For a split-second, Abby saw that moment in her mind—the shadow moving across the glass, high overhead. *It was just a trick of the light, that's all.*

"Yeah, besides that. Even the glasses clinking together—"

Hayden turned to look at her. "Clinking together? As in *ding ding ding* clinking together?"

"Yeah, I mean... kind of, but it... that could have been someone driving by with a lot of bass on their stereo, vibrating the glasses or something."

"Abby, do you—"

"Which makes more sense? Some teenager blaring rap music or ghosts haunting the building by rattling the glassware?" Abby crossed her arms and stared at Hayden with a smirk on her face.

He drove onward in the quiet and she saw him shift his eyes to glance at her several times before he cleared his throat and spoke in a calm tone. "Maybe you're right, okay? But I just… I think maybe we should stay at my place tonight is all."

Abby smiled at him and he turned.

"What?"

Her smile widened. "If you wanted me to spend the night with you, you could've just asked. Didn't need to go through all this elaborate—"

"Yeah, yeah."

"I mean, big points for the effort, but—"

"Shut up, we're almost there." Hayden glanced at her with a smile and Abby turned to stare out the window.

She felt color rise in her cheeks and wondered at that. How she'd known Hayden for so long and was now blushing at the thought of spending the night with him.

"Hey?"

She looked at him, failing to keep the smile off her face as he gave her a slight nod. She slid her hand over to his, laced fingers, and gave it a squeeze.

Hayden crested the hill of the road they were on and the happy expression on his face dropped as he braked the car. Ahead was a thick tower of smoke, billowing from a bright column of flames engulfing his apartment.

Emergency vehicles surrounded the place, every light flashing brightly. People gathered around the closed rear doors of an ambulance while firemen sprayed water against the flames.

"Hayseed…" Abby felt sick to her stomach at the sight of the burning building.

A harsh breath escaped Hayden. He groaned and then whispered under his breath. "Oh my God."

ABBY LED HAYDEN to the passenger seat of his old Buick as if he was a sleepwalking child.

The remains of the building were still smoldering as she drove away, a group of firemen still keeping watch for any errant spikes of flame. The entire upper story had been burned away to nothing but a few thick timbers on the outer wall, and the flooring had caved through onto the ground level.

Hayden remained quiet on the drive back to Abby's apartment, sitting with his hands in his lap, a vacant expression on his face. When they arrived in the parking lot, Abby walked around to his side and opened the door for him, and he barely flinched. After getting him inside, Abby brought him to the couch and guided him to lie down. She took the throw blanket from the back of the couch and spread it over him, and then leaned down to put her hand against the side of his face.

He looks like I did in the past. After Nick got good and wired and slapped me that very first time. Christ, I looked exactly like that in the mirror. Numb. Absent of emotion.

Abby kissed him and then went to the kitchen and opened the bottle of tequila on the counter. She poured some into two glasses and walked to the living room to sit down.

"Hayseed?" She spoke softly. "I have a drink for you if… if you want it."

He didn't even blink, and Abby stared at him a moment longer before taking a drink from her glass.

"I don't know what..." Hayden's voice sounded small in the large space. He turned to her, looked at her with faraway eyes, but took the glass of tequila from her and held it. "I lost everything." He sat up on the couch and the blanket fell to his lap.

Abby moved to sit beside him. She put her glass down on the coffee table and rubbed Hayden's back.

"I've gotta..." Hayden's breath was shallow and rapid. The color bleached from his face and he put his hands palm down on his knees.

"I'm so sorry..." Abby put her arm around his back and held him. She put a hand against his cheek and gently turned his head to look at her as she whispered. "I'm so very sorry, babe."

He stared into her eyes and as his expression began to crumble, Abby pulled him into an embrace. His arms wrapped around her and she felt his face nuzzle against her neck and shoulder. She brushed a hand over the back of his head. "I'm here. *Shhhhh... I'm here.*"

Abby held him that way for a long while, until his breathing slowed, but it was Hayden who pulled away. His eyes were red and glassy. He gave her a nod and a weak attempt at a smile, and then drank from his glass of tequila.

"I don't even have a pair of socks to my name." Hayden released a short harsh laugh and shook his head.

"We'll figure it out." She curled up to sit cross-legged on the couch, and rubbed her hand on his shoulder. "Stay here with me. We'll figure it out."

"Yeah?"

His eyes were still wide and a little frantic-looking, but at least they seemed to be aware of his surroundings again.

Abby nodded and brushed her hand against the back of his neck. "I'll help you, I promise."

He pursed his lips and exhaled slowly through his nose.

Abby could tell he was fighting to hold his expression together. She uncrossed her legs and sat up, gently took the glass from Hayden's hand, and stood up before him with her hands outstretched. "Come on... come with me."

Hayden looked up at Abby and took her hands. He stood and followed her lead down the hall of the apartment to her darkened bedroom.

When they reached the edge of the bed, Abby turned to him, stood on tiptoe to wrap her arms around his neck, and kissed him. Hayden's hands rested on her back and slowly moved down her spine to rest on her waist. His grip tightened and he pulled her close.

She kissed him, groaned into his mouth, and then pulled away, breathing heavily. Abby reached for the bottom of Hayden's shirt and lifted it, helping him take it off over his head. He gave a weak smile as he let his clothes fall to the floor, and then he helped Abby out of her T-shirt. Hayden paused and stared into her eyes a moment, and then put his hand at the base of her neck and they came together to kiss her again.

Abby unbuttoned her jeans and shimmied them down her legs, stepping free as they landed on the carpet. Her hands worked on Hayden's belt and after unzipping his pants, she eased both his jeans and boxers down. Stretching up to kiss him once more, Abby ran her hands over his chest, down along his ribs and finally around his back. His skin was smooth, and she felt heat rush through her body at the sensations against the palms of her hands.

With a practiced move, Abby reached behind her back and unhooked her bra. She shrugged her shoulders, let the straps slide free of her arms, and moved closer, pressing her bare breasts against Hayden's chest. Electric tingles raced over her skin and she bit her lip and then kissed his neck, tracing her fingertips along his spine.

She pushed forward slightly, he took a step back, and then she took another until Hayden reached the bed and sat down. Abby paused to slip off her panties, and then moved forward, easing Hayden to his back. She straddled him, and then leaned down, kissing him as he put his hands on her hips. The feel of his tongue against hers was enough to make her moan with desire, so when Abby slid herself along his length and back again, she felt her breath hitch in her chest. She reached for his hands and grasped them in hers, leaned forward, and pressed them down against the soft mattress.

Hayden tilted his head back, closed his eyes, and whispered "Abby…"

The rocking motion of her nipples against Hayden's chest made Abby wetter still, and she glided high along his hard member until she reached his tip, shifting her hips on the return stroke, and felt him slide inside her. He released a deep groan of pleasure and his hands tightened against hers.

Hayden's eyes fluttered. His breath was a staccato rhythm. He moved his hips upward to meet her and Abby felt him fill her.

She moaned out loud and felt that beautiful warmth inside, swirling at the base of her stomach, sparks and flashes of lightning coursing through her body. Abby rode him, meeting his body as he bucked against her.

His body tightened, and trembled, and the very thought of how close he was made Abby's body succumb. When she came, it wasn't hard and fast. Her pleasure unspooled in a long, slow, ribbon of ecstasy, and she cried out and leaned down to kiss him, releasing his hands. He moaned along with her, exhaling in small sharp bursts. She stared into his eyes, watching his expression as he released inside her and arched his back from the mattress with a heavy groan of pleasure.

Abby kissed his neck, his lips, his face, and Hayden's arms wrapped around her waist as he continued to slowly thrust inside her. He moaned and held his breath, releasing it in one, long relaxed sigh, and then lay still.

Her heart raced. She closed her eyes and put her head against Hayden's neck, listening to her own breath as it slowed. Smiling, she kissed his skin, and then rose off of him, turning to lie on her side beside him. She put a hand against his chest and smiled. "Hey."

Hayden turned to face Abby, and then he watched her for a moment without replying. He shook his head slightly, whispered as he reached out and brushed the hair from her face. "I've spent too much of my life hiding how I feel about you."

He shifted, bent his arm and propped his head up on his palm. "I know you've got things going on in life. I do, too, especially after…" Hayden glanced away, but then returned to her eyes again. "You don't have to say it back right now, but I don't want to hide how I feel anymore. Not with actions… not with words… not with anything."

He leaned close and kissed her, slow and gentle and full of passion. "We were meant for each other, Abby. I love you, I've *always* loved you."

She smiled and closed her eyes and snuggled closer. It felt beautiful and pure and most of all, it felt *right* as Abby nestled in Hayden's arms. His breathing deepened and slowed and shifted into the unmistakable sound of someone in slumber. It made her smile, hearing him like that, but any small thread of exhaustion inside Abby had vanished as they made love.

She lay there, feeling the afterglow of pleasure flow through her, and closed her eyes, listening to him as he slept. Part of her hoped she would be able to drift off to sleep along with him, but eventually, she gave a heavy sigh and carefully eased herself from Hayden, before slipping out of bed.

Grabbing her panties from the floor, Abby pulled them on, and then pulled her T-shirt over her head as she walked to the living room. She glanced at the TV and considered throwing an old sitcom on until she got sleepy, but she ignored the remote, picked up her abandoned glass of tequila, and leaned against the kitchen counter. Abby looked at the door to her apartment.

Outside those doors and right down the hall, a little girl fell down the stairs and died. All over her love and grief of a plastic toy doll.

Abby sighed and took a drink of liquor, feeling its syrupy warmth. Stepping away from the counter, she glanced toward the bedroom and listened to Hayden's slow sleeping rhythm. She put her glass down on the counter, went to her front door, and unlocked it.

Drywall dust and grit scuffed beneath Abby's bare feet as she walked down the hallway toward the main foyer. It opened into the large main entrance area and she studied the rise of the massive staircase that led upstairs. She looked at the closed elevator doors, and then turned to the stretching length of another hallway.

Toward Dobsen's. His office used to be down that hallway.

Abby stood in the wide foyer, and stepped into the grid of marble squares, dimly lit from the hallway lights.

There. Right there.

Flower had to have died within feet of where Abby stood, and out of nowhere, she blinked tears from her eyes.

Abandoned here and left alone. Dead over the grief of a toy doll.

Abby crouched and patted her hand against the floor. Though just as gritty as the hallway, it felt smooth beneath the layer of dirt.

How many footsteps crossed this floor as people dropped off children? Tossed their Dead Pennies in here forever?

Abby stood and shook her head. Her soft footsteps padded down the dark hallway until she reached her apartment. She shut and locked the door, and wiped her feet on the small rug just inside the threshold.

She went to the couch and sat, sipping from her glass, and after finishing the rest of the tequila, Abby gently climbed back into bed and beneath the covers. She snuggled against Hayden's back and smiled at his warmth.

Chapter Thirty-Four

BBY WATCHED HAYDEN as he stood at the living room window. Curls of steam rose from the coffee cup in his hand and his expression was far away.

"How you doin', Hayseed?"

He turned and smiled at her, stepped from the window and put his mug down on the counter of the kitchen island. "Just going through my to-do list."

"Anything I can help with?" Abby stepped closer, put her arms around him, and felt Hayden's arms wrap her close. She felt him sigh and shake his head.

"Nothing I can think of yet, but that might change."

Hayden gave her a slight squeeze, and Abby felt him nuzzle his chin against the top of her head and breathe in. She closed her eyes and took a breath herself, smiled at the scent of him close to her. "Well if you think of something, anything, just tell me."

"I will, I promise." He gave her another gentle squeeze and pulled away.

"Step by step. One thing at a time."

"I know." He took another drink of coffee, smiled, and put his mug down. "I don't know about you, but I slept like I was in a coma last night." He moved around the island and stepped close to Abby as she leaned back against the counter.

"I slept pretty well, yeah." She grinned at him, put her mug down, and slid her arms around his neck. "Why, were you hoping you wore me out?"

"It might be a long day for me today, but when I get back... *home*..." Hayden slid his hands down her arms to her shoulders, and then down to her waist. "You're mine."

"Is that so?" Her smile widened and she stretched up to kiss him. "Bring it on, choir boy."

Hayden kissed her softly and tightened his grip on her waist. He paused to gently bite her lower lip, and then pulled away. He opened his mouth, but then closed it again without saying a word. Leaning forward, Hayden kissed her forehead and held her for a moment before releasing a heavy sigh. "Okay, I'm heading out to talk to Father Walker and let him know what's going on, and then make some calls to the insurance company, find out what's covered and what's..."

Hurt swam in his eyes. She put a hand out against the side of Hayden's face, watching his pained expression. "One thing at a time. One thing at a time."

He nodded and stepped back, took another long swallow from his coffee mug, and then pulled his car keys from his pocket, jingling them from one finger. "One thing a time." Hayden smiled and winked at Abby as he left her apartment.

After checking email and seeing nothing urgent, Abby sat in the quiet of the living room and finished her coffee. Occasionally, flashes of making love with Hayden would come to her, causing a smile to rise on her face. She shook her head.

Oh, how life can change at the drop of a hat.

Her phone buzzed with an incoming call and Abby glanced at it and saw MOM across the top of the screen. She stared a moment and then thumbed the reject button. Abby still felt the peaceful satisfaction of amazing sex and a morning of sunshine. She wasn't about to let her mother ruin that.

She stretched, yawned, and then walked toward the bedroom, pausing at the threshold to look around. There was no doubt the walls were new construction—fresh drywall and moldings could attest to that—but she couldn't help but wonder what was this space used for years ago.

A light shiver trailed up her back and Abby shook it away as she pulled on a pair of jeans. She thought of the building's entrance from her walk the night before, the spot Flower had died, and the way the light cast across the dirty floor.

An idea occurred to her, and she pulled on a pair of socks and a fresh shirt. In the living room, she slipped on her pair of sneakers as she considered the idea more thoroughly. She looked outside, and saw the sun streaming brightly now, mist rising from the lawn in gentle wisps. Abby took one last drink from her coffee mug, and then stepped into the hallway, turning right and then left at the end, heading toward the pool. Several closed doors lined the wall.

This has to be where the supply rooms were.

She looked left and then right at the row of closed doors, and then started down the line, trying to open them. Nothing was locked, and Abby supposed there was no use locking doors when work was still being done, or on hold.

Most were empty shells of space, nothing more than raw plywood flooring and walls of unfinished drywall. Abby walked further down the hall, stopping at a doorway with a small brass sign. STAFF ONLY.

She tried the handle on the door and it opened easily. Abby paused at the sight of stairs leading down below, and in her mind, she thought of Cora Jean, and then Dr. Dobsen, walking to the basement.

A junction box was mounted to the wall on her right and she flicked a switch, spilling bright light across the short set of stairs. The floor at the bottom looked clean and swept—new cement from the construction rehab. Abby descended a few stairs and leaned down to see. The basement was long and narrow, roughly the size of two mobile homes parked side by side, with bright fluorescent lights humming overhead.

She stepped down to the cement and looked around. Three massive electrical boxes with the panel doors open wide, were mounted against one wall. Clean wiring in zip-tied bundles ran out of the top of the boxes upward toward the ceiling and beyond. Bright white PVC pipes threaded the ceiling above her, each joint and connection smeared with purple pipe adhesive. Against the wall to her right was a large rectangular contraption, and from the pipe sprouting from its top, Abby guessed it was a massive modern water heater for the building.

Making her way a little further, she saw an open doorframe to a darkened room on her left, with a new, unpainted wooden door leaning against the wall beside it.

Tink, tink.

The same sound she'd heard before, came from the room and Abby stepped closer. A metal column sat just inside the room's entrance, and she reached out to an aluminum-collared light to switch it on. Where the main area of the basement was cleaned up, this room was a collection of filth. The two narrow windows on the far side were caked with dust and cobwebs.

A massive iron boiler stretched most of the length of the room, ending with a thick grate, opened and ready to receive offerings. The walls were white but caked with dirt, skim coat of cement peeling and exposing the stone foundation peeking through every several feet of length.

Close to the boiler sat an old office desk, its top edged with a ribbon of aluminum, and the desk itself stacked with several open cardboard boxes filled with folders and papers.

Oh god, this is where Dobsen burned the files.

Abby stepped further into the room. It was damp and smelled of mold.

Mewww.

Abby snapped her head toward the sound of the kitten. More cardboard boxes were on the dirt-caked floor around the desk. She took a step forward, pulled out her phone, and turned on the flashlight. As she looked down, the showering metallic sound rained down behind her.

Nothing. There was nothing there.

Mewww.

Abby snapped around and trained her light into the boxes. The first held more dust-covered manila folders in a short stack. She moved her light to the next box and saw a thick mat of papers, black mold spread across their surface, a brown gelatinous rind of some sort of fungus along the outer rim of the box itself.

"Ohhhh fucking hell..." Abby winced and turned away, the beam of her flashlight shining over the monstrous shape of the boiler. She took a breath and bit her bottom lip.

She felt a cold, moist pressure on the fingers of her right hand, a suckling sensation, like the mouth of a newborn calf seeking nourishment. Abby jerked her arm upward, but there was nothing there. She swung her flashlight back toward the boiler.

And that's when the shape began to unspool in front of her. A dense, mercurial spill of black crawled from beneath the belly of the iron boiler. It expanded and then quickly tightened again into a form complete with gangly, reaching arms and the bulbous protrusion of what passed for a head that shuddered in its motions and turned toward her.

Abby screamed and ran toward the hum of the fluorescent lights. A rind of ice formed along her spine and the back of her neck. Her sneakered feet smacked against the cement and she raced up the stairs two and three at a time before she burst into the hallway and slammed the door shut behind her.

She put her back to the door, her hands flat against it, and let out a trembling breath.

"Look, I don't mean you any harm, okay?" The words tumbled out of her in a shaky tone.

No footsteps coming after her. No strange shadows. Only silence. Normalcy. Nothing but the hallway stretching out in either direction, and the bright sunlight streaming through the windows into the pool room.

It's broad daylight. What're you, six years old or something? Running from the Boogeyman?

Abby leaned her head back against the door, stared at the hallway ceiling, and then laughed out loud at herself. Her pulse stopped beating in her eardrums and Abby shook her head and walked back to her apartment. She used her foot to nudge the door closed behind her, and headed toward her cold mug of coffee, silently scolding herself once again.

"Jesus, Abs, why don't you just go buy a Ouija board and…" Abby whispered out loud to herself and froze with the handle of the microwave in one hand and her mug of coffee in the other.

"A Ouija board." She glanced at her laptop and then put the mug of coffee in the microwave and punched in ninety-seconds.

She rummaged in her purse and found, folded and tucked into the side-pocket, the sheet of paper the girl at the coffee shop had given her with the written instructions on what to search for online.

GHOST SCRATCHES GIRL AFTER OUIJA BOARD GOES WRONG AT HARPER'S GROVE

Abby opened her laptop, loaded a new browser window, and ran the search. A long list of links to video clips showed up, all sharing the same still-frame icon of a girl's bandaged face.

"I'm going to regret this, I just know it." Abby sighed, clicked on the first link, and a video window popped up on screen.

Shaky and handheld, the footage showed the beam of a flashlight along with the sounds of footsteps from multiple people as they walked along a narrow hallway.

"Shhhh! Did you hear that?" The person operating the camera came to an abrupt stop and voices cut in as the camera angle swung around to show a teenage boy and girl who had been bringing up the rear in the hall.

"You mean the sound of your mom gettin' fu—"

"Shut up, Ronnie!"

The boy looked annoyed but remained quiet for a three-count before he pulled his hoodie up over his head and spoke again. "This is so lame. Why don't we just go back to the party and—"

"I knew you were chickenshit."

The camera angle swung around again and the footage showed forward motion down the hall as the boy replied. "I *ain't* chickenshit, this is just—"

The video flickered and the video cut to footage of Ronnie and the girl from earlier, along with a third girl, all sitting on the floor. Considering how still the footage was, the camera had to be resting flat on top of something. Five candles formed the points of a pentagram in the middle of the group and Abby could see faint chalk lines running between them. A Ouija board sat in the center of the pentagram.

"Alright, let's all place our hands, *lightly*, on the planchette." The new girl in the footage, a thin brunette, appeared to be the leader of the experiment.

She was the camera operator in the hallway, Abby thought.

In unison, the three of them began chanting in low voices. "Come through, come through, I ask of you. Show me, show me, come to be."

After the fourth repetition, the brunette inhaled and exhaled slowly. "Is there anyone here?"

The candles flickered but the planchette remained in place. The girl's voice broke the silence again. "If there's anyone here, I command you to come forward and show yourself."

Ronnie lifted his head and glared at the brunette, but focused back on the planchette.

The other girl, a blonde with her hair pulled back in a ponytail, jerked one hand away from the board and snapped her head to look at something off in the darkness. "Not cool!"

"You broke the circle!" The brunette straightened and crossed her arms.

"What was it?" Ronnie ignored the brunette and asked the blond girl.

"Something…" She pulled her other hand away from the planchette and wiped her bare forearm. "Felt like someone—"

The planchette flipped over onto its back and the brunette girl's mouth dropped open. She released a harsh laugh and put her hands in front of her as if she was trying to feel the air.

"*Fuck* this shit." Ronnie pushed himself to his feet and held a hand out for the blonde.

The brunette turned to look at him, an amused expression on her face. "They're here."

"Who, crazy bitches?" Ronnie pulled the blonde to her feet beside him. "*Surrrre are.*"

"No, Ronnie. They're—"

The camera angle somersaulted toward the candles and all three teenagers began to scream. Abby watched the remaining blurred footage of them running down a hallway. There was another flicker on screen as one recording session ended and another began. This segment showed Ronnie and the brunette standing together beneath what appeared to be light from a street lamp.

"I'm not messin' around, Laura, you got *jacked* up. Like... we gotta get some bandages on that, *now*. I think you need to go to the hospital, no kidding." Ronnie leaned his head to the side, looking at the brunette's crying face while she held her long hair up. "You sure this didn't happen when we were running or some—"

"It fucking happened *before* we hauled ass out of there." The girl shook her head and turned toward the camera, stepping closer to show the side of her face. "See this? This *just* happened to me."

A long gash ran along the girl's face from the side of her chin up to her cheekbone and rivulets of blood streamed down the opened seam of flesh. "Do *not* fuck with Harper's Grove, people. It is *nooooo* joke."

The girl stepped away from the camera and the footage paused on a freeze-frame of her bloody face wound for a few seconds before it cut to an all-black screen.

Abby sighed.

Okay, so the footage doesn't look like a few kids acting out an independent horror movie. But it just feels like such... such...

"Bullshit." Abby scrolled down to read the comments beneath the video clip. It seemed like quite a few people shared her same skeptical mindset. Quite a few "HOAX!" and "Nice fake blood!" comments. She scrolled farther and paused.

Usr38898: I went to school with Laura Welles!

Abby pulled open a new tab in her web browser and went to work. She only paused once to retrieve her coffee from the microwave, but even so, it took less than a half an hour to find what she was after, or more accurately, *who*.

"The internet is both a wonderful and terrifying thing." She shook her head and stared at the laptop screen showing a satellite map and address of Laura Welles.

Chapter Thirty-Five

WHAT'RE YOU DOING, *Abby?*

The GPS on her phone voiced that she should turn right a half-mile ahead. Abby had been driving through a sprawling countryside of farms and pastures for the last ten minutes and was beginning to wonder if the directions were as unbelievable as the video she'd watched. She thrummed her hands on the steering wheel.

Abby turned right onto a gravel road and slowed her car. The bullseye on her phone screen let her know the address was close. She chewed on her bottom lip and stopped the car along the side of the road.

What are you trying to get out of this?

Answers. I want answers.

Dust from the gravel swirled around the car and got caught up in wind, twirling away from her. The radio was off, but she tapped the steering wheel again with a drumbeat from a song she couldn't remember the name of.

Answers to what questions, Abs?

She ignored the voice in her head and drove on until she saw a wooden sign hanging from a dead tree. The sign was painted dark brown, the lettering: LOCUST POINT COMMUNITY routed out and painted white. It reminded her of signs she might see at the entrance to a campground, but Abby turned into the road and drove into the collection of trailers.

An old Chevelle, painted only in gray primer, rested on top of cinderblocks in one trailer's driveway. Two young boys were sword fighting with pieces of a window screen frame. Abby glanced at the street number and drove on.

An ancient looking man sat in a wicker lawn chair with a chicken on his lap. He took a puff from a cigar and raised his hand in a greeting. Abby shook her head and slowed the car. Her phone announced she had arrived at her destination. Across from her, a shiny black El Camino was parked by a rusting turquoise trailer. A man wearing dirty sweatpants and a dark gray hoodie walked away from a woman standing in the driveway, got in the El Camino and wasted no time driving away.

Why do I feel like I got here at the ass-end of a drug deal? This was a dumb idea.

Abby sighed, got out of her car, and walked toward the trailer. The woman caught sight of her and turned away, heading toward her porch. A faded blue Volkswagen Rabbit sat in the patch of gravel drive.

"Miss?" Abby called out after the woman, who ignored her and continued onto her slanted wooden porch. "Miss?"

The woman opened the trailer door and stretched one hand inside and out of sight as she turned to face Abby. "You a cop?"

Abby blinked at the woman, looked over how she was dressed, and then at the woman again. "Do I *look* like a cop?"

"Can't be too sure these days." She glanced across the street at Abby's car. "Guess not. Even pigs can afford better unmarked cars than that." The woman remained where she was, one hand hidden from view inside the trailer. Her eyes narrowed as she gave Abby a thorough inspection. "If you ain't a cop, what do you want?"

Abby put her hands, palms out, in front of her and took a step closer. "I'm trying to find Laura Welles. I just want to talk with—"

The woman threw her head back and cackled, the rough laughter of a heavy cigarette smoker. "Laura Welles," she shook her head. "I haven't been called that, *not once*, since high school and—" Her eyes sharpened and she eyed Abby, tilted her head slightly, studying her. "You're here about the video, ain't ya?"

"I just want to—"

"Nope. No ma'am. No thank *youuuuu*." Laura pushed the trailer door open and took a step inside. "Been made the fool too many times over—"

"I believe you." The lie tumbled out of Abby's mouth before she'd even considered it. A trick she had learned from Nick probably—sometimes you learn to say *exactly* what people need to hear.

The woman paused, pursed her lips together, and then turned back to Abby, eyeing her over again. "You a goddamn reporter? Like for the *National Enquirer* or some shit?"

"No, I... I'm... I'm writing a college paper, that's all." Abby watched the lady's eyes, the way she studied her. "Listen, I..." Opening her purse, she pulled a twenty-dollar bill from the zippered pouch and held it out in front of her. "I can pay you for your time if you want, I—"

Laura turned and yelled inside the trailer. "Stevie? You still in the goddamn bed? You gotta leave for work in *ten fuckin' minutes* or you'll be late for the *second* time this week! Get the fuck up!" She slammed the door closed and leaned against the weathered two by four porch railing.

"Keep your money, college girl." The woman coughed, a harsh phlegmy sound. "Fuckin' wish *I'd* went to college. Maybe I wouldn't be in this..." She cleared her throat and stared at Abby.

"First of all, I don't know who Laura is anymore. Just call me Gillie." She stepped from the porch close to Abby, and turned her head to the left. "Look at it now. Take a good look." Laura turned to face her. "You can take a picture if'n you want. That's what that night left me with." She turned her face to the left again.

A line of scar tissue curved along the woman's face from the right side of her chin to the top of her right cheekbone. "People stopped calling me by my Christian name years ago. Started callin' me Gillie 'cause of this big ol' fish gill on my face." She shrugged. "Pissed me off for a while, but then I said fuck it and accepted it."

She stepped back onto her porch and then a grin slid onto her face. "Coulda been worse, right? Coulda called me Fish." The woman snorted a bitter laugh, leaned against the railing, and then moved to sit down on the crooked stoop. "So, here's the deal,

Lucille. You ain't a cop and you ain't no reporter, so... alright, I'll tell ya."

She reached into her robe and deep down, Abby already knew what the woman was retrieving as she watched Gillie produce a plastic packet and a glass pipe from her robe pocket.

Gillie held them out in her palm and cocked her head. "I'm gonna hit this pipe and get right first, and then I'll talk to you, tell you what you wanna know. That a problem?"

Abby swallowed hard and shook her head. "Nope."

Nodding as if her answer didn't really matter, Gillie readied her glass pipe and took a hit.

What the hell are you doing here, Abby?

The scent of it, the utter ritual of it all, made Abby's stomach turn. She watched the phantoms of meth smoke rise from the pipe stem and saw the glaze hit Gillie's eyes, how the woman's jaw shifted back and forth almost immediately as the drug hit her system.

Gillie exhaled the smoke and a soft wind carried it along the trailer. She coughed, spit over the side of the porch, and shook her head. "Tastes harsh. Bad batch came through 'bout six months ago, made with battery acid. Damned near tore up the trailer park, set people crazier than shithouse rats." Gillie laughed, the noise choppy, sifted through a cheese grater.

"Good shit." She held the pipe to her lips and took another hit.

The thought of watching Nick smoke flashed in Abby's mind, a memory of the only time she had tried it. After a night of too-many drinks and not enough sleep, she had finally given in to Nick's repeated passive aggressive pleas for her to try it, to *experience* it together. The way it made her heart slam, the world narrow down pinpoint fine, how it twisted time and made her focus on something so specific, the universe on the head of a needle.

She'd never done it again, not once.

"Okay, college girl." Gillie shifted back and forth on the porch stoop. "So, you've already seen the video, but you... *Youuuu* wanna know the behind the *sceeeenes* shit, huh?" The woman pointed with her index finger and nodded as she smiled conspiratorially. "Am I right? *You betcha I'm* right."

"I—"

"Let's see." Gillie nodded and stuffed the meth pipe into the pocket of her robe again. "Well..." She leaned her elbows on her knees and rubbed the palms of her hands together. "The three of us, me, Ronnie, and Sheila, all left the party and went on out to Harper's Grove. Was *my* idea to bring the Ouija board, and what a fuckin' mistake *that* was."

"What do you think it was that did it? That scratched you." Abby stepped closer to the trailer porch.

"Some kinda..." Gillie waved an arm as she spoke. "Damned ghost or demon or somethin' pissed off. Hell, can't blame anythin' for bein' pissed off up there. All them kids."

Abby watched the woman shift back and forth where she sat, the meth working her system. "You knew about the place before you went up there? About how bad it used to be?"

Gillie nodded and coughed, rubbed her fingers along her throat. "'*Course* I did. My Gramma DD told me all about it. She worked there years ago. Told me all about that shithole. Goddamned shameful the city ain't done nothin' 'bout them Dead Pennies still there."

Hearing yet another person say the phrase *Dead Pennies* made a chill curl up inside Abby's guts. "What do you mean still there?" She felt herself reverting to how she'd been at times with Nick, the ever-patient sober person dealing with someone under the influence. "Harper's Grove was shut down a long time ago."

"For a college girl, you ain't so damned smart, are ya?" Gillie's expression was unimpressed. "I *know* the damned place was shut down. Not talkin' 'bout *livin'* kids, girlie. Talkin' 'bout the *dead ones* buried all over the grounds."

Cora Jean telling her about watching Milk get buried came to Abby's mind. She said nothing in response to Gillie, knowing from dealing with Nick in the past that the woman would continue talking all by herself.

"By the time Gramma DD started working, she guessed there was at least seventy-five kids buried there at Harper's Grove. By the time she left, hell, it had to be almost double that. Men up there doin' the goddamndest things. What, you think they bothered practicin' safe sex on them kids?" Gillie scrunched up her face and snorted. "If'n they got one pregnant, so what? Cut them babies out barely after their little hearts started beatin', goddamn sons o' bitches."

Gillie hawked up and spit to the side of the porch. "Ain't even Christian ground! What kind of—"

"Is your grandmother still alive?"

"Naww." Gillie shook her head. "DD passed on few years back. Stroke." She worked her jaw back and forth, and then freed the glass pipe from her robe pocket.

The trailer door opened up and a heavyset man in a white tank top glared at Gillie. "You know it's fuckin' Saturday, right?" He scowled at Abby and then retreated into the trailer's darkness again. "I don't fuckin' work today, ya dumb b—"

"Don't you start talkin' shit today after—" Gillie gritted her teeth and stood up from her porch. She stuffed the pipe back in her robe and snapped her head to Abby. "Don't go there. Don't go in that place. It's goddamned—"

"You going on 'bout your goddamned ghost story again? Jesus Christ, let it—"

"Fuck you, Stevie!" Gillie yanked the trailer door open and marched inside, slamming it shut behind her. "Just 'cause you ain't got no one asking to interview you, you don't—"

Abby heard the screaming begin and she stared at the closed trailer door. Something smashed inside the trailer, the sharp crack and shatter of breaking glass, and Abby walked away to her car, wondering how long it would've taken with Nick before she had ended up in a life like Gillie's.

Chapter Thirty-Six

WHAT THE HELL *do I do with this? A bunch of dead kids buried in a... a potter's field is what Cora Jean called it.*

Abby rolled her window down and let the breeze flow in over her. In the rearview mirror, dust kicked up along the gravel road.

Do you reallllly think some ghost or some kind of... demon attacked Gillie? That Hayden's drone footage of the old man caught—

A snapshot of the shadow beneath the boiler filled her mind's eye, swirling and growing.

—some kind of a ghost crawling down the wall?

Abby swerved to the shoulder of the road, jammed her foot on the brakes and pulled the car to a stop. A cloud of dust blew past her in a whirlwind and she gripped the steering wheel. "What, getting away from a junkie boyfriend too easy? You have to throw yourself into some after-school mystery? This is *bullshit*, Abs! Complete and utter bullshit!"

She sat there, breathing heavily, trying to process everything that had occurred over the last week of her life. Tapping a finger on the mirror, she scolded her reflection. "Stop. Spooking. Yourself."

Abby turned on the radio and hit the SCAN button a few times until she heard Mick Jagger in the middle of singing *Satisfaction*. With the music blaring in the car, Abby turned from the gravel onto the main road, leaving a trail of dust and her inner voice behind her.

———————

SHE'D HOPED TO see Hayden's car, but the parking lot was empty when she got back, and Abby briefly wondered how his day was going. She ran through a mental checklist of food in her apartment, thinking of what she could make for dinner, and decided on ordering a bunch of Chinese takeout instead. Anything to take stress off of Hayden and make him relax after having everything he owned destroyed in the fire.

She punched in her access code and fought the urge to glance at the area where Flower had died. The heavy door closed behind her, and Abby continued to her apartment.

Okay, so check emails. Get a list of Chinese food to order later. Check wine supply. Or maybe margaritas instead. Shit, no, I'm out of tequila.

Abby went to her laptop and checked her email, read edits on a press release from a client, and she immediately began making revisions on the file to get it back in their hands.

Ding-ding-ding-ding-ding-ding—

She snapped her head toward the kitchen cabinets. The glasses behind the closed doors made sounds loud enough to rattle the wood. Abby rose from her chair and stared at the origins of the noise.

—*ding-ding-ding-ding-ding-ding.*

The sounds stopped dead. The rhythm echoed in her ears, inside her mind, and Abby felt her heart beat hard against her ribs.

A moist, spongy sensation flicked over the first two fingers of her left hand, and Abby flinched away from the invisible source. The hair on the back of her neck stood on end as a chill branched out over her skin.

Silence. There was nothing but the incredibly loud silence.

The fan on her laptop kicked in, and Abby jolted in place. She waited, and looked around the room. Nothing.

Cautiously, Abby took a step forward, and then another, and walked to the table to sit behind her laptop again. She opened a new web browser tab and searched for The Divine Covenant Seminary school's website. A few moments after that, Abby picked up her phone and called the number for Father Walker.

Chapter Thirty-Seven

ABBY CHEWED ON her bottom lip. "Father, I... I'm not one to believe in these kinds of things, but I can't ignore there's something strange going on around here. Could you... I mean, would you maybe... this sounds silly, I know, but everything I've seen on TV or in the movies says if you get the place blessed, it'll help—"

"When Hayden showed us that video footage, I got the feeling you're pretty skeptical of things like this, but Abby, if tossing around some holy water and blessing the grounds will help put you at ease in any way, I'll do that for you."

Father Walker's tone was serious, without a trace of humor in it, but Abby still felt like an idiot, a scared child spooked by shadows in the corner, and pushed ahead with the reason she had called him in the first place.

"I'd *really* appreciate that, Father. There's something else I..." Abby cleared her throat and chewed her bottom lip again before continuing. "I was talking to a woman earlier today and she told me, whether it's true or not, I don't know, but this woman told me there are lots of bodies buried here."

"Lots of places like Willowbrook had their own area for burials and—"

"Unmarked graves, Father. Lots of them. It sounds like these deaths were covered up."

The priest on the other end of the call remained silent for a few moments, save for the sound of his breathing.

"Father Walker?"

The man let out a heavy sigh. "There used to be many places like Willowbrook, hell holes where children were discarded, and kept away from society. Ireland had their laundries with pregnant, unwed, young women. England had their own version. Russia... these sorts of places existed everywhere. So many unmarked graves. You feel it at these places, feel the sadness, the grief, a sense of mourning, but sometimes, you feel the anger, too. Enough bad things happen in the same spot, and the shadows begin to gather, and sometimes that pain, that... *rage,* starts up some sort of engine, makes the place itself come alive."

An icy whisper trailed along Abby's spine. She looked round the living room, but everything remained quiet.

"Yes, Abby," Father Walker cleared his throat. "I'll come by to bless the grounds for you. My last class is at four o'clock and I'll gather some things and be over not long after."

Abby put her phone into her jeans pocket and crossed her arms. Part of her mind wanted to rationalize things, to blame the dinging glassware on a close-by train rumbling the cabinets, somehow making the sound louder than what it really was. She wanted to chalk everything up to an overactive mind dealing with the blur her life had been over the last week.

But inside, she knew differently.

She picked up her laptop and moved to sit on the couch, so the kitchen cabinets and the door to her apartment were both easily in view.

Chapter Thirty-Eight

THANK YOU FOR coming, Father."

"My pleasure." The priest gave Abby a nod and walked through the front entrance and into the foyer. He withdrew a small glass bottle from the outside pocket of his suit jacket, and paused at the bottom of the wide stairwell leading upward.

"Cora Jean told me—"

"Later, tell me about it later." Father Walker gave her a slight smile. "Let's begin."

Abby followed him as he sprinkled holy water in the foyer, whispering a prayer as he walked. He paused again at the foot of the stairs, and began to ascend, keeping a hand on the railing as he climbed the steps and sprinkled droplets every few feet.

From Cora Jean, Abby knew what awaited upstairs, and part of her was afraid to see the settings of everything she had heard, but she put a hand on the railing, took a deep breath, and followed Father Walker.

Beyond the double doors on the second floor, Abby saw apartment spaces planned out, areas lined with aluminum wall studs and bare plywood floors. Unopened buckets of joint compound lined one wall like a row of sentries, and a waist-high stack of drywall rested on a wooden palette. Abby watched the drops of holy water mark the dusty floor as Father Walker walked across the corridor.

The moment they crossed the threshold back into the stairwell, Abby heard the sounds from upstairs.

Ding-ding-ding-ding-ding.

The fine hair along Abby's arms and the back of her neck rose with a chill.

Father Walker never broke stride, even as he turned to look toward the source of the noises. He walked on, with Abby in tow, and continued whispering his prayers as he stepped into the upper-most corridor.

It was dark on the floor, and she crept toward the row of tall windows covered over with cardboard taped to the frames. Abby pulled one sheet of the filthy cardboard down, another, and sunlight spilled in through the wire mesh glass. From the edges of her vision, it seemed as if shadows retreated and curled away into the far corners of the room.

The corridor smelled of unwashed, donated clothes. Black mold speckled the walls below the windows and around the elevator door on the far side of the room. There was a quality to the air in here, a heavy sensation, like breathing during a heavy fog that filled your lungs.

It's a time capsule, Abby thought. *This is where Cora Jean was, where it all happened.*

An old desk, stacked with folders and paperwork, sat to her left. A series of doors—some missing the doors themselves—lined the space beyond the desk. To her right, Abby saw two wheelchairs, one folded, and one open, both caked with dust.

One of those was Milk's.

Frost spread over the back of Abby's neck and she crossed her arms.

Father Walker sprinkled holy water and Abby heard the end of a whispered sentence.

"…flow through and fill this building up with your spirit."

From an open door on Abby's left, a blur of shadow erupted from the room and rapidly moved across the ceiling. She screamed and ducked, and the figure moved past her and flapped against a window. A pigeon perched on the windowsill, twitching its head and studying her, while it issued soft cooing noises.

Fucccccck. Abby took a deep breath and ran a hand through her hair.

Mews.

Abby raised her head up at the sound of a kitten. Another chill rippled through her body.

Father Walker turned toward the sound, but continued reciting his prayer. He paused at each doorway, shaking his bottle and whispering prayers, before he moved onto the next room and repeated his actions.

It was subtle but noticeable to Abby, and the tight feeling of the corridor began to ease. It wasn't as if it had been replaced with some-thing better, but rather it was the absence of what had been there, as if the bad air was slowly leaking away. Abby took several deep breaths and watched as Father Walker turned from a doorway at the end of the corridor and walked back toward her. He gave her a nod and continued toward the stairwell.

Downstairs, on the ground floor, he resumed his prayers and sprinkled holy water as he walked down the hallway. Abby followed him until the intersection at the end, and stopped.

"I'll uh… I'll wait here, Father."

The priest glanced at her and she could see the curiosity in his expression, but he continued down the hall and into the poolroom, the *natatorium* Hayseed had called it.

Abby thought of the homeless man falling through the skylight, and the shower of glass that had rained down. The blood. She chewed on her lower lip and leaned against the wall.

Moments later, Father Walker emerged back into the hallway.

"Could you um… could you go downstairs?" Abby raised a hand and pointed at the door to the basement and the boiler room. "Through that door."

She must have shown something in her eyes, some dead giveaway of fear, because Father Walker stopped walking and tilted his head slightly, studying her with that curious expression again.

"Of course." He opened the door and Abby watched him recede down the stairs, the sound of his scuffing footsteps fading as the door closed behind him.

She wished Hayseed was here, and wondered how he was handling everything today. He had held himself together fairly well for a person who had everything they owned burned to a crisp, but Abby was sure it was taking a toll. It had to be.

He'll live here with me while he figures it out.

Just thinking about the idea made Abby smile, and she reminded herself about ordering Chinese food later. The silence in the hallway was so quiet, Abby's ears rang. But it was calm too, peaceful and somehow comforting, like hiding among the back bookshelves of a library.

The door to the basement swung open quickly, startling her, but Father Walker stepped through and offered her a smile. "Anywhere else?"

Abby shrugged, almost embarrassed, but seeing the priest smile put her at ease. It was the first time since he had started his ritual that he hadn't looked as if he was at a funeral. "My apartment?"

His smile grew wider. "Show me the way."

Inside, Father Walker walked the length of the apartment and ran through his prayers. Abby watched the sprinkles of holy water as he went on, and when he returned from her bedroom, he let out a long breath and stood in her living room. "And that's that."

"What about outside? I have a good idea where the unmarked—"

"I walked the grounds before buzzing your doorbell." Father Walker put the almost empty bottle into the pocket of his suit jacket. "I've blessed everything I could. Can't hurt."

"I can't thank you enough, Father." Abby moved toward the kitchen counter. "You're right, you know, about what you said on the phone. I *am* pretty skeptical about these kinds of things, but..." She shook her head. "Would you like a drink, Father? Water? Wine? I can make some coffee."

"Thank you, Abby, but no," the priest gave a light laugh. He cleared his throat and his light expression turned serious. "Cora Jean, she told you the things that happened here?"

Abby nodded. "The abuse, the... absolute hell of it all."

"We can only hope those souls can be at rest now." They were both silent for a few moments, and Father Walker released a sigh. "Relax, Abby. Have yourself a glass of wine, and take a breath tonight. I've got to get going, essays to grade tonight."

Abby smiled and walked toward him, put her arms out, and gave the man a hug. "Thank you again, Father."

"My pleasure." He turned toward the apartment door. "When you speak with Hayden, tell him he's in my thoughts."

"I will. You want me to walk you out?"

Father Walker turned. "I've navigated the jungles of Haiti, I can make it out of here alright."

He gave her another smile and Abby closed the door behind him.

The air does feel lighter. Maybe whatever was here is gone, Abby thought.

Or hiding.

The secondary thought made her bite her lower lip and walk toward the kitchen counter to pour a glass of sangria. Abby glanced at the floating clock screensaver on her laptop. She'd have to order takeout soon.

And why hasn't Hayden called or texted today?

Have you?

Abby sipped from her wine glass and silently scolded herself.

Holy shit, Abs, he's got a lot on his plate. If you ignore the night of the dead homeless guy, you've slept together once, and you're acting like a needy girlfriend. Order takeout. It'll still be hot if he gets here soon, and if he gets here later, well, there's nothing like leftover Chinese food.

After another sip from her glass, Abby set it down on the counter, and walked toward her laptop to pull up the website for Jade Garden, the takeout place in the town's main shopping plaza. She was reading the online menu when she heard two knocks at her door. Abby smiled automatically and thought to herself *"Nice timing, Hayseed."*

She swung the door open, still smiling, ready to give him a big hug, but her mind tripped a fuse at what waited for her in the hall.

"Well hello, my beautiful queen. Miss me?"

Chapter Thirty-Nine

ABBY KEPT HER eyes closed, but she heard the footsteps moving around her living room, the pauses here and there, the sound of a snicker, the noise of a bottle being lifted from the kitchen counter, cap unscrewed, and then the gurgling as someone drank from it. More steps, and then the sound of St. Nick as he sat down heavily into the plush living room chair.

It reminded her of the last night she and Nick had spent together, barely a week ago, but it felt much farther in the past, almost as if the memory was of someone else's life.

She had been on the couch with her laptop, swapping emails with a marketing director in Los Angeles when she heard the knock at the apartment door. It had become a habit of Nick's that started off cute, but had quickly become annoying and cumbersome. She glanced at the door, ignored it, and then there was a second knock. Abby sighed, set her computer on the couch, and walked to the door to open it.

"Why do you knock at the door? You live here, you have an actual key." Abby stared at Nick as he stood in the hallway and smiled at her.

"You're supposed to announce your presence before a queen."

His eyes were glassy, pupils down to pinpoints.

Abby stepped to the side and Nick walked in and shrugged off his jacket. *"Whatcha doin' baby?"*

"The usual," Abby closed the door and flipped the lock before sitting on the sofa again with her laptop. *"Educating a professional on the nuances of how to avoid looking like an idiot on social media."*

Nick pulled a beer from the refrigerator and twisted the cap off. *"You're so damned smart, Abby. You really are. I'm..."* He took a swallow from the bottle. *"I'm really proud of you."*

Abby didn't reply, or even glance at him, only wondered how high he was and what the night would bring. Sometimes he was calm and internal, other nights he was an unpredictable snake, prone to strike at the slightest thing.

"You in for the night?"

He took another swallow and slowly set the bottle down on the kitchen counter. *"What's that supposed to mean?"*

"Nothing, I just..." She kept her attention on the laptop screen. *"Was just wondering, is all."*

She could feel the scrutiny, as he remained silent, staring at her. He sniffled and cleared his throat.

"For a while, yeah. Got some business a little later."

"Mmmm." Abby gave a slight nod and pretended to read the email on screen.

Nick released a snort of disdain, grabbed the bottle of beer and walked down the short hall into their bedroom.

Abby glanced up to see the door close behind him, and exhaled a breath she hadn't realized she'd been holding inside. She forced her shoulders to relax.

Shouldn't be like this. It's like walking on eggshells around him all the time.

She heard the flick of a lighter and the sound of it made her sick to her stomach. Even from behind the closed door, the smell would reach her soon, the syrupy sweet smell of the meth smoke.

He was using more often lately, always justifying it somehow. "It's part of it all, baby. Just to gain trust of the people I sell to. Sometimes I gotta do a little to sell a lot, that's all."

Except he couldn't see the change taking place inside him. The bright look of boyish mischief she used to see in his eyes was gone, dimmed and dull and replaced by a need she would never be able to satisfy.

Abby wrote a reply to her client, read and rewrote it, and then closed her laptop. She leaned back against the couch and stared at the ceiling. She suddenly felt tired and drained. She let her eyes close.

How the hell did I get myself into this?

It was close to one in the morning when she heard Nick come out of the bedroom, and Abby kept her eyes closed as he walked into the living room. She felt him pause and then he took several steps toward the TV cabinet.

Abby opened her eyes, and watched as Nick knelt down, reached beneath the furniture, and withdrew a brown paper bag. He stood up and turned to see her staring at him. His expression was that of a child, caught with their hand in the cookie jar.

"Look, Abby, I—"

"I've asked you over and over not to keep that shit—"

"Where am I supposed to stash it, huh? The fuckin' dumpsters behind Subway?" He shook his head and raised his voice. *"It's not like I'm standin' on a fuckin' street corner sellin' this shit. It's bass players and fuckin' artists from South Street."*

Nick exhaled heavily and softened his tone. "This isn't a lifestyle, Abs, it's... it's only temporary."

"I don't think this..." Abby sat up on the couch, glanced at him and then looked down. "Nick, I'm not sure this is working—"

"Baby," Nick stepped closer and knelt in front of her. "Look, let's go away in a couple weeks, okay? Someplace warm like Bermuda, Jamaica maybe. Just the two of us, okay? We'll sit on the beach and sip drinks with umbrellas."

Her chest buzzed inside, tight and full of tension. Abby swallowed and gave a gentle nod.

"You're my queen." He reached out and brushed his hand against the side of her face. "I belong to you, and you belong to me."

She forced a slight smile and looked into Nick's eyes, saw the absence there. Abby reached down and rested her fingers against his hand holding the bag she knew contained packets of meth inside.

"I think maybe you might belong to this, instead."

Nick tried to pull away, but Abby held tight.

"Let go, Abby."

"You first."

"Fuckin' let go!" Nick's free hand lashed out, whip crack fast, and Abby felt fireworks in her head.

The side of her face exploded and her breath escaped in a hot rush from her lungs. She blinked and saw bursts of light. Nick stood above her, looking down.

"Oh, for fuck's sake, Abby. I'm…" He leaned down toward her. "I'm sorry, it was an accident. You know I'd never—"

"Don't fuckin' touch me."

He reached for her and she flinched, put her hand against her cheek, throbbing with pain.

"Abby…"

"Just go." She lay down on her side and closed her eyes, taking slow, easy breaths. Nick remained where he stood for a moment, and then she heard him put on his jacket and leave the apartment.

She cried for a while after he left, but it was more out of frustration than pain. At some point, she drifted to sleep again, and when she woke, Abby heard Nick snoring in the bedroom. Quietly, she padded down the hallway and stared at him on the mattress, glanced at the open plastic bag on his nightstand. Several pills lay beside it.

How much longer before he overdosed, or a deal went bad? Or whoever Nick was buying from noticed he was shaving off a little of each package?

Abby crossed her arms and stared at him as he slept.

It was time to leave. This was over. This has to be over.

"I know you're awake, Abby."

Nick's voice, speaking quietly, but carrying a hard edge to it. She kept her eyes closed as he continued speaking.

"I used to listen to you breathe at night when you slept." He paused and Abby heard the sound of liquid sloshing in a bottle and him drinking from it. "Used to watch you lying there, so peaceful, like... some kind of angel or something."

Abby swallowed and winced as her throat caught. She remembered his hand around her throat, squeezing. She opened her eyes and glared at him. He smiled, his expression almost embarrassed. His eyes were off, glossy as polished marbles. Bloody scuffs ran along the right side of his face, and his lower lip was busted.

He's higher than a kite.

She pushed herself up on the couch. "How did you..."

"Dontcha love technology?" Nick coughed laughter, reached inside his leather jacket, and then held her phone out in front of him. He tapped it against his leg. "I put a simple little app on your phone, and like magic... I know exactly where you've been, and where you are."

He smirked and stared at her phone. "But like a lot of things, this has already served its purpose for me."

He gripped the phone and slammed it, screen first, against the coffee table, brought it down several times, and then tossed it to the carpet. Nick leaned back in the chair with a grin on his face, and lifted the bottle of sangria. "I'm yours and you are *mine*. Remember, my queen?"

Abby's stomach swirled inside. She had seen Nick high before, seen him borderline overdosing, but this was different. His eyes shifted, wild and scared, but also held a confidence there, a certainty of violence. Abby moistened her lips and Nick quickly stood up from the chair and raised his arms as if he was presenting the living room to her.

"This place! Holy shit, baby!" He pointed at her. "Surprised you didn't go to your mother's though. *Ohhhhh*, that cuntsicle must have shit kittens when you didn't run home to the nest again, right? Though I'm sure she had plenty of happy things to say about me, huh?" He upended the bottle and took two swallows. "Bitch never liked me anyway."

"She liked you fine when you weren't stoned out of your mind."

Nick glared at her, and that bright sheen on his eyes sharpened. He sniffled and shook his head. "No, no. You're not turning this around on me right now. You just fuckin' left. Walked out without even giving me a chance, without a fuckin' word."

Despite the situation, Abby felt anger flow through her veins. "Why the hell not? What, because you said you were *gonna change?*" She glanced at Nick's arms, down at his sides. "How many days you been sucking on that meth pipe *this* time?"

His expression hardened and she watched him clench his teeth, and then Nick nodded, snorted a laugh and shook his finger at her. "Smart girl, Abby."

"What happened to your face, anyway?"

"Got jumped the day after you left." Nick walked to the kitchen counter and uncapped the almost empty bottle of tequila. "Had my supply taken. Owe the wrong guy now."

"I told you—"

"Sure did, didn't you? You told me so. And it was time for me to get the fuck outta Philly before I ended up dead in the Schuylkill." He tilted the bottle of Jose Cuervo, took a swallow and grimaced, and then tilted his head at her and grinned. "Smart. You're *soooo* fuckin' smart. This is all your fault, anyway."

"How in the *hell* is it—"

"You had my head all fucked up, not focused. *You* did that when you left me." He nodded and grinned with tequila-dampened lips. "*Your* fault. That and the priest."

The sickness in Abby's stomach turned to slushed bits of ice, and Nick must have seen it on her face. He raised his eyebrows and nodded in an *aww shucks* gesture.

"Fuck was Father Pokesalot doin' here anyway? You join a prayer group or somethin'?" He snickered and raised the bottle to his lips.

"Nick... what did you do?"

"Shame, really. Seemed like a nice guy." He looked down at the floor, a frown on his face, and then he cleared his throat and glared at her. "Throw some things in a bag and keep it simple."

"Nick, what—"

"This has been fun, baby, it really has. But it's time to go. We've gotta hit the road."

Abby stood up from the couch and crossed her arms. "I'm not going anywhere."

Nick smiled at her and shook his head, mocking her, and then he sat the tequila bottle on the kitchen counter. He reached behind to the small of his back, pulled out a pistol, and held it in down at his side. "Playtime's over, baby. Don't make me use my *Daddy means it* voice."

Chapter Forty

ABBY STUFFED TWO pair of jeans, some T-shirts, and bras and panties into her backpack. She glanced at Nick as he leaned against the bedroom doorframe and watched her, and then she held his gaze, glaring at him. Nick snickered, stared at the small amount of tequila that remained in the bottle, and tilted it for a drink. He turned and walked down the hallway toward the living room.

Her hands shook as she pulled the top of her backpack closed and zipped it shut.

I have mace in my purse. Maybe I could spray him and run as soon as we get into the hallway, find someplace to hide.

Think you can you outrun that pistol, Abs?

She clenched her teeth and felt her heart beating in her chest. As she shifted the backpack on the mattress, her eyes caught the edge of something beneath Hayden's pillow. Abby's heart flipped over and her breath rushed from her lungs.

Hayden's phone. He'd forgotten it when he left this morning.

A quick glance toward the hall, and Abby grabbed the phone and stuffed it into the back pocket of her jeans.

"Find everything you need?"

She snapped toward the doorway, saw Nick standing there again, and she swallowed hard, nodding.

"Good, 'cause we gotta hit the road." Nick sniffled and wiped at his nose, then waved her forward with his hand.

"I… I still need things from the bathroom." She heard the tremor in her voice as she spoke and hoped Nick wouldn't notice it with the alcohol in his blood.

He sighed and nodded and waved her forward again. "Just hurry it up."

Abby slung the strap of her backpack over her right shoulder, knowing as it hung down, it would cover her back pocket. She walked into the hallway and immediately turned into the bathroom.

Nick stepped back and leaned against the wall, watching her as she pulled her deodorant, a pack of razors, and her makeup bag, putting them all into the front pouch of the backpack. She turned toward the shower, reaching for her shampoo and conditioner.

"Fuck that shit, I said keep it simple. We'll buy that stuff when we get where we're going." Nick lifted the bottle of Jose Cuervo and motioned toward her. "Come on, let's go!"

Abby nodded and paused with her hand on the strap of her backpack. She stared straight ahead for a moment and turned to Nick. "I have to pee."

He sighed, frustration evident on his face, and nodded toward the toilet. "Go!"

Abby stood in front of the toilet and stopped with her hands on the zipper of her jeans as she stared at Nick. "Do you mind?"

"Nothin' I haven't already seen before." Nick scoffed and shook his head.

She stood her ground, cocked her head, and sharpened her expression.

"Whatever." He shrugged and raised his hands as he stepped to the side of the doorway, out of sight. Nick released a heavy sigh and she heard his ring clank against the glass bottle.

Unzipping her jeans, Abby pulled her panties down and sat on the toilet. Keeping an eye on the doorway, she reached down and withdrew Hayden's phone from her rear pocket.

The screen showed notifications for the text messages she had sent him earlier in the day, along with two missed calls and a voicemail from Detective Simmons.

Abby swiped her thumb across the notifications, thankful and screaming inside that Hayden didn't have a password lock on his phone. She tapped the phone icon at the bottom of the screen.

"I don't hear any pissin' going on." Nick's voice was starting to slur, picking up that underlying, unpredictable sharpened edge of a blade. Even though he was turned away from the bathroom, the side of his face shown at the doorway.

Her heart was a piston behind her ribs. Abby put the phone down at her side, and closed her eyes, willing her bladder to work. After a few moments, it gave way and the sound of her urinating broke the quiet of the small bathroom. Nick moved and he was completely out of sight once again.

"*C'monnnnn* baby. *Fuccccck*. Wipe, and let's go!"

Pulling the phone back in front of her, Abby swiped to the phone call screen and pushed 9. As she hovered over 1, the phone buzzed in her hands. Abby flinched and a yelp almost escaped her lips. She fumbled behind her to the toilet handle, pushed the lever down to flush and cover the buzzing sound.

The screen showed a call coming in from Detective Simmons. Abby pushed the green *Accept* button and moved the phone down to her side, hidden by the commode, as Nick moved into the doorframe, watching her.

She glared at him. "Give me a break, I'm on my period, okay?"

Nick's gaze slowly ran over her body, down from her face and over her bare thighs.

Abby stood, realizing Nick wasn't going to look away this time. In one smooth motion, she reached for her panties, and set Hayden's phone down on the bathroom rug, behind her right foot and the cover of her jeans. As she lifted her panties, Nick exhaled slowly, and grunted approval, as if satisfied with his appraisal.

"I have *truly* missed you."

Reaching down to grab the back of her jeans, Abby pinched the corner of Hayden's phone with her thumb, hiding it behind the denim fabric as she pulled her pants up over her rear. She shimmied side to side a little, feigning adjustment of her pants, and slid Hayden's phone into her back pocket again.

The toilet gurgled and hissed as water refilled the tank. Abby buttoned her jeans and zipped them shut.

Chewing on his lower lip, Nick shook his head slightly before grinning at Abby. He grunted his approval of her again and motioned with his head to come with him.

"Where are we going, Nick?" Abby slung the backpack over her right shoulder and followed his lead down the hallway.

"Someplace warm. Someplace safe." Nick laughed as they stepped into the living room.

Abby walked toward her laptop, and Nick shook his head.

"Won't be needin' that."

She turned toward him. "That's… that's my job. That's how I make—"

"Won't need to work anymore, baby. Money I've got will go a long way where we're going."

Abby bit her lip and shook her head. "What money?"

"Things went down. Doesn't matter, now." He snickered, and put the bottle of tequila on the kitchen table.

"Nick? Did you…did you kill someone?"

He studied her for a moment, and then stepped closer, reached out a hand to brush her hair from the side of her face. Nick leaned down to kiss her and Abby turned away.

Nick chuckled a humorless laugh, and kissed her cheek as he slid his arm around her back and quickly down to her ass before Abby could twist away from him.

"*Luuuuuuucyyyyy*, I'm—"

Hayden's voice rang out from the hallway, and Abby turned to see the door of her apartment swing open wide. He took two steps inside, used his foot to nudge the door closed behind him, and froze, a wide smile on his face, a new bottle of Jose Cuervo in his left hand, and a bouquet of flowers in his right.

"Hommmme." The smile faded on Hayden's face as he glanced at Nick, and then turned to Abby.

Nick drew his pistol, leveled it in front of him, and pulled the trigger.

Chapter Forty-One

ABBY SCREAMED AS Hayden stumbled backward and fell against the door. He stared down at the dime-sized hole in his chest, and his eyes rolled back to show the whites. The bottle of tequila and the flowers fell from his hands and tumbled to the carpet. Hayden slid down the door slowly, leaving a bright red smear behind him.

Blood flowed from the wound, soaking his black T-shirt. Abby ran toward Hayden, grabbed a blanket from the back of the couch, and then knelt and pressed the cloth over the bullet entrance.

"No, no, no, no." Abby murmured and held the blanket against Hayden's chest, saw his blood coat her fingers. Hayden coughed, and bright red spittle slicked his lips.

"Hayseed?" Abby watched his chest rise and fall, the breaths becoming shallower. She whispered. "Hayden?"

Nick snorted with disgust. "Jesus fuckin' Christ, Abby. Been barely a week and you got some fuckin' guy showin' up with booze and flowers?"

Abby gritted her teeth and hissed at him. "You son of a bitch."

She rose from her knees and spun around without thinking, charging at Nick, rage burning inside her. Abby balled her hands and swung her right fist upward toward Nick's face.

His hand came out of nowhere, smashing his pistol against Abby's face, and creating a night sky of stars in her head. She fell to her knees and caught herself from collapsing to the floor.

"You fuckin' kidding me? Over this guy?" He took a step away from her and shook his head, and then fixed his gaze on hers. "Know what? Fuck your bags, fuck your things. Kings don't act well to betrayal, and you're gonna fuckin' learn."

Nick snapped forward, closed the space between them, and grabbed Abby's left arm around her bicep. She jerked it away from him and fell backward, and scooted away from him toward Hayden.

He stepped toward Abby and then stopped, his attention on the carpet at his feet. Nick's eyes widened and he reached to the floor and picked up Hayden's phone. His gaze focused on the screen, he cocked his head sideways and then glared at Abby. "*Ohhhhhh...* you little fuckin' bitch."

Nick threw the phone down the hallway and there was a thud from Abby's bedroom as it landed. He moved beside Hayden's body and pointed the pistol. "Over *this* motherfucker?"

Abby was sick to her stomach as she watched Nick hover over Hayden's bloody body and wave the barrel of his pistol at his face.

Nick moved fast, within arm's length of Abby in an instant. He grabbed a handful of her hair and pulled. Abby screamed and frantically ran her hands over his balled fist, trying to grab onto him as he jerked her to her feet.

"Time to hit the fuckin' road." Nick used one foot to kick Hayden's shoulder, and his body fell to the side, away from the doorway. His fist still gripping tightly to Abby's hair, Nick pushed her forward. "Open the door."

Abby did as she was told, swinging the door open wide.

Nick paused, jerked her around to face him. "*This* motherfucker? For real?"

Nick leaned and spat in Hayden's face. "How you like me now, you pathetic little prick?"

Ding-ding-ding-ding-ding-ding—

Nick snapped his head around, staring at the chorus of sound in the apartment. Anger bleached from his face, as he tried to find the source. "What...what the fuck is that, Abby?"

The window frames rattled, and the panes of glass joined in as the rhythm grew louder.

DING-DING-DING-DING-DING—

Nick winced at the high-pitched chaos. He tightened his grip on Abby's hair and stepped backward toward the open doorway, aiming his pistol wildly around the room.

—DING-DING-DING-DING-DING—

"What the fuck... Abby, what the fuck is..." Nick held her between him and the living room, using her for a shield. "Did you spike that fuckin' tequila with acid or something?"

—DING-DING-DING-DING-DING—

Nick swung the pistol side to side toward the apartment. Nick yanked Abby's hair and stepped further into the hallway until his back met the opposite wall.

And then, silence.

Nick jerked Abby's hair, moving her head away from blocking his view.

Dead silence.

Abby saw a soft flutter of movement in the hallway, and Nick spun and aimed the pistol with a shaking hand.

"Let her go, son." The voice in the hallway was low and calm. "Easy, now. There's no need for this."

Father Walker held his hands out at his sides, the common body language for *I come in peace,* and stepped closer. The overhead light showed a thick smear of blood along the left side of his face, from his temple down to his jawline, and it continued down his neck. An open wound along Father Walker's face trickled blood in a thin stream.

"You're a tough ol' bastard, aren't ya?" Nick snickered. "Don't you have some little kids to molest or something?"

"Whatever this is, you're only making it worse than it needs to be." Father Walker raised his arms, opening them wide. "Let her go."

Nick thumbed the hammer back on his pistol. "You might be a man of the cloth, but you take one more step and I *will* put a fuckin' bullet in you."

"Father," Abby put her hands up toward the man. "Just step away. I'll be all right."

"Yeah, Father. Up against the fuckin' wall and keep your hands where I can—"

A frigid current of air came from the apartment, and the sound of whispering, but amplified, as if someone was telling secrets over a loudspeaker. One voice over another, a group of sound, layered and smothering each other so nothing specific was intelligible, only the *idea* of whispering itself. No specific words could be heard, but the tone was there, the anger was impossible to ignore. And then, as before, the noise ended abruptly, leaving nothing but the chilled air around them.

"*Fucckkk.*" Nick gritted his teeth.

It's them, Abby thought. *Oh my god, it's them.*

In that instant, Father Walker grabbed for Nick's hand holding the pistol, shoving the barrel toward the ceiling.

The hall exploded as Nick pulled the trigger, and he slung Abby toward the wall. She spun and slammed into the drywall and fell to her knees. In the dim light, starbursts of pain speckled her vision, but she saw the motion beside her.

Nick swung his fist into the old priest's face, and the man's grip fell away. Bringing his pistol down, Nick slammed the hard steel against Father Walker's face. He cocked his hand back and brought it down again, bashing the weapon against the old man's cheekbone. The priest fell to the hallway floor, both sides of his face wounded and bleeding profusely.

Nick leaned forward and grinned at him.

"Really are a tough ol' bastard." A smile cut across Nick's blood-spattered face and he stood, the silhouette of him large and towering in front of the ceiling light. He took a step forward and stopped, stared down at Abby.

"Let's get the fuck out of this creepy ass place."

Abby's face crackled with pain, a high voltage swarm, pulsing with a heartbeat of its own. Her lips were bloodied and she could taste it. She blinked several times, tried to focus on Nick's outstretched hand, and then reached out. The already darkened hallway swirled in front of her.

The sound of something sliced through the air above her, and Abby heard a dull *thunking* noise. Nick let out a grunt and groaned as he fell to his knees, balanced for a precarious moment, and then fell face first to the hallway floor.

Hayden stood behind Nick's prone body, holding a fire poker in his hand.

Dark splotches danced in front of Abby's eyes, and she felt herself swallowed up into shadow.

Chapter Forty-Two

FUCKING ASSHOLE! DID you think I was going to just let you come down here and *fucking—*"

"Hayseed?" Abby tried to open her eyes and the sight of her living room ceiling skewed like a funhouse mirror.

Quick footsteps approached her side, and Abby turned to see Hayden kneeling down beside her.

"Abs?" he whispered and put his hand against her cheek.

She forced her eyes to remain focused on Hayden's face, as memory flooded through her. Behind Hayden, Nick's body lay on the living room floor, his face bloodied, and the right side of his head glistening wetly.

Abby's attention returned to the soaked patch of cloth on Hayden's chest.

"Oh my God, Hayden, you…" Abby's breath was ragged, as patched and distorted as her view of the room. "We've gotta get you to a hosp—"

"Abs, let me help you." Hayden slid a hand beneath her back and helped Abby sit up on the couch. The motion and the change in position made the right side of her face pulse with an agonizing heartbeat, and Abby released a low groan. Her mouth tasted of copper.

"I can get you a wet washcloth." Hayden rose from his knees, but Abby waved a hand at him dismissively.

"No, I can… I can get it." Abby shook her head and put her fingers against her temples, rubbing them. She opened her mouth and shifted her lower jaw, groaning again at the throbbing pain. Pushing herself off the couch, Abby stood in place a moment, finding her balance.

She watched Hayden put his hands out at her sides as if he was ready to catch her if she fell. Her gaze went to his bloodstained shirt.

"You've been shot, Hayseed. We need to get to a hospital." Abby reached toward him, but Hayden lifted his palms in front of him.

"Yeah, we will, just… you're hurt, too."

She stared at him, his face pale, but his expression of concern. On the floor behind him, Nick wasn't moving and the hair on the side of his head looked matted with blood. Abby took a step, felt confident she could continue, and walked down the hallway to the bathroom, turned the lights on, and looked at her reflection.

The black eye Nick had previously given her had changed from blue-purple to shades of yellow-green, but the right side of her face was covered in blood. She reached for a rolled-up washcloth from the rack on the wall, and turned on the cold tap in the sink.

After soaking the cloth and gently wiping at her face, Abby saw the imprint of what looked like a Philips head screw on her cheekbone, and then a ragged wound leading downward.

A drywall screw.

Her stomach swirled inside, but she tenderly continued wiping with the cold rag. Abby turned off the water and paused, listening to the sound of a low angry voice from the living room.

"—warned you, didn't I? Yeah, I *fucking did.*"

She peered around the doorway of the bathroom and saw Hayden standing over Nick's body, leaning down, like a parent scolding a toddler. He gave one hard kick to Nick's stomach, and then Hayden walked into the kitchen, and put his hands on the island.

Can't say you didn't earn it, Nick.

Abby stepped back inside the bathroom and the reflection of her battered face. A thread of blood dribbled from the wound and she clenched the washcloth in her hand, watched the pink liquid fall to the sink.

It'll have to do until we get to the hospital.

In the mirror, Abby's gaze drifted lower, to the floor of the bedroom behind her. There, on the carpet, she saw Hayden's phone, and she spun away from the sink and went into the bedroom to grab it. The screen came to life, but it was a silver spiderweb of cracks. Abby pushed the phone icon, but it didn't respond.

She tilted the phone and watched the screen reorient into horizontal mode. A silver crack line ran over the phone icon, but Abby tried to push the icon anyway.

Nothing.

"*Fucccck,*" she whispered to herself.

The phone gave a single but brief buzz, and Abby saw a notification from Facebook on the screen. She stared at the pop-up screen for a moment, at the profile photo Hayden was using on his page, and then she tapped a small, uncracked area of the screen.

The Facebook app opened and even through the busted screen, Abby could read the notification about a friend's birthday.

I'm not on social media because I don't need Big Brother watching me.

Abby stared at Hayden's Facebook page, at his string of posts.

His profile picture, the same black and white photo he had framed on his wall.

"Everything okay, Abs?"

Abby flinched at the sound of Hayden's voice from the hallway.

"Yeah, I… I thought I could call 9-1-1, but your phone's busted. Nick—"

"Oh God, your face…" Hayden stepped into the bedroom, wincing as he looked at her wound.

"Forget my damned face! You've been shot and Father Walker is…" Abby put her hand against Hayden's arm and took a step forward, guiding him toward the hallway. "We need to get you to a hospital."

At the end of the hallway, Hayden walked around the couch to stand beside Nick, and pointed at him. "This piece of shit set my apartment on fire. I know it was him."

"What're you… what're you talking about?"

"He's been sending me threats, pissed that you're with me, now."

"That doesn't make any…" She swallowed hard and put a hand out against the back of the couch. "Why didn't you say anything to me?"

"Because you're safe with me. I just…" Hayden shrugged and shook his head. "I didn't want you to worry about him anymore."

He coughed, the sound a wheezing from deep inside his chest. Hayden walked to the kitchen counter and put his hands out onto the smooth granite top. "How did Nick even know you were here? Have you... have you two still been talking?"

"Hayden, what the hell does... It doesn't *matter*. He tracked my phone, okay?" She stared at him, saw the line of blood on his chest had reached down to his waist, dribbling down onto his pants. "Listen to me, you're not thinking clearly. We *have* to get you to the—"

"No, see..." Hayden gave another slight shake of his head, an expression of disappointment on his face, and he spoke softly. "It *does* matter. Actually, it matters quite a lot."

He straightened, cleared his throat, and spit blood into the sink. Hayden chewed his bottom lip and looked away. "Were you just going to *leave* with him? I mean..."

Hayden gave a slight shake of his head and then looked at Abby with glassy eyes. "I thought we really had something."

Abby felt a scalding droplet run down her cheek, but the expression on Hayden's face, the shadows in his eyes, opened a frozen pit in her stomach.

Chapter Forty-Three

ABBY SWALLOWED HARD, and watched Hayden pace the living room. She stood in place, keeping the couch between her and Hayden.

His eyes look like Nick's when he's been on a binge, wild and like a cornered animal.

"Abs, do you know how long…" Hayden released a breath and smiled as he looked skyward. "How long I've waited…" He ran a hand back through his hair and turned to her, serious, his eyes rimmed with tears.

"In high school, it was easier telling everyone I was going to be a priest than trying to explain I was saving myself for you. For *us*." Hayden shook his head and studied Nick's still body. "*No one* would understand that. Their small minds would be incapable of even *comprehending* that."

Hayden nodded to himself. "The discipline. The absolute *will* of waiting".

The ball of ice in Abby's stomach twisted as she listened and watched as Hayden glared at Nick.

"And now, this piece of *shit,* he wants to come back and take you? His skin stinking of drugs and filth, and he thinks he can just waltz in here after hitting you and hurting you and…" Hayden paused, breathing heavily, and then his head snapped up. "Absolutely fucking not!"

His expression was filled with a blend of pain and rage, and he released another breath, slowly, before turning to Abby again.

"I was *always* there for you." He tilted his head and sniffled, bringing up his forearm to wipe his nose. "Watching you with guys who'd treat you like trash. But there I was, waiting in the wings to patch you back up again, wasn't I?"

He scoffed and smiled. "All that time we just said *Hey* to each other and both you and I *knew* what it meant… our little secret code for *I love you.* But actually saying it out loud? No… no, we didn't even do *that* in private. Too *weird,* right?" Hayden wiped his nose with his forearm again and walked to the kitchen. "All those years loving you, wanting you… and now it's finally *our* time."

He reached for the knife block and withdrew the wide-bladed chef's knife.

"Hayseed—"

"We're here for each other *now*, Abs. That's what matters. No one's ever going to try and take that away from us." He stepped closer to Nick and turned to her, tears streaming down his face. "I love you, Abby. I've *always* loved you."

"Fuck're you talkin' about, altar boy?" Nick sputtered through bloody lips.

"Shut up!" Hayden spun toward him. The knife blade in his right hand gleamed.

"Hayden, don't!" Abby put her hand out toward him. "Look… just… just put the knife down, okay?"

He didn't even turn in her direction.

"Soul mates." Nick spit blood onto the brick fireplace hearth and tried to sit up. "*Puh-fuckin-leeeeeeze.* Little lost puppy with—"

Hayden swung his fist, punched the side of Nick's face, and knocked him to the carpet again. "You junkie piece of shit! You think you deserve her? Seriously? After hitting her?"

"You are one sad, twisted, little fuck." Nick hissed the words through gritted teeth. "You know, I used to laugh at all the messages you'd send to me about Abby. About how you were meant to be, how you've always loved her. Sometimes I'd laugh at them and then go into the bedroom to fu—"

Hayden screamed and kicked Nick in the face, snapping his head to the side. He fell to his knees straddling Nick's body, and his fist landed against his left jaw. Hayden's hand gripped the handle of the chef's knife and raised it overhead.

Abby screamed and started forward, but she stopped when Hayden slowly turned toward her. His face was contorted and frozen with anger. His raised arm trembled in place, but the wrath painted on his face began to dissolve as he stared at her.

"Hayden, stop."

Blood spattered his face, and he nodded slowly. A sharp laugh escaped him. "See, I knew... I just *knew* it." He pushed a bloody hand against the carpet and pushed away from Nick's body.

"Hayden—"

"Shut up, I'm..." He glanced at Abby and then away again, as if he was ashamed of his harsh words toward her. "Sorry, I... just be quiet for a minute. I need to think."

The photo, Abby thought. *Hayden's photo of us at Shepherd's Point amusement park. The same one he's using as his profile picture.*

That picture isn't real. That was the day I found out Dad had cancer.

She watched Hayden, watched the way his eyes shifted predatorily around the room.

He and I were never there together.

"I'm not sure what's..." Abby let out a slow breath and held her hands out toward him in a calming gesture. "I'm not sure what's going on but... just calm down, okay? Please, Hayden, just—"

"I understand, and I'm not angry at you. You don't have the stomach for this Abs, and that's okay. I'm here." Hayden turned away with tears in his eyes and pointed at Nick. "I'll do what needs to be done so we can be together."

"Hayden—"

"He was going to try to take you away from me, from *us* and that... that's not going to happen." Hayden grabbed Nick's arm and pulled him over onto his side, continuing the motion to roll him onto his stomach. He grabbed Nick's hair and lifted his head, and Abby watched as Nick's jaw went slack. Hayden lowered Nick's open mouth against the edge of the brick hearth, straightened, and lifted his right foot.

"Hayden!" Abby screamed as she ran around the couch, and charged toward him. He raised his arm as she reached him, his forearm catching her face, and she fell against him and then to the carpet.

Hayden towered over her, and Abby watched his expression change. His hand tightened on the handle of the knife.

Ding-ding-ding-ding-ding-ding—

From behind the cupboard doors, the chorus rang loud and crystalline.

—ding-ding-ding-ding-ding-ding—

Abby kicked her leg and connected with Hayden's crotch, but from her position on the floor, it was a weak hit. Hayden groaned and then dropped to his knees, straddling Abby's midsection. She screamed as she reached out and tried to scratch his face and eyes. Hayden grabbed one of her wrists, and then the other, squeezed them together in one of his hands and pinned them to the carpet over her head.

The ringing of glass stopped as abruptly as it had started, and a sharp snapping sound, like a breaking branch, cut through the room.

Behind Hayden, there was movement off to the side, and even in Abby's panic, it caught her attention. He followed her gaze and the two of them stared at the mannequin.

Chapter Forty-Four

T HE CRACK WIDENED along the side of the figure's face, and then lengthened into a ragged circle. For a moment, the section of fiberglass wavered like a flap of broken eggshell, and then the shape fell free and tumbled to the floor.

Abby watched as hands made of shadow reached from within the hollow of the mannequin, gripped the sides of the opening, and pulled itself free. A liquid shape emerged, a body of black mercury, swirling and writhing from the fiberglass figure.

A low whimper issued from Hayden's throat, and he dropped the knife to the carpet as the twisting black shape crawled toward him. The sphere of ice inside Abby shattered and flowed through her veins.

The row of kitchen drawers slammed open one by one, like pistons bursting free of their chambers, and utensils began to flip out of the drawers and clatter to the floor. Cabinet doors slammed open and shut and then open again, cracking against their frames. Plumes of smoke curled from their interiors and slid to the floor, behind the kitchen island, out of sight.

The shadows rose from behind the couch, tripling in size from when they were last visible. Two of them moving in unison, shifting like eels beneath river water.

"Motherfucker!" Nick snapped awake, snapped his hand out to grab the knife, and then drove the blade into Hayden's thigh and twisted.

Hayden screamed and dropped to one knee as he clutched Nick's fist. The shadow crawling toward him shifted, the figure's head turned toward Hayden, but the swirling darkness moved from the kitchen island and reached Nick first.

The two figures moved over his body and cloaked his face. His eyes bulged wide as the black mist drifted into his mouth and nostrils. Nick released his grip on the knife handle, and fell to his back as the shadows burrowed inside him. His frightened bloodshot eyes swiveled toward Abby. His mouth gaped open as if he wanted to scream, but Nick didn't make a sound.

His body spasmed, and Nick slowly eased his head down against the carpet. The skin on his face rippled as if something swam beneath the surface. He blinked once, twice, and then closed his eyes and shut his mouth.

The fingers of Nick's hands stiffened and then clawed against the carpet, and he arched his back up from the floor. The movement under his flesh quickened like tadpoles swimming beneath the tissue, and as Abby watched, Nick's eyelids snapped open.

His eyes had been replaced by moist, writhing spheres. A swarm of pale, wriggling maggots cascaded from his eye sockets, and several milky-white kernels crawled blindly across his right cheek. Nick's mouth yawned wide, and a similar mass erupted over his lips and chin. His body convulsed as more larvae worked free of his nostrils, meeting the frenzy at his mouth.

Hayden screamed and kicked away from Nick's body, and dragged himself backward. Blood streamed down his thigh to the carpet, and Abby's gaze traced the trail of red to Hayden's terrified face, and then beyond at the looming black shape descending on him.

The shadow twisted and turned, almost serpentine in nature. Limbs stretched toward Hayden and curled around his chest, spreading upward over his throat and face, smothering him in darkness.

Abby stood frozen, watching the obsidian flow over Hayden. He clawed at his face as the shape draped around him and a muffled scream escaped his mouth. The form shrank in size, drawing itself inside Hayden as the others had done with Nick. A plume swirled around the bullet hole in Hayden's chest and entered the wound, spiraling like black water down a drain.

Hayden's eyes watered, the tears spilling down and catching at his beard. He trembled in place, and a small fissure appeared along his forehead, a winding thread of blood, and then it continued in a ragged oval, encompassing Hayden's face.

A tab of his flesh peeled away along his left temple and Hayden's bulging eyes blinked rapidly. He released a low whine from deep inside his chest, and then the skin of his face tore free in one brutal motion, leaving Hayden's bloody skull and facial muscles exposed and glistening. His lidless eyes turned toward Abby, and a phlegmy coughing sound sputtered from his lipless mouth, opening and closing like he was a fish out of water.

The patch of skin fell to the carpet, and the obsidian shape that had invaded Hayden's body pulled itself free. There was a bulge along Hayden's throat, an obscene ripple beneath his Adam's apple, and then, as they had with the mannequin, fingers forced themselves from his mouth, prying his jaws open wide.

Ding-ding-ding-ding-ding—

Snaking down Hayden's body, the shadow arrived at the carpet, and Abby watched the patch of flesh rise from the floor, hovering there against a black cloud. Hayden fell forward, a large oak taken down to the forest floor. His hands grabbed at the carpet, he shuddered, and then lay still.

"I'm just like youuu. I'm jussst like you."

The voice was an oily whisper, and what passed for the figure's head tilted toward Abby. Arms stretched forward, and fingers that looked like twists of burned driftwood clawed at the floor and pulled itself in her direction.

—ding-ding-ding-ding-ding—

Abby screamed and ran toward the door. She flung it open wide and lurched into the hall and *felt* them behind her, icy trails across her skin.

Chapter Forty-Five

ABBY GLANCED AT Father Walker's motionless, bloodied face as she ran down the hallway toward the main entrance. The urge to grab Nick's pistol from the floor was strong, but Abby forced herself ahead.

A pistol won't do you any good.

Abby risked a look behind her, and saw shadows crawling on the walls, spindly limbs pulling themselves forward like wild animals. Another dragged itself along the main corridor, a misshapen, bulbous form where its head should be.

—ding-ding-ding-ding-ding—

Light, child-like giggling echoed off the walls, along with a wet gurgling sound.

"I'm jusht like you. I'm jusht like you. I'm jusht like youuuuuu."

She glanced behind her and saw the mask of Hayden's face bobbing in the dim light, the grotesque mockery tilting this way and that, studying its prey as it streaked toward Abby.

The overhead lights in the hall swung like pendulums, casting pinwheels of moving shadows. One by one, the lightbulbs shattered, and Abby heard the shards as they rained down. She ran through the darkness toward the dimly lit foyer.

Abby rushed from the hall into the main area, turned left toward the main door, and her heart flipped in her chest. She put her arms out in defense, as the black silhouettes loomed in front of her, blocking her exit.

Chapter Forty-Six

SHE PUNCHED AND clawed at the darkness in front of her, felt it grab her arms.

"Abby!"

She screamed and kicked out and tried to wrench herself free of the steel grip.

"Abby, stop!"

Detective Simmons held her tightly, his face grim and serious. He stared at Abby, and then his gaze shifted over her shoulder. His face went slack and he whispered. "Holy Mary, Mother of God."

"I'm jusht like youuuuuu."

Abby felt the icy sensation, an air conditioner's breeze on sunburned flesh, pass through her, *inside* her, and then continue forward. She watched the twists of shadow flow over the detective and the officer to his right. A swirl of ebony poured over them, and Abby heard the men scream.

The rag of Hayden's skin pressed against the detective's face, but the flesh was inside out, the bloody underside exposing gobs of yellow fat. A jagged bloody line opened up along the right side of the detective's face, twisting down from his temple to his lower jaw, and though he tried to scream again, his attempt was choked off as the shadow filled his mouth, forcing its way into the moist tunnel.

Two shadows whirled in a cyclone around the officer, gnawing his face. He waved his hands, trying to fend for himself, but his hands sliced through nothing but the dark swirling cloud. A bite mark appeared against the man's left cheek and as he opened his mouth to scream, ebony flowed inside him.

The shadows rose like the hoods of cobras, casting death before them, as the men uselessly tried to defend themselves. The wound on the detective's face continued to grow and his eyes bulged wide behind the sagging eyelids of Hayden's face.

Chapter Forty-Seven

OH, DIVINE ETERNAL father, in union with your divine son and the holy spirit, and through the immaculate heart of—"

Abby turned at the sound of the familiar voice, and saw Father Walker standing at the edge of the hallway, reciting his prayer. Spatters of blood covered his bruised face, and he held the crucifix of his necklace in his hand.

"—to destroy the power of your greatest enemy, the evil spirits. Cast them into the deepest recesses of hell and chain them—"

An icy current flowed through the space of the foyer, and Abby watched as a black plume unfurled from Detective Simmons' mouth. The officer fell to his knees, and the darkness surrounding him twisted and stretched away toward the darkened corners of the ceiling. He clutched at his throat and coughed.

"Take possession of your kingdom, which you have created and which is rightfully—"

Detective Simmons choked and sputtered, hands at his throat as the darkness inside him unspooled from between his parted lips. Hayden's flesh peeled away wetly from the detective's face and fell to the floor in a bloody crumple. The current of air grew in strength around them like the prelude to a heavy summer storm.

The mercurial shadows retreated to the dark recesses of the high ceiling.

"—beat of my heart, and with every breath I take. Amen." Father Walker breathlessly finished his prayer, his words echoing off the walls.

"What…" The detective's chest heaved and he wiped a hand over his bloody face. "What in the fuck is—"

"Quiet!" Father Walker whispered, but his single word was said with such authority, the detective held his tongue.

The room was dead silent, except for the labored breathing of Detective Simmons and the officer. No chilled wind flowed around them—there was no movement at all. Abby took a cautious step toward the priest, and then walked until she reached him, gently lifting his arm around her shoulders to help support him.

"I think…" The priest's breath came in rags. He swallowed hard, coughed, and continued. "I think it's over."

Detective Simmons wiped his forearm over his face and looked around the room. "What in the name of all that's—"

A deep, metallic rumbling cut off the detective's words, and the four of them turned toward the other side of the foyer in the direction of the noise.

Lights from within a metal box above the elevator doors flickered, and the number three lit up in a sickly yellow. The rumbling sounds stopped as the panel box sparked and the light shifted to highlight the number one. Something slammed against the other side of the elevator door, and then again, an avalanche of rage from inside the compartment.

The steel casing of the elevator doors bent outward from the impact. The metal dented and bulged, misshapen from invisible fists, and then the noise stopped.

A single, high-pitched *ding!* sliced through the silence, and the four of them watched as the elevator doors rattled open to a narrow gap.

Chapter Forty-Eight

BBY GAGGED AND covered her nose and mouth with her free hand as the stench of rotted meat drifted around them. The temperature dropped, and their shivering breaths were small white clouds. An internal light from within the empty elevator hummed and snapped as the four of them stared, frozen in place, as the doors trembled, and slowly closed.

A heavy breath escaped Abby's lungs, and she tightened her grip on Father Walker's arm. The doors of the elevator slammed open hard enough to crack the wall framing it. A flood of smoky obsidian poured from the recess of the compartment, a black tsunami of chaos, swirling around them in a torrential current. Screams echoed from within its depths, cries of pain and torment, the skewed laughter of children. The sound rose to a thunderous crescendo in the foyer. The river of darkness swelled around them, and Abby watched as the detective and the officer were swallowed. Twists of shadow curled over the walls, climbing insect-like. The room shook, and chunks of plaster from the ceiling rained down as wide cracks broke across its surface.

She screamed and tried to drag Father Walker toward the exit, but felt icy hands on her body, tearing her clothes, clawing at her flesh. Cold teeth in hungry mouths clamped down against her right thigh, and before Abby could yell in pain, another savage bite attacked her left leg, just behind her knee. The sensation was a frozen saw blade against her skin, and she twisted and fell away from the priest, landing on her knees in the vast emptiness.

Tiny fingers entwined in her hair and wrenched her head backward. Abby screamed and swung her hands, trying to fight them off. Father Walker stumbled to his knees beside her, and Abby saw the terror on his face. His crucifix necklace lifted from his body, and then tore away into the whirlwind. Bloody slashes scored his face, gouges from small fingernails.

Abby crawled to the old man, watching as he reached a hand inside his suit jacket. She wanted to shield him somehow, protect him from this madness, but she could still feel the punches and scratching against her own body. Icy fingers traced the back of her neck and then clawed into her skin.

Father Walker withdrew his hand from the inner cloth of his suit, and through the tornado, Abby watched him clench his hand into a fist and reach toward the ceiling. He wore a heavy gold ring, and even in the low light, the red, inset stone gleamed brightly.

The black cloud parted away from his fist, and the sounds erupted from hell itself, agonizing shrieks slamming Abby's ears. Darkness curled away from them, and she fell as she reached for Father Walker.

Spinning around them, the raven mist tightened and raced toward the staircase. The mass coiled upward, taking the screeching cries with it. Squealing and hissing trailed up the stairs, and invisible claws raked the walls, leaving long gouges in the plaster.

Overhead, the lights popped, issuing a shower of sparks. A heavy mechanical thud came from the elevator, and Abby saw the floor of the car had tilted at a broken angle. The light inside the compartment burst, and a mixture of sparks and glass rained down.

Up above, from the stairwell, heavy doors slammed closed, and then it was silent.

The rotted stink of decay had been replaced by something else, a smell like burnt ozone, the air after a lightning strike.

Abby stood and helped Father Walker to his feet. The wounds on her back, and the bite marks on her legs, pulsed with their own heartbeat. The officer and Detective Simmons were a bloodied mess, but they were moving.

Risking a glance behind her, Abby saw flickers of orange light from the darkened hallway, and the smell in the air hit her harder this time—acrid and metallic, the scent of copper and blood.

Chapter Forty-Nine

GOING TO NEED multiple trucks, the whole building is going to—"

Detective Simmons grabbed the CB mic from the officer's hand. "This is Detective Simmons on scene. We'll need the fire trucks and medic, but the building is clear, no one is in danger, so take…your…time."

He handed the mic back to the officer, and then sat down in a patch of grass along the edge of the parking lot. The detective's face was covered in bloody crosshatches, along with a jagged wound almost completely encircling his face. Flames reflected in his eyes, but his expression was vacant.

Abby pulled the pant leg of her jeans up from her ankle and saw the half-moons of bite marks at the back of her ankle. She let the fabric fall back in place, and she stared at the building as flames roared at the upper levels.

The glass of the first-floor windows had all cracked and fallen out, allowing flames and smoke to billow free.

Father Walker walked close enough to be cast in orange light from the fire.

Abby watched as he pulled the golden ring from his finger, turned it over and studied it, and it seemed for a moment, as if he was going to throw the ring into the flames. Father Walker pocketed the thing, let his arms down to his sides, and walked back to join them. He carefully eased himself to sit, pulled his sunglasses from an inner pocket and donned them. Then he withdrew a tightly rolled joint from his suit pocket, and lit up.

The Detective watched as the priest took a long drag and exhaled. "Seriously, Father?"

"Arrest me." Father Walker never even turned his way, only smiled as the other man snickered and shook his head.

"It's Dobsen's ring, isn't it?" Abby stepped close to the priest.

He nodded without looking in her direction and took a puff from the joint. "Part of my collection. Picked it up at a Historical Society auction a few years ago."

"Decided to keep it today?"

Father Walker exhaled smoke. "Sometimes you need some evil shit to fight evil shit."

Sirens blared in the distance, and Abby saw the officer sitting in the open driver's side of his patrol car. He sat with his elbows on his knees, hands clasped together in front of him. The man's expression was shaken, trying to process what he had been through. She nodded at the man and turned to Detective Simmons. "He gonna be alright?"

"Stevens?" He glanced at the police cruiser. "Physically, yeah. Mentally? Hell, I wouldn't be surprised if he resigns and runs off to be a carpenter or something. Christ, I might take his lead."

A portion of the roof cracked and caved in. A column of flames spewed high into the air, and motion behind the third-floor windows drew Abby's attention. Dark silhouettes moved and shifted behind the glass.

Father Walker took another puff on his joint and ran a hand back through his hair.

"Father?" The detective spoke in a low voice, as the sirens grew closer. "Anything you can offer to make sense of this?"

"If you're expecting that old bullshit about God working in mysterious ways, don't hold your breath. This had nothing at all to do with him."

Another segment of the roof caved in, exposing thick timbers covered in flames.

"After the medics patch us up, we're gonna need to talk, Abby." The detective's vacant expression remained, but was layered beneath a seriousness.

Nodding at Simmons, Abby felt waves of hurt rushed through her. She wasn't sure she could even begin processing everything that had happened, wasn't sure she ever would be.

Abby's attention returned to the building, and she watched the silhouettes on the third floor undulate behind the windows.

The fire engines and paramedics arrived, the men scrambling from the vehicles and going to work. Abby watched as the firemen dragged the heavy water hose toward the front of the building and started spraying it down. A thick wave of white steam hissed from the door and windows.

The moving figures up above faded into the flames.

Chapter Fifty

ABBY SET A garbage bag stuffed with clothes in the backseat of her car. The action of setting them down made the plastic at the top puff out slightly, and the air smelled of smoke. She put a box of books into the trunk and the same burned odor lifted from the cardboard.

Packing's a lot easier when you've barely got anything left.

The sounds of a backhoe caught her attention, and she watched as an operator continued digging up the ground. Two uniformed officers stood close by, as they had for the last several days. So far, there had been twenty-six unmarked graves of children, and Abby figured that was barely the start.

She looked up as tires crunched on the gravel of the drive, saw Detective Simmons, and closed the trunk and rear door of her car. Abby watched as he pulled to a stop and smiled at her through the windshield before parking.

"You headin' out, young lady?" He looked at her over the roof of his car, and even though his face was more bandages than skin, his smile widened.

"Nothing left for me here." Abby returned his smile. "Maybe I'll go to Disney World."

He raised his eyebrows. "Florida, huh?"

"It's home."

Detective Simmons nodded and turned to stare at the burned husk of the building. The exterior was tiger-striped with soot, stretching toward the upper floors, and the absent rooftop, save for several thick wooden trusses at either end of the structure.

"Been a cop for a long time, seen some pretty crazy things, but this…" His face took on the same lost expression he'd worn the night it all happened. His glassy eyes scanned over the debris. "The world is…" He scoffed and let his sentence go unfinished.

Abby stepped around the car and stood close to him, reaching a hand out to rest on his shoulder.

His smile returned as his gaze focused on her. "You alright? This was a lot to take in for anyone, considering… Hayden, Nick and," Detective Simmons gave a nod toward the building. "The goddamn Amityville House."

Abby snickered to herself and though she fought the urge, she gave in and glanced up at the third-floor windows of the building. Smoked, broken windowpanes lined up in a row, with nothing behind them except charred wood. "I'm not sure I can answer that question just yet."

The detective shifted in place, put his hands in his pants pockets, and leaned back against his car. "Don't beat yourself up over anything. Just know you're not naïve. People change, and most of the time, there's no way anyone else knows, not even their own family or people who love them."

He withdrew his right hand and tapped his temple with his index finger. "Sometimes people just… go wrong."

Abby released a heavy sigh. "You had mentioned the computer team might have something soon?"

Detective Simmons nodded. "They salvaged some, but the fire took care of the rest. A lot of doctored images on Hayden's hard drive. Photos of the two of you. Some everyday photos, you know, boyfriend girlfriend vacation sort of things. Others…" Simmons shrugged, made a face, and looked away. "More of a graphic nature."

Her insides twisted and a wave of nausea swirled inside her. "Were they shared? Posted anywhere on—"

"No, I don't think so. The computer guys don't think so either. These were for his own… *use.* The photos he shared on social media were the normal ones, made you two seem like you were a couple." Simmons appeared almost embarrassed by the topic of discussion.

Abby shifted, needing to change the direction of the talk. "Is there uh… going to be a memorial service or… something, for Uncle Jack?"

The detective inhaled slowly and nodded. "I spoke to Jacksonville PD, told them about Jack's death, the charge officer told me Jack's wife has been a missing person for a little over a year now. Still an open case."

Abby felt her guts churn and she forced herself to exhale slowly from the gut punch.

"Forensics is looking at Jack's corpse, trying to determine how long it'd been on the first floor of the feed mill. If the place hadn't caught fire, who knows, no one might have ever known he was dead. I told the officer about everything and it's probably going to point them in another direction in the investigation of his wife. My guess is Jack's body had been below Hayden's apartment for at least a few months, so I guess a little longer for a proper burial isn't going to hurt."

The diesel engine of the backhoe revved, and they both turned to watch the bucket dig into a patch of untouched ground, saw the group of men standing along a series of holes in the earth. Abby nodded toward the work being done. "Think *they* waited long enough for a proper burial?"

Detective Simmons winced at Abby and sucked against his front teeth as he looked away, and then quickly turned back toward her, waving his hand dismissively. "Look, don't worry about this right now, okay? It's… you go on, get down to Florida. Start fresh from all this."

"You'll keep me posted on things, though?"

"Sure, yeah. I've got your cell number."

Abby watched as the backhoe bucket dumped a load of dirt off to the side of the hole. One of the men raised a hand toward the driver, and then looked down inside, stared for a moment, and then nodded at the operator, pointing at something in the hole.

"And what about…" A snapshot exploded in Abby's mind, the image of Nick's dead body stretched out on her living room floor, and Hayden, on his knees, his bloody skull glaring at her with lidless eyes. She stammered out the rest of the sentence. "What's going to happen to Nick's… remains?"

"We found a cousin of his in Philadelphia, rude woman named—"

"Carolyn."

"That's her, alright." The detective laughed softly. "We're sending his remains to her. After that, who knows?"

The man near the dig site stepped down into the hole and leaned over. Abby watched as he stood straight again, holding a long bone in his gloved right hand. He put the bone on a plastic tarp laid out on the ground, and leaned down again.

Abby turned toward the detective and gave him an unexpected hug. He put his arms around her and squeezed her back, and it felt safe and good. "Thank you, detective. For everything."

"I could be one of them smartass try-hards and say *I was just doing my job, ma'am*, but I'm not that big of an asshole, so you're welcome." Detective Simmons laughed as he held her, and then pulled away, grinned at Abby, and opened his driver's side door. "You take care of yourself, Abby."

She nodded and held her hand up at him to wave good-bye, stood there and watched as he drove out of the lot and down the street. The breeze chilled her and Abby put her hands into her coat pockets. A flapping sound caught her attention and she looked up at the burned shell of a building. A mourning dove perched on a charred piece of wood.

Ding-ding.

The chilled air moved around her neck like an icy scarf, and Abby felt a scream catch in her throat. Beyond the open entrance of Harper's Grove, lay nothing but darkness.

Ding-ding-ding-ding—

Abby recognized the direction of the sound, and turned toward the street.

The powder-blue ice cream van drove slowly, a tall row of bare sycamore trees as a backdrop.

—ding-ding-ding-ding—

"Son of a biiiiiiiitchhhhhhhhh." Abby whispered through gritted teeth. She closed her eyes as she exhaled and put her head down, trying to force her heart to stop hammering in her chest. The scream she had restrained changed into a harsh laugh, and she allowed it to escape. Shaking her head, Abby opened her car and slid into the driver's seat. She started the car and turned the heater on.

The stereo signal from the college station was weak with static, but the voice of Sinead O'Connor singing *This is the Last Day of Our Acquaintance* drifted from her speakers. She smiled at the song and reached to her left, pulled the seatbelt down and buckled it into place, and then Abby grabbed the door handle, readying to pull it shut.

A glimmer caught her attention on the gravel drive, inches below the open car door. A single penny lay there, half of it twisted and damaged but gleaming and shiny as if it had been chewed on with a pair of tin snips.

Unfit for human circulation.

Sometimes, that goes for both the living and the dead. Abby thought.

Abby yanked the door closed, leaving the penny untouched, and then she patted the dashboard. "C'mon Linda, let's go home."

THE END

ROBERT FORD has written the novels *Burner,*
The Compound, No Lipstick in Avalon, and *Blood Roses,*
a horror-western. He also has a collection of his short
fiction *The God Beneath my Garden,* a novella collection, *Inner Demons,* and the novella *Larva Me Tender.*

He collaborated, with John Boden, on the novel-
las *Rattlesnake Kisses, Cattywampus,* and *Black Salve,*
in the Knucklebucket Thang series.

Robert lives in Central Pennsylvania and is usually hard at work on at least two projects at a time.
You can find out more about his upcoming releases at
www.robertfordauthor.com

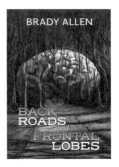

HORROR
DNA
MOVIES
COMIC BOOKS
MUSIC
BOOKS
VIDEO GAMES
IT'S IN
OUR
BLOOD
horrordna.com